MURDER

A VERY ENGLISH
MURDER

VERITY BRIGHT

Bookouture

Published by Bookouture in 2020

An imprint of Storyfire Ltd.
Carmelite House
50 Victoria Embankment
London EC4Y 0DZ

www.bookouture.com

ISBN: 978-1-83888-618-9
eBook ISBN: 978-1-83888-617-2

'Murder is always a mistake. One should never do anything that one cannot talk about after dinner.'
Oscar Wilde, *The Picture of Dorian Gray*

PROLOGUE

Staring up at the imposing facade, Lady Eleanor Swift wondered yet again if her decision to return had been a sound one. Since the letter informing her of her uncle's death and her unexpected inheritance of Henley Hall had arrived, she'd been sure coming here had been what she needed at this point in her life.

But now…

She stood at the double-fronted oak door and looked up at the two narrow towers that flanked the entrance of the vast cream stone mansion. Separated by three rows of arched windows, the towers pierced the grey, overcast sky. The carved Henley family crest, set high on the building's central arch, seemed to peer down disapprovingly at her.

Around the Hall lay two hundred acres of formal gardens and parkland, while behind her the semi-circular drive with its central fountain sat empty of cars. She wondered if her uncle's beloved Rolls was still running? She remembered riding in it along the winding half-mile drive to the Hall's imposing wrought-iron gates and then on to Chipstone railway station. That was years ago, and it was the last time she'd seen it or her uncle.

She sighed. Her last stay at the Hall had been as a thirteen-year-old in the summer of 1904. It had been one of the few holidays from her boarding school when she'd been allowed to come home. Her uncle, however, hadn't been there for more than a week or two. Business had taken him abroad, as it usually did, leaving her in the care of his inscrutable butler, Clifford.

It had been a particularly wet summer, and she'd escaped the monotony by losing herself in her favourite books by day and dreaming up fantastical plans to avoid returning to her even more dreary boarding school by night. And now, after an absence of sixteen years, here she was, once again.

She took a deep breath and pulled on the doorbell, recalling that the last time she'd stood here she'd been too short to reach the bell at all.

As she waited, she stared up again at the Henley family crest. *What were you thinking of, Ellie?*

CHAPTER 1

After what seemed like forever, Clifford, her late uncle's butler, opened the door. He looked as impossibly stiff as the last time she'd seen him. And, implausibly, he looked the exact same age, whatever that was. She couldn't remember a moment without him at the Hall. She was convinced that all butlers were born a certain age at which they stayed until they disappeared in a puff of discreet smoke. For a good servant would never die on his employer, that would be just too inconvenient.

However, he didn't give her the warm greeting she was craving. He bowed stiffly, and said, 'Welcome to Henley Hall, Lady Swift.'

Had he been rehearsing that line? How else could he have infused it with coldness plus a touch of aloof disapproval? But what had she expected? In truth, she hadn't expected anything, not having thought that far ahead.

'Thank you, Clifford.'

Clearly he remembers you, Ellie, she consoled herself. *Although unlike him, I know I have changed considerably. I can reach the doorbell now, after all.*

He held the door and pursed his lips as she stepped over the threshold carrying her somewhat minimalist and wind-blown baggage. 'Forgive me, my lady, did I mishear your original communication? I was given to understand that you would be arriving tomorrow evening by the six thirty train. I intended to pick you up at Chipstone Station in the Rolls.'

'You are correct, Clifford. However, I arrived early and made my own way. And, here I am.'

'Very good, my lady.'

A forceful scratching distracted her attention as the oak door behind the butler burst open. An elderly bulldog lumbered in, jaws flapping, with its claws scrabbling on the wooden flooring between the thick rugs that lined the entrance hall. The dog launched itself onto her lap, pushing her back into a low chair with a thump. Shoving its wrinkled face into hers, it bashed her nose with the leather slipper offered as a welcome gift. At least someone seemed delighted to see her.

Clifford clapped his hands. 'Stand down, Gladstone!' The dog sat obediently. 'This is Master Gladstone, my lady. He was purchased by your late uncle sometime after your last visit here.' He paused. 'It has been a long while since you were at the Hall.'

Eleanor said nothing – she was well aware of how long it had been since she had been anywhere she could call home, however loosely.

Gladstone flopped onto her feet, his stumpy tail beating out a muffled rhythm on the deep pile rug. Clifford changed tack. 'Would you like to take some tea, my lady? You must be thirsty after your long journey.'

'Actually, I would like to get changed and gather my thoughts.'

'There are some papers from your uncle you may wish to read.'

'Papers? It's been almost seven weeks since I saw a half-decent bed. Papers can wait.'

'Very good, my lady. Shall I show you to your room?'

On the elegant landing of the second floor, Clifford stopped by a familiar door. Opening it, he stood to the side. 'Your room, my lady.'

Eleanor stepped forward and in a heartbeat was transported back sixteen years. 'Oh, my!' She looked around in disbelief. The room was obviously cleaned regularly for there was no evidence of dust. And it must have been aired frequently, as it smelt as fresh as new laundry. However, nothing else had changed since she had last stayed there as a child. 'But, Clifford…' she started, and then faltered as his retreating coattails glided noiselessly back down the stairs.

Eleanor stood feeling lost in the middle of the room. She never imagined she'd be given this room. Since she'd gone abroad she had travelled to places and experienced things few women of her age could, or would ever be allowed to. But now, even though she had turned twenty-nine the month before, she felt like a small child. She looked into the mirror on the opposite wall. A slender woman with flame-red curls and world-weary green eyes, dressed in hopelessly unfashionable clothing looked back at her. She shook her head. *Snap out of it, Ellie!*

The pink-and-gold eiderdown puffed behind her as she sat on the side of the bed, running her hand up and down the silky fabric. A giggle caught her by surprise. As a small girl, she had loved this bedspread – she had even tied it round her like a princess' cloak and entertained the dolls on the chaise longue with her witty speeches. Then a few years had passed before she'd visited again as a young adult and she'd hated it.

She looked around again. Between the two vaulted windows were three bookcases with carved elephants. And were those…? Yes! The very books she had devoured on those endless rainy days, with her feet tucked up on the window seat: *Rebecca of Sunnybrook Farm, The Adventures of Huckleberry Finn…* And further along *Arabian Nights, Treasure Island, Around the World in Eighty Days* and *The Jungle Book.* As a child, those stories had seemed so real.

Above the bed, there was a picture of an oasis. A camel train was resting there, recovering for the next leg of its journey. She had drunk in this image for so many hours in her childhood. At any time since then she could have reproduced a perfect copy. Palm trees ringed the water, with dunes of golden sand rising to a light purple in the distance. Under the palm trees stood camels with exquisitely detailed saddlebags with black-and-gold tassels cascading and glinting in the afternoon sun.

It had been the camel drivers in the picture that had captivated her most all those years ago: their swirling, white robes and red chequered headdresses, set against the blackest of eyes. Sitting cross-legged on the bed with her journal she'd written enough stories about her imagined camel-train adventures to fill those bookcases several times over.

And now you've done those things for real, Ellie. You've crossed the Dasht-e Lut, followed the Silk Road and had so many other adventures. And some of them were wilder than you could ever have dreamed of as a little girl.

She sighed. Maybe it was time to stop beating herself up. The books only told half the story. She'd learned first-hand that exploring mountains, deserts and forests, and sleeping under a million twinkling stars, often went with days of hunger, exhaustion and illness.

And even though she had never felt so alive, she'd never known where her next bed or meal were coming from.

She didn't claim to be the first, as she was following in the wake of her heroines: the few brave female trailblazers who had dared to defy convention and the odds and stand toe to toe with their more famous male counterparts. But still, doing it all as a woman was doubly hard.

Was she glad she'd done it? Without doubt. Was it like the books? Not at all! She sighed. If only that blasted letter hadn't come! But in truth, the letter had only been the catalyst. If she was honest with herself, she was already struggling to find the joy she had once found in the life she led. Usually she loved travelling, especially to exotic destinations. After all, she'd made it her life and job, but after living such a lifestyle for the best part of her adult life, the constant uncertainty and discomfort had lost its allure.

Even her journey from South Africa to London hadn't seemed an adventure, more like a fight for survival. She shook her head. In fairness, she thought, a voyage of some nine thousand miles that included two crash landings was bound to be a little wearing even to the most intrepid traveller. That was the trouble with inaugural flights, their unpredictability. And the first commercial flight from Cape Town to London was no different. They'd only spent five days out of the forty-five-day journey in the air. The rest were on the ground repairing the plane with whatever could be found first in the Sudan and then in Bulawayo where they'd crash-landed. But they had made it, albeit a little battered and bruised. She groaned. 'If I never see sand again, I'll be happy!'

She stood up and walked over to the dresser. On it sat a marionette, still twisted up in his web of knotted string. Poor fellow. He'd seen one afternoon of bobbing round and round the circular rug and then another with his limbs being yanked in frustration. His strings had stayed hopelessly tangled from that day on. She sighed. She thought she'd cut any ties that bound her to this place long ago, never imagining she'd return, and certainly not with her emotions as tangled as that poor marionette's strings.

Next to the marionette, Eleanor's least favourite plaything had been the most expensive: a doll's house modelled on Henley Hall. Standing as tall as she was now, the whole front opened to reveal most of the Hall's rooms reproduced in six tiers.

Inside, furniture, paintings and four or five dolls rattled around. There was a man, her uncle she supposed, whose arm had dropped off; two women in maids' outfits who she'd relegated to the kitchen; and a butlery-sort-of figure who ended up in the wardrobe after a particularly difficult afternoon with Clifford. They had fallen out over what young ladies should and shouldn't do. None of his ideas had fitted in at all with hers as she set out to savour her moment of freedom from school rules.

Something caught her eye through the top window of the doll's house. Reaching into the miniature bedroom, she picked up the object. Turning it over in her hands she recognised it as her uncle's fob watch. He'd spent an hour one wet afternoon showing her a trick where he pulled the watch on an invisible string from pocket to pocket.

'Guess which one it's in now?' he'd said.

'That one!'

'Aha! Wrong again.'

She realised this was one of the few fond memories she had of her uncle. Most of the time he'd seemed so distant. And the rest of the time he had been away, his business taking him abroad frequently. As a child she had had no idea what his occupation was, and even now she was still in the dark. She knew he used to be in the army, but he'd retired early. Everything after that was a mystery to her.

She sighed and dropped the fob watch into her pocket, happy to have one positive memento.

As she closed the doll's house, Eleanor reflected on the irony that the one place that could have been home never had been. And yet, now it was. She owned Henley Hall. But as she turned away, she wondered if it would ever truly feel like home, the kind of home she'd dreamed of. Suddenly she felt as stifled as if she was still in that tiny buffeted cabin in the sky. She'd told Clifford that she wanted to gather her thoughts after the trip. *What rot!* Up here, being alone with her thoughts was murder. Outside had always been her haven, her escape, and she needed it right now.

As she got to the bottom of the stairs, Clifford appeared. 'Are you sufficiently rested to meet the rest of the staff, my lady?'

'Meet the staff?' Her thoughts flashed back to the anonymous maids in the doll's house. 'No, Clifford, I fear I am not sufficiently rested. Meeting the staff will need to wait a while longer.'

Throwing on her jacket, she fumbled the buttons with one hand and pulled open the front door with the other. Clifford stepped forward, blocking her way.

'My lady, it is getting dark. It is not safe to wander the grounds at night. There are several—'

Several what she never learned. Grabbing her hat, she strode past him and out into the gathering gloom.

CHAPTER 2

Outside, the weather had gone from a strong breeze to a near gale. Eleanor caught her hat as the wind snatched at it. But it wasn't the noise of the wind she heard as she battled along the drive and towards the Hall's gates: it was her uncle's bulldog. Snorting loudly, his stiff legs made him rock back and forth as he wobbled to catch up with her.

'Gladstone. What are you doing here?' As she bent down the dog licked her nose and forehead in exuberant greeting. 'Yuck!' Glad of the company, if not the slobbery kisses, she warned him that if he did any more licking he'd be sent back to the Hall.

That settled, she set off again to clear her head of those old memories. 'Okay, boy, let's see if we can walk out the stiffness and this grump. If I'm honest, you haven't seen me at my best.'

She sighed. Maybe Clifford hadn't either? And the rest of the staff, well, they hadn't met her at all. A little voice in her ear whispered to her, asking what the point was of meeting them when she might not be staying long enough to remember their names. All it would take was three maddeningly dull weeks on crowded trains and stifling steamers and she'd be back in the world she'd made for herself. A busy, adventurous life. Not one full of stuffed suits and uniforms governed by all manner of ridiculous rules and etiquette.

Maybe there was a flight back to Cape Town she could catch? The passengers had paid handsomely to be the first to fly from Cape Town to London but she doubted many would pay for a return trip. She'd travelled for free as the company she'd worked for owned the plane, but she wasn't keen on another two months of crash-landings and desert survival either.

She had no desire to meet anyone until she was in a more positive mood and the ten-minute walk up the drive to the gates hadn't achieved that yet. Sighing again, she turned right, away from the road down to the village, and puffed on up the hill with her companion in tow. After meandering for what seemed like a couple of miles, the road ended at a junction with a broken sign. As she had no idea where she was going it made no difference to her, so she plumped for the right-hand turning again and kept going.

As she tramped along the deserted lane, she tried to marshal her thoughts. 'Gladstone, my friend, what am I to do? I received a letter telling me of my uncle's death and the unexpected news he had left me Henley Hall. So… I came back, hoping I could belong here, that I could call it home.' She shook her head. 'But, as usual, I feel like a complete stranger.'

Her companion seemed to be finding her woes dull – his keen lollop had become more of a slow shuffle, his head bent forward. He'd even stopped chasing after imaginary rabbits.

There was, however, another reason for the dog's increasing lack of enthusiasm, one that now suddenly struck Eleanor. 'Gosh, I've been so lost in my own silly thoughts I hadn't noticed the rain.'

It had picked up and was now a harsh curtain of cold spite, causing Gladstone to shake his head every few minutes. Lacking any expertise on the saturation tolerance of elderly bulldogs, she worried the poor dog might catch a chill. Or worse, his genetically stiff legs might seize up altogether if the damp got into his joints.

A crash of thunder made her jump like a startled springbok. Gladstone ran to her legs and cowered under her skirt. 'Sorry, old chap.' She slid her scarf off and tied it to the dog's collar, fearful that the next clap might make him bolt. Just then a flash of lightning followed instantly by a loud crack showed the storm was nearly overhead.

She wrestled her uncle's fob watch from her pocket. Ten ten. They'd been walking for close to forty minutes and she had no idea where they were. 'Shelter, Gladstone. There must be somewhere we can hole up until this blows itself out.'

Her soaking hair stung her eyes as the wind whipped it across her face, and her drenched clothes clung to her body. As the boughs of the trees thrashed back and forth, she caught a glimmer of light through the thick hedge. A gust pulled her sideways, dragging the bulldog along with her. But it also parted the branches just enough to reveal a patch of brightness again.

'Come on, boy. Salvation!'

She struggled through the thick undergrowth and squinted through the deluge. The light was coming from some sort of shelter. 'I'll bet you a week's worth of dog snacks, Gladstone, that whoever is in that building will have coffee for me and a blanket for you.' She tried to chivvy the soaked bulldog along, but he was close to mutinying.

Finally she was near enough to see the building was a large, wooden workman's hut. But between her and the hut was a wire fence, and a wretchedly high one at that.

With shivering fingers she tied Gladstone to one of the posts, plopping her hat on his head to keep the worst of the rain out of his bloodshot eyes. 'I'll let them know we need help and come straight back for you, boy.'

He stared dolefully after her as she scrambled up the fence. As she reached the top and pulled herself over, her heart skipped a beat. On the other side of the fence was a sheer drop. *That must be forty foot or more, Ellie!* Just her luck, a quarry! A thin line of trees had hidden the sheer chalk and flint escarpment that dropped to a pool of inky-black water directly below her. Sparse bushes clung to the deep sides of the hewn-out ravine. On the far side, the ground had been levelled out into an area large enough to accommodate quarry lorries turning and the workman's hut.

She started to struggle down, tearing her dress as she did so. As another streak of lightning ripped the sky apart, and a booming clap of thunder rolled away, raised voices came from the shelter. Through the window of the dimly lit hut, she made out a man inside, his arms above his head as if in surrender.

She shook her head and blinked hard trying to clear the rain from her eyes. She couldn't be sure, but… wasn't there something about the man that was familiar? How could she attract his attention? Waving would be more effective than shouting but before she could do either she froze, suspended high on the fence, as a flash and a crack rang out. Lightning? No, that was a shot! To her horror, she saw the man fall backwards.

She scrabbled back down and dropped to the ground, winding herself in the process. It took her over a minute to untie Gladstone, as her fingers were numb with cold. She ducked behind a hawthorn bush, dragging the bemused dog with her. 'Don't you dare make a sound!' she hissed. Eleanor's mind was racing. 'Gladstone, that man might need our help. We have to find a way round this fence. There has to be an entrance somewhere. Come on!'

Keeping low to the ground, she returned to the road, which was now flooded. A car appeared out of the gloom, the headlights blinding her. She hastily stepped off the road, pulling Gladstone with her. The car passed by and disappeared into the darkness.

Even though she was soaked and freezing, Eleanor decided it was safer off the road. Pushing back through the undergrowth, she returned to the fence and followed it, dragging an increasingly reluctant bulldog in tow. Stumbling over the thick grass and snagging her coat on wildly waving branches, eventually the fence was broken by a set of open iron gates. She checked her uncle's fob watch again. Ten thirty. She'd seen the man shot about five minutes after she'd first checked the time at ten ten, which meant he'd been bleeding for fifteen minutes or more… or was already dead. She crept through the gates and across the quarry yard as fast as she dared until she could see the lit hut in front of her. The noise of the storm had receded and she could hear her heart pounding in the eerie silence.

Step up, Ellie! she chided herself. She'd been in similarly dangerous situations before but still had to force her legs to move. Perhaps it was just the icy rain running down her back, but she stopped and shivered at the entrance to the hut.

No sound. No movement.

Gladstone jerked her towards the door and then halted, sniffing the air. Inside there were a few wooden crates, a rough table and a handful of shovels leaning against the wall. Looking down at the dirt floor in the half-light, she could see a dark ominous pool.

'Blood, do you think, Gladstone?' she whispered. And given the amount of blood her instincts had been right. She'd seen a man get shot and die, of that she was sure. But like some kind of macabre magic-show trick, the body had vanished.

Back at the Hall, peeling off her soaked clothes was no easy task. However, she'd been caught in the monsoon rains of India before and half-drowned, so she was happy just to have found her way back. And happy not to have got run down. As they'd been following the road away from the quarry trying to find their way back, a motorcycle had appeared out of the dark. The driver had seen them at the last minute and swerved wildly, narrowly missing them. Regaining control of the machine, he'd sped off into the night, leaving Eleanor's heart thumping and her mind turning: why would anyone be riding so recklessly on a night like this? And on a road that, as far as she knew, only led to the quarry she'd come from and a few, widely spaced farms?

Clifford hadn't improved matters on her arrival back at the Hall, looking her up and down, lips pursed. 'Perhaps on a night such as this, my lady, it would have been wiser to travel in the Rolls? Certainly,' – he'd glanced at the sodden bulldog – 'for Master Gladstone in his advanced years.'

In fairness, she had resembled a tragic waif left to wander the moors, if there had been any moors to wander on in the Chilterns. But she had been in no mood for a lecture. Clifford seemed to be treating her as if she was a small child. Now it was her house and things would change. She'd felt her face flush with anger.

'Are you alright, my lady?'

'Oh, just dandy, Clifford. Not at all soaked, frozen or in need of a brandy after…' She'd hesitated. Why tell him what she'd seen? He'd only drone on about the social incorrectness of a lady being at a murder scene or some such nonsense. 'A warm brandy reviver will be all I require, thank you.' She'd spun round and squelched up the stairs, distractedly towing Gladstone by her scarf. He'd plodded obediently behind her, happy to comply with any wish so long as it didn't involve going back out into the rain.

In the bathroom, she rubbed him down. He wriggled in delight and the mud coating his fur had soon transferred itself to the thick cotton towel.

'Just look at the mess you've made! I'd be surprised if the housekeeper doesn't scold you for the extra laundry.'

The bulldog looked at her in disgust.

'Well, you wanted to come.' Still, maybe Clifford was right. She patted the dog's head. 'You deserve a little luxury for being such a stoic hero. And it's your house as much as mine. More so, actually.'

At that moment the housekeeper, Mrs Butters, arrived with a warmed brandy and a thoughtful plate of thickly buttered toast.

She didn't mention the state of the towels, remarking only, 'I'll fetch a couple more, you'll be needing a hot bath, I shouldn't wonder,' as she left.

Once they were alone again, Eleanor discussed a thorny subject with her newly appointed sidekick. 'The thing is, Gladstone, we witnessed a murder, so we'll have to tell the police. You're up to your ears in this as well.' Gladstone seemed unconvinced about his part in the proceedings, so she hurried on. 'Okay, I'll have to go to the police and, well, you know my views on authority.' She paused, but the bulldog seemed generally unimpressed. With a loud snort he collapsed on the remaining towels making it clear he would have no further part in the discussion.

Undaunted, Eleanor continued. 'You see, I'm not really one for running to the first uniform around. Not had the best experience. Give a man a badge and an official title and he thinks he's the sole decider of right and wrong. Which would be fine if power didn't corrupt.'

She shook her head. 'It would be better if they got more women into the police, Gladstone. There are a few, I've heard, but I doubt if the local constabulary out here are sufficiently enlightened to employ female constables.'

She paused, searching for an alternative plan and came up empty. She didn't really know anyone in the village except Clifford, and that was a very tenuous relationship. And besides, there was something about the man who'd been shot. He seemed familiar and yet… *Who could it be?* She groaned.

'Okay, the police it is.'

Gladstone thumped his tail. Was that his way of agreeing, or code for 'more toast'? Given that she had dragged him through a storm, he deserved a suitable apology. 'There you go, boy, you have the last slice.'

Mrs Butters returned to clear the plate and glass and check if more brandy was needed. She left a pile of fresh towels, and suggested that Gladstone might be better by the fire in the drawing room before leaving.

Eleanor absentmindedly brushed toast crumbs off her new sidekick with one of the fresh towels.

'Mrs Butters is obviously a far more sympathetic character than that over-stuffed shirt, Clifford. Us ladies will have to stick together!'

'Tomorrow morning! What do you mean tomorrow? Why on earth would it wait until then?'

Eleanor was staggered. It had taken her an age to get through to the police. All calls to Little Buckford's only local law-enforcement officer, one Constable Fry, had been diverted to Chipstone. Apparently the constable's wife had surprised him with the gift of triplets and he had been permitted a few days off. The thought of childbirth made Eleanor shudder. Bringing a new life into this world might be the work of God, but the mechanics of childbirth were surely the work of the devil. And triplets! What had the poor woman done to deserve that?

A bored voice asked if she was still there.

'Yes, Constable. The fact that the police force may have three new mini-recruits in the offing is of no consequence. I saw a man being murdered!'

The voice came through the receiver with more force. 'Miss, if there is *no body,* as you have assured me there wasn't, and *nobody* but you saw it, there is no point in *anybody* coming out tonight.'

The line went dead.

CHAPTER 3

The morning brought the clear calm that so often follows a storm. Perhaps it was just in contrast to the fury of the previous evening but the air was strangely still as if life itself was on pause. The shrubs bordering the semi-circular drive drooped forlornly, the London plane and lime trees that had stood proudly on the elevated lawns now hung low. Even the carpet of leaves and twigs that littered the grounds lay motionless.

Eleanor slept fitfully. At 3 a.m. she declared, *This is ridiculous, Ellie!,* rose and spent the early hours rummaging through the books from her childhood.

Breakfast should have been a relaxed affair as the police weren't due until eleven. However, waiting had never been Eleanor's chosen pastime and this morning the ticking of the clock was especially infuriating.

'Can I bring you more tea, my lady?' Clifford asked, seemingly for the hundredth time. He was bearing another plate of something she hadn't the stomach for, despite her normally robust constitution. Was it the lack of sleep? Or seeing a man murdered? Yes, that was it, watching someone die could diminish one's appetite. 'More coffee?'

She shot him a look. Was he playing games with her? 'I'm sure you just asked me that?'

'No, I asked if you wanted more tea, my lady. This is coffee.' He glanced at her cup. 'You have, it would appear, been drinking both.'

She nodded distractedly. 'I'm not too keen on breakfast right now, so I'm making up for it with liquid refreshment.'

Clifford pondered for a moment. 'Perhaps you might prefer breakfast at eleven? Although that will throw the elevenses schedule out. Or I could ask Mrs Trotman to serve breakfast at lunchtime and move lunch to suppertime? However, that would mean waking you up at midnight for supper?'

She was flummoxed. Was that humour? Sarcasm? 'Clifford, how did my uncle ever swallow your unwavering advice on his every daily action?'

'With Darjeeling and lemon, my lady.'

Thankfully at that moment Mrs Butters arrived with news of a 'gentleman policeman' waiting in the hall.

'Thank you, Mrs Butters.' She glanced at the clock on the mantelpiece: five minutes past eleven. 'Please tell the constable I will be there in fifteen minutes.'

'Very good, my lady.' Mrs Butters stayed rooted to the spot. 'Forgive me, my lady, but the gentleman did say he was in a fearsome rush.'

'In a rush, you say? In that case tell him I will be twenty-five minutes. He may wish to take tea on the settle in the hallway.'

Mrs Butters nodded and left. Clifford tilted his head in Eleanor's direction.

'I have waited precisely,' she checked the clock on the mantelpiece again, 'twelve hours for our "gentleman policeman". A small wait on his part is a fair exchange I feel.'

'Very good, my lady.'

She swore she saw the flicker of a smile pass over his face.

The clock ticked on. Clifford tidied the sausages in their salver. Eleanor straightened her cardigan buttons to line up with each other. Helpfully, the pleats of her striped tweed skirt proved more of a challenge, the bolder green lines refusing to match up with the stiffly creased folds. Her single string of pearls slid through her fingers as she counted the jewels, and then recounted twice again. She stole a glance at the mantle clock: twelve minutes past eleven. Only seven minutes had gone by. *You really must learn the art of doing nothing, Ellie, especially now you're a lady of leisure.*

'How fast time flies,' Clifford observed, offering her a get-out clause.

She took it gratefully and sprang up from the table. 'It seems unlikely I will be back for elevenses, Clifford. Perhaps Mrs Trotman could hold over her eleven o'clock delicacies until afternoon tea and move afternoon tea to suppertime as you suggested?' Having chalked up this childish point, she swept from the breakfast room.

'Constable, shall we?' Eleanor indicated the front door.

'Sergeant, if you don't mind, miss, *Sergeant* Wilby.' He tapped the stripes on his left shoulder with a gloved finger. Wisps of his moustache caught in his top lip.

She pinned her hat straight in the mirror. '*Lady* Swift, if you don't mind, Sergeant. Shall we?' *Oh dear, Ellie, you're turning into an abominable snob after less than twenty-four hours back in England!*

Outside, the sergeant's fresh-faced assistant opened the door of the Model T Ford waiting by the steps.

'Thank you, Constable…?'

'Lowe, m'lady. But I'm working hard to alleviate myself up the ranks of the force.' The young constable's accent was even more broad Buckinghamshire than his sergeant's, elongating 'a' to 'ah' and 'o' to 'ohw'.

'Well, jolly good luck to you.'

As Lowe cranked the engine into life with embarrassed difficulty, she spoke to the back of the sergeant's head.

'Is there anyone else coming down? Maybe a detective?' She hadn't meant it to sound so cutting.

'Until we are aware of what we're dealing with, Lady Swift, I saw no reason to waste precious police time,' Wilby said. 'Detectives and the like are highly trained and required on more serious cases.'

'More serious! This is murder we're talking about!'

Wilby turned in his seat. 'Then I suggest we proceed to find out about this here "murder". Drive on, Lowe.'

As the Hall's driveway met the road out of the village, Wilby spoke without turning around. 'Which way, Lady Swift?'

She consciously put her irritation on hold. A killer was on the loose after all. 'Right, up and over, right at the broken road sign, then it should appear.'

'What will appear?'

'The quarry, Sergeant.' She tried not to show her exasperation. 'Did you read over the notes you took last night during our call? It was you I spoke to, I believe?'

'Quarry?' He swivelled his eyes towards her without moving his head, or answering her question. 'I do hope you can identify the correct one. This area has a great many diggings.'

A few minutes later she rather imagined she could. 'There! There's the road junction. Turn right here.'

Trees came and went. Hedges continued about their quiet business. Verges verged. However, since turning right she'd recognised nothing from the night before.

'Lady Swift,' an exasperated voice enquired, 'is it much further?'

'The track is a little hard to spot, Sergeant. A moment, please.' It wasn't easy trying to get her bearings while they were motoring at such speed. 'I know, drive at walking pace, Constable Lowe.' Eleanor heard something muttered from the passenger seat but chose to ignore it. 'Now then, that untidy copse of undergrowth looks familiar.'

However, on closer inspection it turned out to be surprisingly unfamiliar. Lowe did make rather a meal of turning the car in the lane. If he'd waited for a wider spot instead of following his sergeant's barked order, the headlight would have fared better.

'We'll talk about that back at the station, Lowe,' grunted Wilby.

'Sorry, Sarge.' Lowe got back into the car and placed the dented rim case on the floor of the vehicle.

'Lady Swift, if you will.' Wilby was tiring of the whole escapade and rude enough to show it.

'Ah, there!' she said.

The head of the track that led down to the gravelled turning circle finally surrendered its game of hide-and-seek.

Wilby's face reddened. 'You do realise, Lady Swift, that what we have done is driven in this here motorcar for near on twenty minutes to end up where we started! That,' he pointed over her shoulder, 'is the boundary wall of Henley Hall's grounds!'

Eleanor blinked. How could it be? Then comprehension dawned…

'Well, of course, Sergeant, what do you expect? It was pitch dark, there was a violent storm raging and… and I haven't walked these roads for years. Understandably, I may have become a little disorientated and er… walked in a circle.' She cut off his reply with a raised hand. 'Now, Sergeant, shall we avoid wasting any more time and proceed?'

For a moment she was sure Wilby was going to tell Constable Lowe to turn around, but he wilted before her challenging stare and sank back into his seat, merely muttering, 'Proceed, Lowe, and watch the tyres.'

As they bumped in and out of the numerous potholes Eleanor said to the sergeant, 'I was lucky not to turn an ankle last night on this rough path.'

Wilby looked as if he wouldn't have been too bothered if Eleanor had turned both her ankles.

She ignored his look and cast around for any familiar landmarks. Finding none, she shook her head. She'd navigated herself across deserts and mountain ranges and yet hadn't realised that the quarry backed onto her uncle's estate! At the thought, a chill went through her. Before she'd seen the murder as a distant affair, but now she realised the man had been murdered no more than a stone's throw from Henley Hall itself.

CHAPTER 4

At the end of the track, Lowe stopped the car, and both men turned to face her.

'Now we walk,' she said.

'So help me…'

Ignoring the sergeant's outburst, she sprung from the car and spearheaded the way to the fence where she'd first tied Gladstone and tried to climb over. 'There! If you look through the fence to the right you can see a small hut. That's where I saw the man shot.'

Wilby peered through the fence at the drop on the other side. 'That there must be thirty foot!'

'I thought more like forty. That's why I carried on to the gates.'

'The gates?'

Lowe had obviously seen that purple hue to the sergeant's face before. 'If I may, Sarge, I do believe this track along the fence eventually leads to the quarry gates in Old Gateshead Lane. But if we go back and take the road and then Jefferson's tractor cutting, we'd be at them gates in a jiffy. And without messing up your uniform, or the lady's dress, on all this hawthorn.'

'Those gates, Lowe,' said Wilby. 'Honestly, how are you going to file a proper report with faulty grammar?'

'Sorry, sir, those gates, that's where they're to.' He turned to Eleanor. 'I know the way on account of a missing milk delivery I investigated this way last month. Kids was stealing old Jefferson's milk and hiding the empties along the track here.'

They returned to the road and the car. Lowe's shortcut turned out to be just that and they were soon pulling up at the same gates Eleanor had walked through the night before.

'Top work, Constable Lowe.' Eleanor applauded from the back seat.

'Thank you, m'lady, but those gates look mighty locked. We could ask Mr Cartwright down at Pike's Farm.' He turned to Eleanor. 'He's the farmer what owns the land that your uncle's estate backs onto. He might have a key.'

Momentarily, she wondered if she was back in South Africa as an angry trumpeting, reminiscent of an elephant, erupted from the passenger seat.

Chickens scattered in all directions as the car swung into the farmyard. A gaggle of hissing geese surrounded them.

'Morning, gentlemen. Miss.' A stocky man dressed in farmer's overalls stood in the yard. He raised a dusty cap.

Eleanor automatically took charge. 'Mr Cartwright, I presume?'

'That's right,' he said.

'Forgive us conducting the interview from the confines of this fine police vehicle, but unless you can call your geese off, I fear we must peer out at you.'

'Interview?' Cartwright frowned. 'Why am I being interviewed?'

'Relax, Mr Cartwright,' Wilby soothed, doing a poor job of hiding his scowl. 'This is Lady Swift. She has inherited Lord Henley's estate.' Cartwright shot her a look that made her glad there were others present. 'She is helping us in our enquiries. Perhaps you can be of assistance in a potential police matter?'

Eleanor rolled her eyes but bit her tongue – *potential!*

'If needs be,' Cartwright said, 'but I don't see as I'll know much, if anything.'

'It's not what you know, Mr Cartwright,' Wilby said, 'it's what you possess. A key, Mr Cartwright. We are searching for a key to the gates at the entrance to the quarry.'

Cartwright's brows formed a solid hedge across his face. 'Them gates is always locked.'

'Those gates,' mumbled Lowe.

Eleanor's minimal patience was wearing thin. 'That's as may be, Mr Cartwright, but do you have a key or not?'

Cartwright scratched his head. 'I got a key somewhere on account of it being my land but I leased that whole patch to the quarry company, though they've not worked it for some time. Not sure they'd be too pleased at folk poking around.' He looked pointedly at Eleanor.

'No doubt, Mr Cartwright,' Eleanor agreed, 'but if they knew there had been a murder—'

'Reported murder,' Wilby corrected.

Oh dear, this uniformed buffoon was getting extremely tiresome. She smiled at the farmer. 'Mr Cartwright, we would be most appreciative of the use of your key.'

'Best I meet you up there in a moment then.' Cartwright strode off towards the farmhouse.

Finally, it seemed things were going the way of an actual police investigation: a witness, two policemen, a murder scene, and even the means of accessing it.

After Cartwright unlocked the gates, Lowe drove through and pulled up facing the workman's hut. Wilby climbed out of the vehicle.

'Lady Swift, please just show us what you think you witnessed and where you think you witnessed it.'

'For your official police record, Sergeant Wilby, I don't *think* I witnessed anything. I *know* I did.'

Cartwright followed them across the yard to the entrance of the hut.

'Was there a light inside this here hut?' Wilby asked.

'Yes, through the window I saw a man with his arms up in front of him. Then,' she hastened on, 'I was about to try to gain his attention when—'

'Could you identify the man in a line-up?'

'I could not be certain of that, regrettably, but there was something about him. I'm fairly sure I'd seen him before.'

Wilby seemed unconvinced. 'And where would you have seen this here gentleman before?'

Eleanor thought hard. 'I-I really can't say.' She shrugged.

Wilby's face registered disbelief.

She glared at him. 'First, I forgot to say, I heard shouting… well, raised voices.'

Wilby leaned forward. 'Did you hear what they were saying, I wonder?'

'The wind… I… no, I didn't.'

'Lowe!' Wilby turned on his heels and made to climb back into the car.

'Halt!' Eleanor was a long way past the end of her very limited patience. 'Sergeant Wilby, I have not, as you are acutely aware, finished telling you the full set of events. Am I to have to go to your superiors and report that you left a murder scene,' she emphasised, 'without gathering at least half the facts?'

'Lady Swift.' Wilby twitched his moustache as if it were trying to stifle a sneeze. 'We of His Majesty's Constabulary are most busy and would appreciate you telling us the facts a sight faster.'

Eleanor bit back a caustic reply and continued with her account. 'First came a shot and the man fell backwards.'

'What time was this?'

Eleanor thought for a moment. 'I left the Hall about nine thirty and checked my watch just before I saw the light in the hut. It was ten ten, but it was about another five minutes before I saw the man shot, so roughly ten fifteen.'

'A question. Was there any more lightning when this "shot" was fired?'

'No.'

'And what did you do then?'

'I took evasive action and grabbed Gladstone as I did so.'

'Gladstone?'

'My uncle's… my bulldog.'

'So you grabbed this dog and when you stood up again?'

'I went back to the road and nearly got hit by a car in the dark.'

'Dark.' Wilby pulled a small notebook from his top pocket and wrote what appeared to be three short lines. 'Then you thought you would be a good Samaritan and see if the poor fellow who you thought was dead needed any help?'

'I wasn't a hundred per cent certain he was dead. Because I wasn't standing next to him when he died… I mean, when he was shot. And yes, I thought I would do the decent thing and double check. But when I got there, it must have taken me at least a quarter of an hour, there was no body.'

'You mean nobody?'

'No. You know perfectly well I mean that the body was missing. And there was nobody there either. I looked in the hut too.'

Lowe gave a quiet whistle.

Wilby shuffled over to the hut and gave the inside a perfunctory glance. 'Did you see anything else that might clarify the events of your story?'

Eleanor's eyes narrowed as she called back. 'I saw a patch on the ground. Gladstone thought the patch to be most interesting and I struggled to pull him away from it. I am sure it was blood.'

Wilby glanced around the dirt floor of the hut. 'Am I missing this patch of yours, perhaps? The ground appears to be clear of any perceptive stain.'

'Perceptible, you mean. Perceptive is what the police are supposed to be.'

Wilby flipped his notebook shut and climbed into the car. 'Thank you for your time, Lady Swift. We have recorded your report and will be in touch if any *actual* evidence turns up.'

Eleanor turned to Lowe. 'Thank you for the lift. I shall, however, walk myself home as…'

She was about to say 'as it's not far' but felt there was no need to point out that small detail again.

'As I fear any more minutes spent in the company of your sergeant might lead to a second murder occurring. And this time there will be quite a sizeable body! Good day.'

CHAPTER 5

That afternoon, while she was taking Gladstone for a walk around the garden, Eleanor realised something odd: she was furious and disappointed at the same time. 'Clifford knows perfectly well why I had the police round, as I told him the full story this morning, but he hasn't said a single word about it. You know, Gladstone, I simply can't fathom that man out.'

Gladstone's look suggested he'd rather be chasing a ball, if it was all the same to her.

'Fair enough, boy, go find a ball and we'll see if we can run a little of the fat off you.' At the 'b' word, the bulldog's ears picked up, and he loped off into the undergrowth.

She sat on one of the stone benches and gazed out over the grounds. The gardens had been designed by a friend of her uncle's, who had a taste for exotic plants. Peppered with bergamot and ornamental grasses, the striped lawn at the back of the house ran down from an imposing balustrade that encircled the entire back of the house. Beyond this, less formal greenways sloped away, intermingling with beech, sweet gums and pin oaks.

Dotted around the lawns were marble statues, her favourite being the girl in the pinafore. During her rare childhood visits, she'd often sat cross-legged on the grass and confided her troubles to her silent marble companion.

The music of the trickling water that cascaded from the central stone fountain pulled her back to the present. It felt odd to own it all now that her uncle had passed away. She'd known he had no other relatives once his sister, her mother, had… disappeared. The Swifts had been one of the few aristocratic families to ensure that their estate and title passed equally to male and female heirs, so she was already Lady Swift. The Henleys had made the same provisions, so she supposed she could theoretically call herself Lady Henley, but she would always be Lady Swift, in memory of her parents.

She'd never expected to find herself being the last surviving member of her family.

Even odder than owning all these grounds she surveyed was to think that a man had died just beyond them. She slapped her forehead, realising what Clifford had been trying to warn her about as she ran out of the door last night! If the estate was surrounded by quarry diggings, it would indeed be a dangerous place for the unwary, especially in the dark.

She shivered. And dangerous for other reasons too. Because out there, just beyond the safety of the estate, a killer had been lurking.

A cough made her start. She glanced up. *How does he do that? He just appears from nowhere.*

'Good afternoon, Clifford.'

'Good afternoon, my lady. Perhaps you are sufficiently rested to formally meet the rest of the staff?'

Eleanor groaned. She hated formal. 'Let's say an informal meeting in fifteen minutes?'

'Very good, my lady.' He left with his customary half-bow.

The whole meeting-the-staff episode was less painful than Eleanor had feared. As she entered the sunlit morning room, they shuffled into an untidy line along the walnut display cases. Clifford indicated for the first person to step forward. 'Mrs Butters, the housekeeper.'

Mrs Butters' diminutive height, cuddly figure and soft, round face gave her the air of everyone's favourite aunt. She beamed a motherly smile at Eleanor.

'Yes, of course, Mrs Butters, we have met,' said Eleanor.

Mrs Butters giggled. 'It was a pleasure to meet you, my lady. We were all so excited at your coming to stay… to live at the Hall.'

'Thank you.'

Clifford swished her back into line with a deft waft of his hand. 'Mrs Trotman, the cook.' Clifford's head barely moved as he indicated for her to step up.

A pristinely aproned woman, the shape of the perfect English pear, met Lady Eleanor's gaze with a quiet smile. 'Welcome, my lady. It is a joy to meet you. We all hope you will be very happy here at Henley Hall.'

'Why, thank you, Mrs Trotman, I do too,' said Eleanor. 'And I must congratulate you on your paprika relish, it dressed the sausages perfectly at breakfast.'

The cook blushed and with a muttered, 'Most kind, my lady,' she stepped back into line.

'Polly, the maid.' Clifford gestured to a gangly streak of a girl, barely fifteen, Eleanor guessed. The young girl jiggled nervously on her willowy legs and curtseyed awkwardly. 'Welcome, your ladyship. 'Tis an honour to meet you.'

'Thank you, Polly. It is a delight to meet you too.'

The man with a weather-sculpted face and rough hands didn't wait for Clifford's cue to step forward. 'Joseph Wendon, my lady. It's been my passion to care for the gardens for nigh on twenty year for his lordship, your late uncle, God rest his soul.'

'Thank you, Joseph. I've already enjoyed them a great deal.' Looking along the line of welcoming faces, she continued. 'My late uncle was most fortunate to have the blessing of such dedicated and skilled staff. I hope we will continue where he so unfortunately had to leave off.' She was nowhere near deciding whether to stay or dash back to the safety of her old, chaotic but familiar life, but it seemed better not to reveal that.

Clifford broke the silence. 'There is one more member of the staff, my lady, regrettably he is not with us today.'

'Oh, yes, and who is that?'

'Silas, my lady. The gamekeeper.'

Joseph's smile widened. Polly blushed. Eleanor simply nodded, having seen no sign of game or a gamekeeper since her arrival.

Clifford coughed and stood a little straighter, if that was possible. 'On behalf of all the staff, may I offer you our sincere condolences at the passing of your uncle.'

All eyes looked expectantly at her. She wasn't prepared for this.

'Thank you for your kindness. However, I imagine it is you who miss him more than me.' That hadn't come out right. She hurried on. 'I would have loved to have made the funeral but I didn't receive the details of Lord H—, of my uncle's death… and funeral arrangements… until it was too late. I was out in the Veldt, the bush, exploring new routes for safaris…' She shrugged. 'It can be difficult to be found out there. Communication is sometimes a little hit and miss.'

Clifford inclined his head. 'We quite understand, my lady. Your uncle and I spent some time in South Africa.' At Clifford's flick of one finger, the staff filed out.

Out of nowhere Eleanor found herself asking, 'What did you call my uncle, Clifford?'

'Lord Henley, my lady.'

'I mean when it was just the two of you?' she pressed.

Clifford hesitated. 'Tex.'

'Tex?'

'Your uncle spent some time in the United States. He was a great fan of the silent movies, particularly of westerns.'

'My uncle really was quite the English eccentric, wasn't he, Clifford?'

'Yes, my lady. The Henleys have always been on the cutting edge of unconventional. And perhaps the Swifts too?'

'Perhaps, Clifford.'

He held the door respectfully as Eleanor wandered out into the hallway.

'Forgive me, my lady.' Mrs Butters was waiting. 'May I speak with Mr Clifford?'

'Of course, go right ahead, Mrs Butters.'

'Mr Clifford, were you planning to venture into the village this afternoon? I can't be waiting for Mr Penry's boy to deliver tomorrow. If you're not going, I'll send Polly, and just hope she manages better this time.' She smiled wryly.

'No, Mrs Butters. My schedule does not include venturing into the wilds of Little Buckford today.'

'Oh, no matter, Mr Clifford. Just asking.'

Eleanor snapped to. This was her chance to get out of the stifling atmosphere of the Hall.

'Mrs Butters, my schedule absolutely includes such a venture. I will complete the errands.'

'Oh, my lady, I couldn't!' the housekeeper flustered. 'Thank you kindly for your offer but that wouldn't do at all.' She faltered at Clifford's deep inhalation.

'I insist. I wish to become acquainted with the village and its undoubtedly interesting and colourful inhabitants. Leave me a list. I shall depart in twenty minutes.' Without waiting for a reply, she made her escape upstairs to grab a jacket.

CHAPTER 6

After passing through the gates, Eleanor adjusted her stride to make it easier for her increasingly faithful sidekick to keep pace. Life at the Hall might be looking up, but there was the matter of a cold-blooded murderer on the loose. With the police as hopeless and disinterested as a flapper in a nunnery, she'd have to tackle the investigation herself. And a trip to the village would give her just such an opportunity.

At the brow of the hill, she paused and looked around. The view across the valley was one of peaceful beauty. The only sound was the piercing whistle of red kites. It was an eerie call, but she felt strangely comforted by it. It took her back to the few childhood days she'd spent wandering the grounds of Henley Hall, wishing there was something tangible to do with the summer holidays.

Below her, Little Buckford nestled among the fields and woods like a picture postcard. From the medieval flint church, the short high street ran the length of just seven small shops and a reading room, before meeting the village common and the well-populated duck pond. A series of cobbled lanes ran off in three directions to the higgledy-piggledy clusters of thatched roofs dotted between apple orchards and neatly planted vegetable gardens. Murder surely had no place here.

Eleanor breathed out deeply. 'Murder or no murder, the country air is good for the soul, Gladstone. And walking is excellent for the health. But slow. I think I shall look to buying a bicycle. I used to cycle a lot, you know.'

Gladstone jerked his head up.

'Hmm, good point. I don't think there is a basket large enough for such a sturdy beast as yourself. I'd certainly get my fitness back though, pedalling you up these slopes.' She looked beyond the village at the distant landscape, an unbroken swathe of green fields and copses peppered by clouds of white flowering blackthorn. 'It's funny, this all feels so familiar and yet I came so few times growing up.' She sighed. 'Come on, my trusty sidekick. Let's go investigating!'

The curtains in the first three houses on the opposite side of the street to Eleanor all twitched in unison. Eleanor smiled. She was used to drawing curious looks. And none more so than in a sleepy village like Little Buckford where nothing much happened. Except, it seemed, murder.

She swung into the first shop on Mrs Butters' list. The sign outside promised 'Penry's Butchery, the finest cuts'.

'Good afternoon.' She smiled at the aproned heifer of a man behind the counter.

'Good afternoon, Lady Swift.'

She wondered how he knew who she was. 'You must be Mr Penry?'

'Dylan Penry at your service, m'lady. It is a great pleasure to have you visit my humble shop.' The lilt of his sing-song Welsh accent was charming.

'I can see you run a most well-provisioned and spotless place of business, Mr Penry. Here is a list Mrs Butters has entrusted me with.'

Penry's eyebrows shot up. 'Well, that's quite the thing, Mrs Butters sending you on errands.'

'Yes, it is unusual, I suppose. However, I volunteered, so the slight is upon my character, not Mrs Butters.' She placed the list on the wooden counter, noting the neatly stacked wrapping papers and perfectly wound string on its bobbin.

'Right so, m'lady, let's see what we're up against today then.' Taking up the list with his sausage-like fingers he read the paper carefully. 'Mrs Trotman will be after making one of her specials, I see. I'll be back in a minute.' He lumbered out of view into the rear of the shop.

While waiting, Eleanor admired the shelves of fine pickles and sauces. In the three glass-fronted cabinets lay trays of precisely sliced meat cuts, displayed like works of art, each separated by a thin line of fresh green herbs. An extensive selection of fine crust pies filled one section of the window, offset by links of sausages framing the display area.

Penry lumbered back into the front of the shop, with his hands full of carefully wrapped packages. 'That's almost all, m'lady. Just the finest of chops in addition.'

Never one to hesitate, Eleanor saw her opportunity. 'The Little Buckford community are lucky to have such a fine establishment as yours. Tell me, do you deliver to the outer edges of the area?'

'Well, Mrs Penry drives our van on the round, Wednesdays and Saturdays.'

'And does she drive past Henley Hall? I passed what I believe was a quarry that way.'

'A quarry? Most of our outlying customers are to the south of the village, no trade out past the Hall. Indeed, your late uncle could have been said to be our most northerly customer, you see.' He laughed at a joke that escaped her entirely. Once he'd contained himself, he continued. 'I've no idea about the quarries, except there's a few and the wagons have gone quiet these past six months or so.'

With an innocent air Eleanor enquired, 'I ran into a Mr Cartwright out that way, the quarry was on his land. Do you know him?'

Penry stiffened at the name. 'Thomas Cartwright has no need of my butcher's shop.' He strung up the last of the parcels with an extra-sharp twist of the knot.

Eleanor's eyes glinted. It seemed Mr Cartwright was not wholly beloved in Little Buckford. 'Really, Mr Penry? I find it hard to believe that Mr Cartwright would have no need of your excellent shop. Is he, perhaps, a vegetarian?'

'Good Lord, no!' Penry shook his head. 'There's nothing wrong with Thomas Cartwright in that department. He's still got all his own teeth and can chew meat just fine.'

Eleanor smiled weakly. 'I rather thought vegetarians avoided meat on moral, rather than dental, grounds, Mr Penry?'

The butcher looked uncomfortable. 'I hate to disagree, m'lady, but you're surely not suggesting a man in full control of his mental faculties would voluntarily avoid eating all meat? Why, the poor man would be dead within a year at most.'

Eleanor felt she needed to get the conversation back on track. 'Well, if Mr Cartwright isn't a vegetarian, why has he no need of your shop?'

Penry shuffled his feet behind the counter. 'The fact is, Thomas Cartwright may, or may not, have need of my shop, but either way he's not welcome here. I may not understand the morals of those new-fangled "vegetables", I mean, those—'

'Vegetarians, Mr Penry?'

'Thank you, m'lady, those vegetarians, but I understand the morals of Thomas Cartwright even less!' He placed her packages on the counter. 'Now, I almost forgot the most important package of all.' The conversation about Mr Cartwright was obviously over. He wrapped a giant knuckle bone in brown paper and handed it to her. 'For Master Gladstone.'

'Thank you, Mr Penry. It has been delightful meeting you. Now, I must be off to continue my walk.'

'Your feet will always bring you to where your heart is.'

She turned back to him, surprised.

He smiled. 'It is a Welsh expression, m'lady. Good morning.'

*

Walking back to the Hall, she observed, 'So, it seems Mr Penry considers Mr Cartwright a man of lax morals. Lax enough, perhaps, to commit murder? What we need to establish, Gladstone, is where exactly Cartwright was at the time I saw the man shot. We shall have to investigate further. You know, Gladstone, I think women are naturally good at this detective lark. I believe I mentioned that the more progressive police forces in this country have a scattering of brave ladies among their ranks.' She stopped in her stride and fixed the bulldog with a withering look. 'Although I'm told that the women officers are only allowed to patrol the streets in pairs with…' she spluttered '… with two male officers walking some yards behind them!'

She decided her companion looked suitably shocked. 'Exactly!' She set off again with Gladstone shaking his head, possibly in disbelief, though it might just have been her rather too forceful pull on his lead. 'They say that behind every great man is a great woman. But it seems that behind every trailblazing female constable is a lumbering male nanny!'

Eleanor's thoughts on the British police force were interrupted by the sound of wailing as she entered the front door of the Hall.

'Polly, what on earth's the matter? Has someone been hurt?'

All the young maid could manage was to jiggle from leg to leg and mumble, 'Oh mercy, your ladyship!'

The poor girl was obviously in shock. Did one slap servants if they were hysterical? Eleanor wished she'd had more training in these matters. While working in the bush she would certainly have slapped one of her guides if they had come over all histrionic, but here?

Clifford materialised, saving her from having to make what might have been a rash decision.

'Not hurt, my lady. Dead.'

Polly wailed louder. Clifford clicked his tongue and she scurried away down the corridor.

'Dead, you say?' Eleanor gasped. 'Not one of the staff, surely?' She had no idea how to engage new help. This would be a disaster.

Should she take charge and administer sweet tea, or whatever else might calm her remaining staff's nerves? Could one administer brandy to one's staff? She shook her head. *You have so much to learn, Ellie.* She tuned back in to Clifford, who was waiting patiently.

'Er, who exactly is dead, Clifford?'

'Mr Spencer Atkins. A most tragic loss.'

So it wasn't one of the staff! Before she could rejoice, a thought struck her: maybe she was being a tad insensitive? 'Did you know the man, Clifford?'

'Yes, my lady. Mr Atkins was a good friend of your late uncle.'

A memory flashed into her brain. Of course, she remembered him. A tall and angular man with an earnest expression that didn't quite fit with his bright-blue eyes and the wilful tuft of hair that continually escaped his best efforts with the brilliantine.

Several times when she was staying, he'd turned up to dine and play cards with her uncle. And he'd always gone out of his way to include her. Well, not when they were smoking cigars and drinking port, obviously, but, on the whole, she remembered him as a more sympathetic character than her uncle. Indeed, one summer when her uncle had been absent for the whole holiday, Atkins had unexpectedly turned up one wet afternoon with a jigsaw puzzle. He and Eleanor had spent several fun hours together, lying on the floor in the morning room among various puzzle pieces.

'But, Clifford, how did it happen?'

'An apparent accident. Mr Atkins was cleaning his shotgun when it went off.'

Eleanor froze. An image from the night before flashed across her eyes. 'Clifford, do you have any recent photographs of Mr Atkins?'

'Naturally, my lady.'

She waited expectantly until he returned with a framed print.

Eleanor stared at the photo. Yes, he had more lines around his face than she'd remembered. And his hair was thinner, as was he. But the man smiling back at her from the photo was definitely the man she'd spent those carefree hours with, sprawled on the floor among puzzle pieces.

And definitely the man she'd seen shot at the quarry.

CHAPTER 7

The news of Mr Atkins' death had obviously hit the household hard. Clifford had kept his professional air of detachment, but the kitchen had been unusually quiet, while Polly's eyes had been red-rimmed whenever Eleanor passed her in the hall. Eleanor wanted to hug the young girl, but felt she'd already broken enough house rules and worried the young maid would just be mortified rather than comforted.

In truth Eleanor was struggling to come to terms with Atkins' death herself. Especially as she suspected he hadn't died accidentally while cleaning his gun, but rather had been murdered, possibly by the mysterious motorcyclist at the quarry. She'd tried to find out more details about Atkins' death from Clifford, but it seemed the police hadn't released any further information as yet, except that the body had been discovered at seven that morning by Mr Atkins' housekeeper when she arrived for work.

With Clifford being out doing whatever it was butlers did, the housekeeper arranged breakfast the following morning. Eleanor found Mrs Butters was in a subdued mood but as genial a presence as ever. Despite the somewhat heavy atmosphere, as the housekeeper busied herself about the salvers, easy conversation flowed between them.

'Tell me, Mrs Butters, when was the last time Mr Atkins was at the Hall?'

The housekeeper paused in checking the sausage salver. 'Let me think, now. I believe Mr Atkins came round for dinner only a few days before…' She paused and shook her head sadly. 'Before your uncle himself passed away.'

The housekeeper was obviously upset.

Eleanor hesitated to speak, but if the police believed the death to be an accident, then who was there but her to establish the true facts? She owed it to the man who had taken the trouble to befriend her on his visits to the Hall to see justice done and his murderer caught.

'And what was Mr Atkins' connection with my uncle? Was he a business partner, or just a friend?'

Mrs Butters replaced the lid on the salver. 'Mr Atkins worked in London a lot of the time, in some government office, I don't know which. Mr Clifford would. Your uncle knew him because they were neighbours. Well, nearly. Mr Atkins' house is straight up the road past Cartwright's farm. I think they first met at a shooting party at Langham Manor.'

'I see. Was Mr Atkins a good shot?'

'I really couldn't say, my lady, you'd need to ask Mr Clifford, he'll know.'

'Thank you, Mrs Butters, I'll do so on his return. One last question, did Mr Atkins' job have anything to do with quarries?'

'Quarries! I wouldn't have thought a man of his standing would have been found dead in such a place, my lady.'

And yet he was, Ellie!

She took a gulp of coffee and decided she'd revisit the murder scene straight away while everything was still fresh in her mind. 'Thank you for a wonderful breakfast, Mrs Butters. And please thank Mrs Trotman. I fear I may burst if I am tempted by another morsel of her yummy fare beyond what's already on my plate.'

Mrs Butters laughed. 'Your late uncle often said that very thing. And most often at breakfast too.' She placed a stack of plates on an oval silver tray.

'Well, my system needs a kick after that mountain of sausages,' Eleanor waved her full fork, 'and Clifford isn't here to chide me for mucking up the meal schedule. So,'– she smiled at the housekeeper – 'if it won't put you all out too much, I shall sail out the front door and return whenever I am done.'

'What a delightful idea, my lady. Please enjoy your day. Food as befits whatever time you return will be easily prepared in a trice.' Balancing the overladen tray, Mrs Butters left with a cheery smile, pulling the door closed behind her with the front of her shoe.

'Gladstone, my friend, I fear you should stay behind and catch up on your sleep.' The drumming of his tail let her know he agreed.

She fed him a corner of toast she'd saved. 'The thing is, Gladstone, one thing I've learned since I was, well, orphaned I suppose, is you need to look after yourself. It's obvious no one believes me about the man I saw shot in the quarry, so what's the point of telling them that it was Atkins when they're all convinced he accidentally killed himself?'

The bulldog was too busy licking up toast crumbs that had fallen from his jowls to reply.

Eleanor, however, took this as tacit agreement. 'Exactly, and if you want something done, do it yourself. Mr Atkins was good to me the few times I met him, more so than my uncle or that stuffed shirt, Clifford, so I owe it to him to see justice done.' Gladstone looked up at her with his doleful eyes and licked her nose. She patted him on the head. 'It's good to have an ally, Gladstone, even if a rather licky one. I have a feeling I'm going to need all the help I can get to solve this mystery.'

As she closed the front door of the Hall behind her, the air outside was giving up the last breaths of a crisp dawn frost and yielding to the warmth of the morning sunshine. A deep blue gave the sky that rare promise of an endless summer soon to arrive. Once out of the Hall's grounds, she set off toward 'Murder Quarry', as she had dubbed it.

As she walked, she wondered if she could really solve a murder case. True, she'd been in some serious scrapes before, but she didn't have the foggiest clue about solving a murder. *Where on earth does one start, Ellie?* Well, the murder scene would be a good place, so she could tick that box straight away as she was already heading there. Feeling pleased with herself, she counted off on her fingers the questions she needed answers to: why was Atkins at the quarry that night? Had he come to meet the man who murdered him? Who was the second man at the quarry? Was he the motorcyclist who had almost run her down? In which case, Atkins' murderer and the mysterious motorcyclist were one and the same person. Surely all she had to do then was find the motorcycle and that would lead to the motorcyclist and the murderer!

She mentally patted herself on the back. This crime solving was easier than she'd first thought. Then she remembered the next question she needed an answer to: what had happened to the body?

As she strode on, her mind turned this over. After a few minutes her head hurt and as she'd come up with no real answers, she turned to the matter of suspects. Well, it was early days, but Mr Cartwright was certainly looking like a contender. Why had he said the quarry gates were always locked? On the night of the murder she'd walked right through them. True, they'd been locked when she arrived the following day with the inept Sergeant Wilby and Constable Lowe. Yes, that morning 'them gates' had been locked alright. But the night before…

Eleanor's pace quickened. She'd decided she would show the police how it was done and interview Thomas Cartwright herself. After all, if she left the murder investigation in their incompetent hands, Atkins' murderer would never be caught.

Maybe she should make another foray into Little Buckford as well, under the guise of running some more errands for Mrs Butters. She needed to find out more about why Cartwright was persona non grata, certainly to some of Little Buckford's inhabitants.

As she continued to her new destination of Pike's Farm, the hedgerows twittered with the chatter of various birds. Different birds were singing their hearts out. However, Eleanor couldn't distinguish any of them. In fact, the only bird she could name was the brave robin redbreast who was fluttering curiously alongside her.

Ah! Thinking of birds, there was the small matter of Cartwright's vicious geese. Eleanor had spent her early childhood and large parts of her adult life in countries where the majority of the animals were trying to either kill you or eat you (or both). Since, by the time you worked out whether or not an animal was dangerous, you could be dead or a mummified snack, she had a somewhat jaundiced view of wildlife in general.

Spying a stout length of hawthorn, she picked it up and swished it in the air. 'Perfect! Let's see those pests try any of their geesey ways on me!'

Thirty minutes later she stood at the entrance to Pike's Farm. The farmhouse itself was a fine example of the local flint dwellings of the Chilterns: a large building with a hotchpotch of angled roofs and outbuildings. The immediate wall boasted one small round window, bordered by a circle of red bricks and flanked by two recently repainted iron cross braces either side.

She looked around the yard, which was surprisingly free of pecking and hissing guards. A row of higgledy barns lined the right flank, while the central driveway continued straight on to a sturdy gate that secured the first of Cartwright's fields.

Unfamiliar with the protocol of seeking a farmer on his property, she looked around, dismissing the house. He was unlikely to be sitting with his feet up having tea. Was it lambing season? Then again, did Cartwright even have sheep? Or was this an arable farm? Eleanor didn't have the patience for these kinds of questions and plumped for searching the barns instead.

In the first outbuilding, she found a stack of straw bales and a barn owl watching her from its lofty perch on a rafter. In the second, there was a stack of poultry feed and a dead rat.

'Lovely!'

She was coming out of the second barn when she caught her breath and ducked back inside. Looking around, she spotted a shaft of light coming through a split plank in the barn's side. By bending down and squinting through the crack, she could clearly see across the yard to the far outbuildings. In the shadow of the largest, a man was handing Cartwright a large brown-paper-wrapped parcel in exchange for a sum of money.

She couldn't see the man's face as he had his back to her, but what she could see was a motorcycle leaning against the wall inside the outbuilding. It did look rather like the one that had almost run her down. As to the man with the package, she couldn't say if he was the rider that night. It was so dark and squally, and the rider had had on a large, shapeless rain cape and goggles.

Cartwright and the mysterious stranger looked up at the sound of a low-flying plane. Eleanor lay flat against the barn wall, hoping they hadn't seen her. Once the sound of the plane had passed, she peeped through her spyhole, only now the outbuilding door had been closed and both men had disappeared.

'I presume you've come for an insight into the farming life, Lady Swift?' Cartwright was leaning in the doorway, looking unimpressed by her unannounced visit. All she could think of was to be engrossed in studying the dead rat. 'There are some traps in the next barn you might like to see?' he offered.

She turned. 'Why, Mr Cartwright, what a splendid idea. But I fear even though we are now neighbours you are far too busy serving our community's agricultural needs to be wasting time showing me the workings of a model farm such as this.'

'You'd be right on that. So, to what do I owe your gracious visit then? Would it be summat along the lines of more murder business?'

'How shrewd you are, Mr Cartwright.'

His lack of surprise at seeing her was unnerving. Did he know she'd seen his clandestine trade with the mystery man?

'Folks call me Thomas as a rule.'

'Excellent! Now, Mr Cartwright, have the police called to ask you any further questions?'

'Nope. Why would they? I can't see nothing of the quarry down here. Look for yourself. Middle field rises up so you can't see over the brow.'

Eleanor couldn't argue with that. In the distance lambs called. Ah! Mystery solved – a sheep farm. 'I appreciate you are busy, Mr Cartwright, so forgive me for detaining you.' She tried a smile. Cartwright's expression remained as hard as the stone wall he was leaning against. Eleanor shrugged – she hadn't come to make friends. 'I have been feeling perplexed by something you said to Sergeant Wilby and myself.'

Cartwright shifted slightly. 'And that would be?'

'As you know, when we went up to the quarry, the one that borders my uncle… *my* grounds and you followed the police car, the gates were indeed locked. However, only the night before, at around ten thirty I think, I had walked through them unhindered. How could that have been? It has got me wondering because I thought I heard you say they are always locked.'

'No idea. T'aint no business of mine. Like I told you, I leased that land to the quarry firm long time ago. What they do over there's none of my affair, long as they don't upset the livestock. They said gates had to be locked to stop fools' – he looked pointedly at Eleanor – 'from falling in the pits and messing with the machinery.'

'What a good job I'm not a fool then, Mr Cartwright, because those gates were definitely open that night.'

'If you say so.'

'I do, Mr Cartwright. And I wonder, Mr Cartwright, if you own a motorcycle?'

The farmer looked at her quizzically. 'What would I be doing with a motorcycle? You can't round up half a dozen stray sheep and take them back to the farm on a ruddy motorcycle, can you?'

'Indeed not, but you might have one just for the fun of it.'

Cartwright grunted. 'I'm a farmer, Lady Swift, not one of your entitled set. I don't own anything for fun. Everything I own has to earn its keep, and a motorcycle ain't going to do that on a farm.'

'Quite, Mr Cartwright. I have one more question. Where were you the evening of the murder between say, ten and eleven thirty? Perhaps you saw or heard something?'

Cartwright glared at her.

She tightened her grip on the geese stick. In an emergency she was adept enough at defending herself to take a man's eye out with such a weapon, but Cartwright's eyes followed her action and seemed to find it more amusing than threatening.

'If you must pry, I had my tea with the wife and then I settled into sharpening a box of hand tools by the fire.'

'So you were indoors *all* evening?'

Cartwright nodded and gestured towards the road. 'Now if you'll be so good as to remove yourself from these premises, I'll be getting back to my business.'

'Thank you for your time, Mr Cartwright. You've been most helpful in my investigation of the murder.'

'It's a rummy kind of murder without a body, and no cartridge cases left at the scene I'd say.'

Dash it! She hadn't thought of that. 'Are you saying you don't believe there was a murder?'

'I'm not saying anything either way. I wasn't there, after all. Just seems an unlikely set of facts. Now as I said I'll be getting back to my business.'

She nodded. 'Of course, I've taken up enough of your time already.' She half-turned to go, but then stopped. 'Oh, by the way, did you hear the news about poor old Mr Atkins?'

Cartwright's eyes narrowed. 'I heard, alright. Man always was a fool.'

Eleanor stiffened. 'That's no way to talk of the dead, Mr Cartwright. He was a neighbour of yours, I believe?'

Cartwright looked at her coldly. 'Lady Swift, I say what I think. The man was my neighbour and a worst neighbour you couldn't have. I wasn't surprised when I heard, he had no idea how to handle a gun.'

'But you obviously do, Mr Cartwright. Especially a shotgun, I would think, being a farmer?'

Cartwright nodded. 'Now as I said, for the third time, I'll be getting back to my business.'

Eleanor was desperate to ask him why Atkins had been such a bad neighbour, but it was obvious Cartwright considered their conversation over. She'd just have to ask Clifford later, he was bound to know. He knew everything.

The roar of a plane that skimmed the roof of the farmhouse interrupted her thoughts. Cartwright shook his fist at the sky. 'Oh, but there'll likely be a real murder sometime if he don't stop that!'

Eleanor had shielded the sun from her eyes and was still staring at the plane as it turned over a field somewhere behind the barns. 'Who is that?'

'It's that young fool who pays to use the next field for his flying antics but I'll have to consider stopping that arrangement after all his shenanigans. He drives that plane so as to scare the sheep, I'm sure of that. Shame, mind – he pays well enough for it.' Cartwright brightened. 'You should ask him, young moneybags. He's got the bird's-eye view up there. Always hanging his beaky nose out of the cockpit, staring at my missus. If anyone knows anything about goings on at that quarry, it'll be him.'

'Capital idea, Mr Cartwright, I'm most grateful.'

'And I'll be most grateful not to find you sniffing round my barns in future, Lady Swift. I'll be sure to keep the geese out from now on.' Cartwright turned without a word and strode up the central driveway.

She shivered at the image of a pack of Cartwright's geese bearing down on her, hissing and flapping those hideous wings. Or was that turkeys? Whatever, she'd rather face a charging rhino, at least rhinos didn't attack you in flocks.

'Charming fellow, that Cartwright.' She addressed her remarks in the general direction of the dead rodent. 'And quite definitely at the top of my suspect list!' In fact, if she was honest, he was the *only* person on her suspect list, apart from the mysterious motorcyclist. But perhaps she was about to add another…

CHAPTER 8

The plane's landing place was easy to spot as Eleanor trudged across the field looking for a way into the makeshift airstrip. A gap in the hedge, where two hawthorn trees hadn't yet grown together, presented an opportunity. She squeezed through, shielding her face with one hand and holding her hat with the other. Glancing down at her mud-spattered boots and ripped dress, Eleanor wondered if Mrs Butters had an above-average tolerance for a housekeeper. She might be needing it.

On the other side of the hedge the sun seemed brighter and her dress even more torn. She squinted across to the plane. Ah! Movement! She wasn't too late. She swished through the swathe of long grass and umbrellas of cow parsley bordering the field. The shorter grass, which had presumably been cut low to make a rudimentary landing strip, made for speedier progress and she soon reached the plane.

Resplendent in its coat of vibrant blue paint, with its intricately carved wooden propeller, it looked as majestic and dainty as a dragonfly. Between the two sets of short, wide wings, sat the teardrop cockpit from where the muffled clang of what sounded like tools was the only response to Eleanor's hollered 'hello!' Peering round the front of the plane she could see a pair of green flannel trousers tucked into tan leather boots, and a torso bent over into the cockpit. 'I say, good morning!' she tried again.

The pilot turned to her, the straps of his aviator helmet hanging loosely against his chiselled jaw.

'I say.' He grinned. 'Now it *is* a good morning.'

Eleanor thought the morning was improving too as she cast a discreet eye over his athletic frame, broad shoulders and boyish good looks.

'Excuse the interruption,' she called up. 'I need to ask you something.'

'Coming right down.' He jumped backwards, landing close beside her.

'Lancelot!' He held out a hand, pulling off his helmet with the other. The ends of his tousled blond hair quivered in the breeze.

'Eleanor.'

'Sorry about your uncle.'

Naturally he knew who she was, everyone did. Shaking hands, she couldn't help staring at his eyes, so unusual, steel grey or were they blue? Either way, his silk scarf set them off magnificently.

'You've made quite a trek to snag me in the middle of this glamorous rurality.' He gestured round the field, his shirtsleeve rolled up past his forearm. 'It must be something frightfully exciting.'

'Oh, quite. Exciting, yes… no.' *Get a hold of yourself, Ellie!* 'A few nights ago, I saw a man murdered over there in the quarry.'

To her surprise, Lancelot didn't react. *Was murder such a common occurrence around here?* she wondered. She pointed in the quarry's direction. He gently took her wrist and slid it to the right.

'Over there, perhaps?'

The touch of his hand on her bare skin was unexpectedly thrilling, and her quickened pulse threatened to give her away. 'Don't be obtuse. You know where I mean; you can see everything from up there on the wing. Even Mrs Cartwright, apparently.'

Lancelot guffawed. 'I see you've been speaking to Cartwright.'

'He prefers Thomas.'

'Absolutely. Cartwright's a pain in the behind, always fussing about something. Ranted on about his blessed sheep, then his roof, then his wife. He's a finicky old nuisance but I do need this field.'

'Indeed, for your "flying antics" no less.'

'What a delight to hear you have discussed me in such detail, and before we'd even met.' He ran a hand through his hair. 'But you didn't come here to discuss Cartwright. What was it you wanted to ask me about this sensational murder?'

Eleanor wrenched her mind off Lancelot's hair and back to her investigation. 'Oh, I thought you might have noticed any recent activity round the quarry. Cartwright mentioned to the police that there has been little excavation for some time, but there was plenty of activity that night and no mistake.'

Lancelot threw his head back and laughed. 'You really are a most intriguing creature. Traipsing across fields to accost dashing chaps you've never met, cavorting round murderous quarries at night and sleuthing all on your own. I shall call you Sherlock! Tell me, Sherlock, what wheeze have you got up your sleeve for this afternoon? Sneaking into Parliament, dressed as the prime minister and delivering his four o'clock address to the chamber?'

She couldn't help feeling he was mocking her. 'Women politicians aren't a joke. And you really are insufferably smug and asinine.'

'My dear girl, what a great pair we'd make.' Before Eleanor could think of a suitable comeback, Lancelot continued. 'Now, what can I tell you about the quarry? Apart from the fact it is north-west of where we're standing, not south-west. There are lots of diggings, some frightfully deep and dangerous-looking holes that genteel ladies should avoid. Although…' He glanced at her muddied, torn state. 'You look like it might actually be your idea of fun. Unfortunately, I've seen no one moving about there, not for some time just as Cartwright told you. As for the evening of your "murder", what day and time was that?'

'Saturday night. Around ten fifteen in the evening.'

'Then I'm afraid I was at a masked ball.'

'Where exactly was this masked ball? And when did you arrive and leave?'

He chuckled. 'I'm afraid that's classified information.'

Eleanor frowned. 'This is serious! Can you prove you were at this ball?'

'Yes, but where would be the fun in that? You'd have all your answers and you'd have no need to quiz me again later.'

Eleanor took a deep breath. 'So there's no chance you were in that quarry between, say, ten and eleven Saturday evening?'

Lancelot grinned infuriatingly. 'No chance.'

'So, no chance either that you saw someone dragging a body away then?'

Lancelot looked at her quizzically for a moment before understanding dawned. 'There's no corpse, is there? Oh, this is too rich, are you really sure you saw a murder?'

The playboy pilot had been entertaining Eleanor, but she bristled at this remark. 'Quite sure. I'm convinced of what I saw. The fact that the police are too idle to do anything about it only makes it more imperative that I continue, what was it you said, oh yes, "sleuthing". Now, do you own a motorcycle?'

He gently held her shoulders and turned her round. A motorbike stood only a few yards away on the other side of the plane. So that was a yes! Then again, he hadn't tried to hide it. What did that mean? She sighed to herself, maybe this detective lark was more difficult than it looked.

A thought struck her. 'Have you ever seen Cartwright on a motorbike?'

Lancelot guffawed. 'Cartwright? On a motorbike? That I'd love to see!'

'I'll take that as a "no" then. Last question and you can get back to fixing your plane.'

He nodded. 'I'm all ears.'

'Did you know Spencer Atkins?'

Lancelot's expression changed to a serious one. 'I heard about that, poor bloke. Wasn't surprised though, he wasn't great with a gun.'

Her heart quickened. 'So you knew him?'

'Not really, bu—. Hang on, why are you asking about him?'

Suddenly it didn't seem such a great idea to tell a potential suspect that she knew Atkins' death was no accident and he was the missing body. 'Oh, no reason, I just thought it was a shame. I knew him… a little. Anyway, have you any idea who might have been responsible for the murder in the quarry?'

Lancelot stroked his chin in thought. 'Well, it could be the work of the notorious Sand Gang, I suppose. They could be your starting point.'

Finally a lead! 'The Sand Gang. Who are they?'

'A ruthless bunch, local mafia, in a nutshell. If the police aren't taking you seriously, I guess you've no choice but to fly solo. Are you going to march up to a higher authority with your murder exclusive?'

She took this as a challenge. 'Yes. That's exactly what I plan to do. I wonder who that higher authority is? Who do you think?'

Lancelot rubbed his forearm and flexed his fingers. 'Surely that would be Mayor Kingsley? Chipstone's the biggest place round here for miles.'

'Indeed. Then I shall thank you for your assistance and be off to visit Mayor Kinsey.'

Lancelot laughed. 'Kingsley,' he corrected. He glanced again at her. 'Are you on foot? Chipstone's a fair few miles.'

'I've walked further, thank you.' She turned to go.

'Come on, Sherlock,' Lancelot said. 'I'm heading into town. I'll give you a lift.' Hopping back up onto the wing, he leaned inside and returned with a leather jacket over his shoulder and another helmet, which he threw across the grass to her.

'Are we going by plane?' Eleanor's eyes widened with excitement.

'Oh, you are too much. Please do come and entertain me more often. Of course we're not going to fly in Daphne. Well, not unless the authorities have installed a runway at the town hall and I missed the news. No, thought not, so we're relegated to arriving on my other trusty machine.'

Daphne! He had named his plane Daphne.

'Hang on a sec.' Lancelot disappeared into the cockpit. He emerged a moment later with another set of goggles. Eleanor caught her breath. With his goggles and aviator helmet on, Lancelot looked dangerously familiar. Was he the mysterious motorbike rider that night? It seemed far-fetched seeing as she had no real idea what the rider had looked like, but he was here, only half a mile from the murder site and – she glanced past the plane's wing – with a motorcycle.

But she'd been sure the motorbike she'd seen at Pike's Farm a few moments ago was the one at the quarry. It certainly looked similar. But then again, so did Lancelot's. The thing was, all motorbikes were pretty much the same when you came down to it. She looked at the motorcycle again. Oh, who was she trying to fool, she wouldn't recognise one bike from another. She'd only ridden one once, in the wilds of Persia, and she'd had no idea what that was. Nevertheless, Cartwright wasn't alone any more on her suspect list.

Despite this, she dismissed any thought of danger. Even if this dashing pilot was the murderer, he wasn't about to kill her in broad daylight. Besides, everyone in the county seemed to know who she was. He'd have to be a fool to think he'd get away with it.

She looked over at Lancelot. He was standing with his jacket, helmet and goggles on backwards, chuckling at his own brilliant joke. *On the other hand, Ellie, you could be in real danger!*

*

Lancelot had suggested that Eleanor should hold on to him tightly as the clutch was behaving oddly. Maybe because of a recent crash, she thought. With her skirt tucked behind her legs, she was enjoying the sensation of speed and the wind buffeting her face. The scream of the motorbike engine and the flaps of their helmets made conversation impossible. With her arms round Lancelot's chest, she hoped he was as clueless about the murder as he appeared to be. At the same time she was acutely aware of how hugging him was making her feel. If she wasn't careful, life in Little Buckford might take on a whole new sheen, albeit an unwanted one.

She shook her head and loosened her grip as much as she dared. *Pull yourself together, Ellie. You haven't come thousands of miles just to fall in love again. Especially not with a murderer!*

CHAPTER 9

Perhaps it was just the reckless act of jumping aboard this powerful machine, which was being ridden by a man she'd only just met, that had her heart racing. With each burst he gave the motorbike's throttle, she gripped a little harder, trying not to grin like a simpleton.

The six miles to Chipstone flew by in a blur of hedgerows, farm gates and a sprinkling of farmhouses set back off the road down muddy lanes. Soon they were flying through the slightly rundown outskirts, past rows of terraced flint houses, dodging children and dogs playing in the street. They entered the bustling high street filled with fluttering awnings and ladies chattering over their shopping bags. Having narrowly avoided a fox terrier as it stole a bun from the baker's barrow, the motorbike finally stopped and idled outside the town hall, which had a brightly painted clock tower.

'Right ho! Here you are,' Lancelot called over his shoulder.

Eleanor pulled off the soft leather aviator helmet and goggles Lancelot had given her and shook her red curls. 'Thank you, kind sir.' She mock curtsied.

'Pleasure. Always happy to help out in an investigation.' He winked. 'Well, I'll see you at the Manor.'

'The Manor?' No one had said anything about a manor.

'When you come to dine at Langham Manor, silly.'

Eleanor frowned. 'No one's mentioned luncheon.'

'Oh, don't worry about that. Mater will have made sure your invitation is waiting.'

'Lancelot…?' She realised she had no idea of his last name.

'Fenwick-Langham. I'm the wicked only son of Lord and Lady Fenwick-Langham.'

She frowned. 'Oh! So you must be… Lord Fenwick-Langham as well?'

Lancelot laughed. 'Officially, yes, but you must know "lord" is only a courtesy title? It's given to all sons of lords. Pater's the real lord. I won't inherit the title properly until the old man kicks the bucket.'

She nodded as if she'd known that all along.

'And you must be Lady Swift. Would you prefer I addressed you as such?'

Eleanor blushed.

'I'll take that as consent to carry on calling you Eleanor and you can call me Lancelot, so long as the servants don't hear.'

Eleanor found it irritating that she couldn't tell when he was joking and when he was being serious. It was a trait people had often accused her of. 'I haven't accepted your parents' invitation yet. I might be busy.'

Lancelot snorted. 'You can't say "no" to Mater, trust me, it really isn't worth the battle. Goodbye, Sherlock.'

With a cheeky salute, he slipped the motorbike out in front of a coal merchant's wagon, giving a cheery wave in return to the man's angry rebuke.

Please don't let him be the murderer, Ellie! She sighed and walked up the steps.

Eleanor and bureaucracy went together as comfortably as a munitions store and a lit match, so it wasn't long before fiery words were flying round the reception area.

'What do you mean I can't see the mayor? Move aside this instant!'

'The Worshipful Mayor Kingsley will not receive unsolicited callers,' the tweed-suited clerk repeated.

'His most worshipful…' Eleanor gave up. '… mayor whatever would be failing most appallingly in his duties should I be turned away.'

'But Mayor Kingsley—'

'Does he possess a first name? Are you allowed to call him by it in secret?'

The clerk appeared horrified. 'Miss, forgive me, but I ask that you speak of Mayor Kingsley with respect or I will have no choice but to—'

The roar of a deep voice and the stomp of angry feet drowned out his words. 'What in the name of thunder is going on here?' A ball of a man emerged from the office, the veins in his thick neck standing out. 'Perkins! What the deuce is this commotion?'

Before the clerk could stammer a reply, the man noticed Eleanor and switched track in the blink of an eye. He smoothed his thinning side parting, unnecessarily as it was already held fast with brilliantine. 'Well, well, a visitor. Show the lady in, Perkins.' Smiling at Eleanor he left with a, 'One moment, my dear.'

At the door to the mayor's office, the clerk pushed it open enough for her to pass through and announced, 'Er…'

'Lady Swift,' she coaxed.

'Lady? Oh, I didn't realise.'

Kingsley gestured for him to be silent. 'Good morning, Lady Swift.' He pulled out a pocket watch strikingly similar to her late uncle's. 'Although I do believe it's nearly noon. Perkins, tea immediately and properly hot. I'll deal with you later.'

'Yes, sir.' Perkins scurried out, without chancing a look at Eleanor.

'Please do take a seat.' Kingsley indicated a buttoned, leather library chair in one of the window recesses. 'Such a pleasure to meet you. I can only apologise for the preposterous treatment you've received upon your arrival.'

Eleanor waved away his apology. 'Thank you, but please excuse me arriving unannounced. I wouldn't trouble you in such a way if it wasn't a matter of urgency.'

'I am sure not, my dear. Do make yourself comfortable first.'

There was a nearly imperceptible tap at the door.

'Come,' Kingsley bellowed, making Eleanor jump.

A rabbit of a woman ventured in, pushing a tea trolley with quivering hands. She placed the cups and refreshments on the ornate rosewood table.

'The coat, woman, take Lady Swift's coat!'

Eleanor stood with her back to the poor creature and let the coat slip from her shoulders. The woman took her coat and scuttled back out. She noticed in the far corner a mannequin standing guard on a section of herringbone floor, resplendent in the mayor's ermine-trimmed scarlet robe. A bicorn hat of silk adorned with black feathers sat on top of the dummy's neck. In a locked case hanging on the wall to the left were the town's silver mace with its sparkling gold top and the civic sword. *How funny, that grown men dress up in costumes like little boys*, Eleanor mused.

Perched on the edge of his oak desk, Kingsley made a great flourish of signing some papers before putting down his pen. 'Forgive me, my dear, life in the mayoral office is a busy affair.' He crossed the short space and more than filled the chair next to Eleanor.

'I imagine it is,' she said. 'So I'll come straight to the purpose of my visit.'

He leaned forward. 'It is always a pleasure to make time for a lady with a businesslike approach.'

'Quite. Now, Mayor Kingsley, I bring grave news. There has been a murder.'

He stiffened. 'A murder?' He heaved himself out of the chair and paced the floor. 'That won't do at all. A murder, indeed. On the whole, my constituents are reasonably law-abiding. I can only assume the perpetrator must have come from over the border.' He sat back down. 'The Oxfordshire contingent are quite a rabble.'

'Perhaps so, Mayor Kingsley. I wish I could say that the police have a line of enquiry in that direction. However, being as inept as they are, they have made no enquiries at all.'

He adjusted his position and swung one leg over the other knee, picking a piece of imaginary lint off as he did. 'This sounds most grave indeed. Please do give me all the facts, my dear.'

She started her story from the point when the storm had been raging overhead and she had seen the light in the quarry yard's hut. Kingsley sat silently throughout, save for a few surprised grunts when she described the shooting.

'So I reached the hut but there was no one there. And the man I saw shot, well, there was no corpse. It had simply vanished,' she concluded.

He ran his tongue over his lips. 'Lady Swift, what an incredible tale. How very intrepid of you.' He shook his head. 'Now tell me,' he held her gaze, 'what did the police say?'

'They made it abundantly clear that they believed it was nothing more than a fabrication on my part, as if I were some mad, attention-seeking old crone.'

'A fabrication!' He thumped the arm of his chair. 'Let me assure you, Lady Swift, that I do not hold such a view. It is obvious to me that you are a level-headed and observant young lady.' He took a sip of tea, looking thoughtful. 'Tell me, my dear, were… were you able to see any useful details? Such as, perhaps, the face of the killer? Or victim?'

'As I said I never saw the killer and I only got a glimpse of the victim.'

'So you couldn't identify either of them if you saw them again?'

She realised he was leaning forward in his chair, staring at her.

'Alas, not with any certainty.' She'd decided not to disclose her belief that the victim was Atkins until she had some positive proof. It seemed unlikely anyone would take her seriously otherwise.

Kingsley leaned back and studied her. 'And there is the inconvenient lack of a corpse?' He shook his head slowly. 'It's as if the event never happened.'

She nodded.

'I assume you've discounted the idea that the victim may simply have been injured?'

'With the amount of blood, yes.'

'Blood?'

'I found a large stain where the man was shot. Too large to believe anyone could have survived.'

'It is indeed a puzzle.' He sucked his teeth. 'It is as if the event never happened,' he repeated, resting his elbows on the plump padding of the chair's arms. 'However, my dear, you have been treated shabbily by our law enforcement officers. I will see to it immediately that they are given a severe reprimand.'

'Thank you, but the matter of the murder is my only concern.'

'Indeed, indeed. I shall ensure the police start a full investigation into the events you saw.' He held up a finger and pursed his lips. 'And, I shall monitor the investigation closely myself.'

She was impressed. Here was a man who, despite his brusque manner, was to be applauded for his direct approach. She rose to leave. 'Thank you, Mayor Kingsley, I appreciate your time today.'

'An absolute pleasure, my dear.'

They crossed the floor and at the door, he held out his hand. 'Thank you again for bringing this to my attention. It really is most helpful of you.'

She shook his hand and started off down the hallway before halting. Spinning around, she asked, 'Oh, Mayor Kingsley, one last question.'

He looked up from adjusting his chain.

'Where can one buy a…' She glanced at his stubby legs, rotund body and bright-red cheeks and nose. 'Oh, never mind.'

CHAPTER 10

Chipstone's town hall clock struck a quarter past one as Eleanor stood below, running over her recent meeting with the mayor. *Finally, Ellie, someone whose thinking isn't mired in the dark ages when it comes to taking a woman seriously! With the mayor taking an interest in the case, things should start happening.*

She paused in her reflection and looked around trying to remember the instructions to Bevan Brothers the man outside the town hall had given her. The shop was at the southernmost end of town, just after a sharp turn east. Or was it west? Over the years Eleanor had travelled much of the civilised, and uncivilised, world alone on her trusty bicycle. Having perfected the art of asking directions even when she couldn't speak the local language, she'd also developed the peculiar habit of forgetting them instantly.

She glanced around. 'East or west? This is ridiculous! Isn't this why people lived in small rural backwaters like Chipstone because you don't have to go on an expedition just to purchase a bicycle!'

Had it been able to reply, Chipstone might have balked at being called a rural backwater, as it rather prided itself on being a bustling market town in the heart of the Chilterns.

But fortunately it couldn't, so there was no offence taken. Eleanor, however, continued to let off steam. 'What on earth is wrong with using left and right?'

'I couldn't say, miss,' a bright voice answered. Eleanor looked down. A young boy of about ten stood with his cap in hand, in a waistcoat that was neat and clean but missing two buttons.

'Pardon?'

'I thought you were asking me a question… since there's no one else here, miss.'

'Yes, I can see how you would have thought that. However, I do have a question for you. Actually two. What's your name?'

'Alfie, miss.'

Eleanor realised she had now used up one of her two intended questions without asking either of them. No matter, she doubted if the boy would notice. 'Now, Alfie, would you like to earn a penny?'

The boy slapped his legs in excitement. 'You bet, miss.'

'Excellent. Then can you point me to Bevan Brothers?'

'Actually, begging your pardon, miss, but that's three questions. Is it a penny each or a penny for all three?'

This child was not to be underestimated. In fact, if she needed a team of street urchins like the one used by Sherlock Holmes, then Alfie would be a good choice to head it up.

The child was looking at her expectantly.

'To answer your question, it's a penny for all three. Deal?'

'Deal!' Alfie extended a small, unexpectedly clean hand. Eleanor shook it. 'Well,' he said, 'you want to know how to get to Bevan Brothers. That's easy.' He turned to face the opposite end of the high street to the one she and Lancelot had entered the town by. 'Do you see that chimney over there? The tall one with the smoke blowing out the top?'

Eleanor nodded, bending down to the boy's height and squinting where he pointed. 'Yes.' 'That's Barnes' Paint Factory. Me dad used to work there. I still help out sometimes. Now follow my finger along, you see where them buildings stop?'

'I do.'

'Well, that last roof, that's Bevans.'

'Brilliant!' Eleanor straightened up. 'You have been most helpful, and a well-earned penny it is, young man.' Eleanor opened her purse and smiled as she handed over the coin.

'Thank you, miss. Anything else you need, miss?'

She shook her head. 'No, thank you, Alfie.' But as he was about to go, she dropped another penny into his hand.

Alfie stared at it wide-eyed. 'What's that for?' he asked.

'Call it a retainer fee. If I need any more information when I visit Chipstone, I'll know where to come.'

'Thank you, miss, but the deal was a penny. We shook on it.' The boy handed the penny back and sprinted down a path that ran along one side of the town hall.

What a splendid young chap. She turned her attention back to the matter of Bevan Brothers.

Now, head for the chimney, then the last roof.

'What could be easier?'

A glance at her uncle's fob watch showed two twenty, an hour since she had uttered those fateful words. Well, getting lost in the backstreets of Chipstone was certainly easy, it seemed. What had happened to that blasted chimney? It had simply disappeared when she'd crossed the road to peer into a dress shop when a dazzling emerald silk scarf had caught her eye. Even though she'd never admit it, it set her pulse racing as much as the recent ride on Lancelot's motorbike. Despite her apparent disregard for fashion, she occasionally dreamed of pulling off the effortless elegance she'd seen in ladies parading through Paris, London and Milan. Then she'd noticed another gorgeous accessory shop further along. In fact it was as if someone had dropped a trail of coloured sweets along Chipstone's winding backstreets.

Emerging from the last shop clutching another exquisitely wrapped packet, she pictured herself sashaying along in her new organza choker with matching fascinator somewhere fantastically elegant with a deliciously handsome escort. Maybe someone with tousled blond hair and grey-blue eyes? She pulled the gold ribbon from the parcel and tied it around her wrist with a giggle.

Eleanor wrenched her thoughts back to the job in hand. *No falling for the enemy, Ellie!* Lancelot was still a suspect.

She stood on the pavement, scanning the skyline for any sign of a chimney or roof that might be Bevan Brothers. Seeing none, she chose a random street and emerged a few moments later on the high street opposite Chipstone's police station, with its typical blue lamp over the door.

Eleanor's quest for Bevan Brothers receded into the back of her mind. She had intended to let the mayor deal with the police, but now she had arrived on their doorstep it seemed the perfect opportunity to move her investigation forward. *After all, never send a man, however helpful, to do a woman's job, Ellie!* She strode towards the building with renewed purpose.

Approaching the entrance, Eleanor tutted at the small huddle of uniformed men smoking in the adjoining alley. 'Good to see the town is crime-free, gentlemen,' she called before climbing the steps to the station's door. *Please ring the bell* a sign instructed. Ignoring it, she pushed the door and strode in.

'Sergeant Wilby, please.'

There was a scuffle as the two policemen behind the desk tried to appear awake and busy.

'Bell not working, miss?' the leaner of the two chided.

'I really have no idea. Now, Sergeant Wilby, if you please.'

'Well, I don't think Sergeant Wilby will be too pleased at being called out unexpected like,' his chubbier colleague ventured.

'I have no doubt of that. Shall I find him myself?' She set off down the corridor, throwing open the first door she came to.

'Miss! Please take a seat. We will have Sergeant Wilby with you in just a moment.' The first policeman was already hurrying up the stairs.

'Good.' Eleanor returned to the front desk and waited with the sweetest of smiles.

A moment later she heard an unmistakable voice. 'What is the meaning of this?'

She turned to the approaching sergeant who faltered on realising who his visitor was.

'Brice, Fry, make yourselves scarce, and no listening down the stairwell!' Wilby barked. 'Lady Swift,' he groaned. 'To what do I owe the pleasure?' Wilby's expression revealed that the only thing that might actually give him pleasure would be to manhandle her back into the street.

One of Eleanor's great strengths was her decisiveness. Unfortunately, it wasn't always matched by a capacity to think ahead. Now she was in front of Sergeant Wilby, she had little idea as to how to extract any pertinent information from him. *Think, Ellie, think!*

Ah! She remembered Lancelot's words. Mayor Kingsley was the highest authority in the area; a man like Wilby would be bound to be terrified of him. She looked him coldly in the eye.

'News of my recent meeting. With the mayor.'

'Mayor Kingsley?'

'You have more than one mayor?'

Wilby shook his head.

'I thought not, so it's a pointless question on your part, I fear. Anyway, Mayor Kingsley was fit to burst when I told him about your dismissive treatment of the murder I witnessed and reported to you. He will be taking severe steps to rectify the matter and then will be monitoring your activities and attitude personally. I thought it might be helpful for you to be forewarned. The mayor appears to have a most fearsome temper, wouldn't you say?'

Sergeant Wilby was ashen by the end of Eleanor's speech. 'I'll call his worshipfulness now and explain that's not how it is at all, really not at all.' He moved towards the desk.

'There's no point,' Eleanor bluffed. 'He went out. Probably to call upon your superiors, I expect.'

Wilby squirmed. 'But, Lady Swift—'

'But nothing. I have a few, simple questions for you. Do you think you can manage that?'

Wilby nodded sullenly.

Again, Eleanor decided not to pass on her belief that the man she had seen shot in the quarry was the same man who had apparently died by accident in his own home. Besides, she didn't trust Sergeant Wilby, but that distrust was largely born of her upbringing. After her parents' disappearance and her uncle's, as she saw it, failure to take her in as his own, she'd developed a general distrust of humanity as a whole. Her naturally positive side fought against it, often leaving her hopelessly see-sawing between deciding whether to trust someone or not.

'Have there been any reports of any other deaths in the last twenty-four hours, excluding that of Mr Atkins?'

'No.'

'You seem awfully sure. How can you be so certain?'

'Because I have been on duty twice in that time, both being long shifts.'

'Ah, that would explain your dishevelled appearance.'

Wilby looked down at his uniform.

Eleanor started imperceptibly, her mind whirling. Maybe Sergeant Wilby had been reluctant to attend her call that night because he was the cause? Perhaps he'd been too busy cleaning his uniform – of blood? After all, it had been Sergeant Wilby who had refused to come out when she'd reported the murder originally and who had also refused to take her seriously when they finally did go to the quarry. But why would he murder Atkins? For the moment she had no idea, but Wilby was definitely elevated to her suspect list.

She looked shrewdly at the sergeant. 'Has anyone from your department returned to the quarry and looked for further evidence of a murder?'

'No.' Wilby gritted his teeth.

'Has anyone from your department checked all the registered owners of motorbikes in the area and interviewed them?'

'Again, Lady Swift, no.'

'Mmm. Is there even the modicum of a chance that given my statement, you've established the exact time of death? Or the murder weapon used?'

A sound like escaping gas alerted her that Sergeant Wilby was close to snapping.

'No, how could I given there was no murder!'

'Has any evidence come to light that Mr Atkins' death was, perhaps, not entirely accidental?'

Wilby breathed hard. 'We investigated Mr Atkins death thoroughly and have come to the conclusion that his death was *entirely* accidental. Mr Atkins died some time between seven thirty in the evening after his housekeeper left and four in the morning *at his home,* not in a blooming quarry!'

She decided to go for broke. 'Ah! But he could have been killed in the quarry and then his body transported to his house and arranged to look like an accident. I don't imagine Mr Atkins' house is very far from the quarry, nowhere is very far from anywhere round here, and on those back roads at night 'the murderer would have been unlucky to have come across—'

Wilby leaned forward. 'An interfering busybody? With nothing better to do, perhaps, than—'

Eleanor raised her hand, silencing Wilby. She noted the sergeant's ashen colour had switched to near beetroot in a matter of moments. She obviously wasn't going to get anything further from him, so she might as well have some fun. 'With nothing better to do, perhaps, than show the Chipstone police that if they want to join the twentieth century, they need to employ women in their ranks?'

Wilby exploded. 'Lady Swift, if you will!' He indicated the door with a jerk of his arm.

Eleanor tossed her head. 'Well, I shall report back to Mayor Kingsley but he won't be at all pleased. In fact, it seems I have no choice but to solve the case myself!'

She swept from the station's reception area and strode out the front door, petulantly pulling the doorbell on her way.

CHAPTER 11

Oh, the joy of moving at more than walking pace! Eleanor cycled out of what she now knew was Chipstone's most southerly end, her goal achieved. It had been easy to find Bevan Brothers' Cycles, as it turned out to be only a stone's throw from the police station.

Once inside, she had dismissed the Bevan brothers' attempts to sell her a fashionable lady's bicycle. She knew what she wanted: a sturdy, no-nonsense, go-anywhere machine. The perfect transport for her investigations.

Actually, the perfect transport would be the Rolls. Disappointingly, it wasn't the one she'd remembered from her visits to the Hall as a child, but a newer, altogether more imposing model, a 'Silver Ghost', it seemed. But since she hadn't learned to drive any motor car, and Clifford would no doubt make irritating comments should she ask him to chauffeur her on her investigations, a bicycle it was.

But there was the problem of her new sidekick, Gladstone. That basket on her handlebars would bear little more than the weight of a rabbit. And a runty one at that.

The poor road surface made the journey considerably harder than Eleanor had expected. For the last few years she'd explored new routes for the travel company, adventures for rich tourists in Persia, China, India and, most recently, South Africa. Unfortunately, using her trusty bicycle had been too slow and erratic out there, and the local guides she had to use preferred the relative speed and safety of a motor. Consequently, she wasn't fully fit for cycling and, within a few miles, she had become quite sweaty and unladylike. At least her modesty, or what she had of it, stayed intact. The Bevan brothers had thoughtfully provided clothes pegs to anchor her skirt either side of the bicycle's frame. Several of these, however, now littered the road, as they had pinged off when she was pushing down hard on the pedals on a steeper section. A black car crawled past, giving her a wide berth.

Unluckily for Eleanor, the county was famed for its hills, and none more so than the final climb up to the Hall. *Come on, Ellie, you've got this far, just one last bit.* Moving at a snail's pace through the gates and hauling on the handlebars, at last she creaked and wheezed up the drive and came to a shaky halt. She wondered if the Hall gates were always open, or if Joseph or Silas closed them at night. Perhaps with a murderer loose it would make sense to lock them, but then again, it wasn't as if anyone at the Hall was in danger, was it?

'Congratulations, most impressive!' A broad-shouldered man in a blue wool overcoat stood with his bowler hat in his leather-gloved hand. The black car that had passed her was parked near the steps to the house.

'Thank… you.' Eleanor dismounted from her now stationary bicycle, trying to hide her breathless state.

'I'm Detective Chief Inspector Seldon. Oxford CID. Forgive me, madam, have we met?'

Eleanor clapped her hands. She had found the novelty of being recognised everywhere tiresome, and this chap's ignorance of her was rather refreshing. 'Lady Eleanor Swift.' She wiped her hand on her skirt and held it out across the handlebars.

The detective pulled off his right glove and shook her hand firmly. Since her return to England, Eleanor had noticed how many men shook a lady's hand as if it were made of fine bone china. The detective seemed to have no such reticence.

'What brings you to see me, Detective? Sorry, Detective Inspector?'

'Actually, I've come to see Lord Henley.' He smiled. 'And "Inspector" is fine.'

'Gosh, you must be frightfully late for your appointment.'

'I beg your pardon but I haven't made an appointment. This is more of an unscheduled visit.'

'Then might I suggest you schedule an appointment in future? My uncle, Lord Henley, passed away this February.'

To his credit, DCI Seldon remained calm in spite of his social faux pas. 'My sincere apologies. I am actually stationed in London at present. And, of course, my condolences. How insensitive of me.'

'Indeed. Now whatever you wanted to see my uncle about, you'll have to deal with me in his place. Come inside, I shall scrape a little of the countryside from my face and be with you before you've had time to sit down.'

Eleanor leaned her bicycle against the steps and gestured for him to follow her.

Mrs Butters opened the door, revealing straight away that Clifford was obviously off on one of his butlery errands. 'Hello, my lady. Before I forget, the Reverend Gaskell called to introduce himself. He's the Vicar of St Winifred's. He couldn't stay and said he will come back some other time.'

'Not to mind, Mrs Butters, may I trouble you for some tea? We have a visitor.'

'Right away, my lady.' Mrs Butters trotted off, retying her apron as she went.

'Inspector.' Eleanor gestured towards the oak door. 'How are you with dogs?'

A few minutes later Eleanor reappeared, her face shiny from the rough scrubbing she'd given it in the visitor's washroom. 'I see you've met Gladstone.'

DCI Seldon grunted, gesturing to Gladstone's prostrate form sprawled across his lap. There was a leather slipper hanging from the dog's mouth.

'Now, that is the finest canine welcome you'll ever receive, I'm sure, Inspector.' Eleanor giggled as she took up the chaise longue opposite.

'Not to mention all the licking.' He grunted again.

'Apologies, he hasn't quite learned the full etiquette of greeting new people. And I fear, at his advancing years, he's unlikely to. Now, to business.'

The inspector's brow furrowed. 'With respect, Lady Swift, I am not sure you will be able to assist in my enquiries. Not unless I am mistaken and you were well acquainted with Mr Spencer Atkins?'

'No, I was not well acquainted with him, but…' She hesitated. Unlike Mayor Kingsley and Sergeant Wilby, this man had something trustworthy about him. 'But I did know him from my childhood. I was saddened to hear of his passing.'

'I am sorry for your loss.' he said, running the palm of his hand along Gladstone's side.

A thought struck her. 'Inspector, kindly explain to me why…' She paused as Mrs Butters heralded the arrival of tea with a polite knock. The housekeeper placed it on the occasional table between her and the inspector before leaving.

'Tea, Inspector?'

'Thank you.' He nodded with minimal enthusiasm.

Eleanor poured a cup and passed it across the table. 'Help yourself to milk and sugar.' She racked her thoughts a moment. 'Where were we? Oh, yes. Was I misinformed as to the nature of Mr Atkins' sad demise? Something to do with his shotgun, am I right?'

'Yes, a fatal wound from his own gun, fired accidentally whilst he was cleaning it.'

'Whilst he was cleaning it? Really?'

'Yes, rather careless. People get complacent.'

'Do you get complacent, Inspector?'

'No, I do not,' he said stiffly. He shuffled his feet, wiggling Gladstone into a more comfortable position. 'You seem particularly interested in this, Lady Swift.'

'Forgive my rather blunt question, but why are you, a Detective Inspector, investigating an accidental death such as this? Unless, of course, you suspect foul play?'

He looked at his hat and gloves squashed under Gladstone's front legs. 'Mr Atkins was an influential man on account of his position. In such a case it is police protocol to conduct routine enquiries.'

She narrowed her eyes at this politician's answer. Plenty of words but they contained nothing but hot air. She snapped to. 'His position?' Clifford hadn't mentioned what Spencer Atkins had done for a living.

'Yes, he was an influential… government official.'

'Do go on, Inspector,' she encouraged.

He hesitated a moment. 'May I ask, Lady Swift, how long have you been here at Henley Hall?'

She looked up at the ceiling. 'Three, no four days, I think.'

'And do you intend to remain in Little Buckford?'

Again she hesitated, still undecided as to whether she should stay or go. And then she remembered she had a murder to solve. 'I intend to stay, certainly until I have completed my own investigations.'

DCI Seldon frowned. 'Your own investigations?'

Eleanor looked at the man opposite her, and suddenly noticed his soft brown eyes, kind hands and gruff voice. She caught her breath. Was there something in the water out here in the countryside? What was happening to her? Falling for every man who appeared was the job of giddy-minded women with over-tightened corsets. She'd come here for altogether different reasons.

She was sure she was right though; there was something peculiarly trustworthy about this one. So much so, that she decided to break her recent decision not to tell anyone about her suspicion that the dead man at the quarry was Atkins. 'I don't believe Mr Atkins shot himself, accidentally or otherwise. I believe he died elsewhere at someone else's hands.'

DCI Seldon stared at Eleanor long and hard before putting down his tea with a sigh. 'I see, well, perhaps you would be so good as to enlighten me as to what you are basing your theory on.'

'I believe he was murdered in the quarry that borders the grounds of Henley Hall. His was the corpse I couldn't find that night.'

The inspector failed to hide his irritation. 'The corpse you couldn't find? I must insist you be a little clearer.'

'Clearer? If the police had come out that night, they would perhaps have apprehended the perpetrator by now and everything would be perfectly clear.'

'Lady Swift. May we go back a few steps, I am not quite following this.' The inspector wriggled forward in his seat, sliding Gladstone on to the floor. 'Sorry, old chap, legs are really quite numb,' he muttered. He turned back to Eleanor, closer than before. She felt the heat rise in her cheeks. 'Now, start at the beginning. What night? What murder? Which police?'

'The murder in the quarry that I reported three days ago.'

DCI Seldon pulled his notebook from his breast pocket. 'Did you report the incident to the Little Buckford or Chipstone police?'

'Chipstone. Little Buckford has but one constable and he was apparently detained by the inconvenient arrival of three offspring in the space of half an hour.'

For the first time, he seemed to be trying to hide a quiet smile. 'As I mentioned earlier, Lady Swift, I'm based in Oxford and sometimes London. Local reports rarely come across my desk, not unless there's a serious murder involved.'

Eleanor jumped in. 'And what constitutes a "serious murder", Inspector? Is it possible to have a "trivial" murder?'

'It is a standard police term. "Serious murder" is a phrase we use when there are sufficient facts to warrant a full-on murder investigation. As public servants we are duty bound to justify our use of time, resources and manpower. I gather the Chipstone police did not feel sufficient facts had arisen in the report they took from your statement.'

Tired of defending what she knew she'd seen that night, her tone was terse. 'My statement was quite clear. I saw a man shot in the workman's hut in the quarry yard at around ten fifteen on Saturday. When I arrived at the hut, there was a large pool of blood but no corpse. Oh, and a man on a motorbike then nearly ran poor Gladstone and myself down while we were trying to get back home.'

'No corpse, you say? I see. And the blood?'

'When the police finally turned up the following day that too, had conveniently vanished.'

DCI Seldon took a long breath. 'And was there any other evidence of this murder? The gun in question, spent cartridges?' He held out his hands. 'Anything?'

Eleanor sighed. 'No.'

'Then that probably would have prevented the event from being tagged as a "serious murder".'

'That's because the police are buffoons with badges!'

He snorted through his tea. 'I'm a policeman. Am I a buffoon with a badge?'

Eleanor laughed, she was beginning to like this detective. 'It's too early to tell, Inspector, I'd have to get to know you better.' She did a tiny double take. Where had that come from?

DCI Seldon put his cup down. 'Today is not the day for that, as I have a full schedule. If you would care to repeat what you reported to the police, I will open up a new line of enquiry at a later date, if that suits you?'

A knock at the door interrupted Eleanor's reply. 'Yes,' she called.

Clifford stepped into the room and bowed. 'Please forgive my intrusion, my lady. I merely wanted to alert you to the news of my return. Is there anything you need?'

'No, thank you, Clifford. I believe the inspector and I are almost finished here.'

DCI Seldon rose from his seat. 'Lady Swift, thank you for your gracious hospitality and for assisting in my enquiries. Goodbye, Lady Swift.' DCI Seldon collected his battered hat and gloves. The two men left the room.

As the door closed, Gladstone joined her on the chaise longue. Eleanor poured herself another cup of tea and helped herself to a slice of Mrs Trotman's fruitcake. She cosied up to Gladstone. 'You don't mind, do you?'

Gladstone gave the impression that he wouldn't mind so long as she shifted over and fed him some.

'Surely I'm supposed to be top dog, Gladstone? Although I fancy Clifford thinks he's the one in charge.' She bent and rubbed the dog's belly. 'But then again, perhaps you think you should be top dog? I suppose we could share the title.' She fed him the last edge of her fruitcake, making sure it had no raisins in it. 'Mrs Trotman tells me that even though you love them, they don't agree with you.' Eleanor lay back on the chaise longue and sighed. 'I think I have the same problem with men, Gladstone!'

Eleanor heard DCI Seldon's car purr down the drive. She was still smarting from his apparent lack of interest in her investigations when Clifford returned to the drawing room.

'So, Clifford, did you and the inspector have a hearty chuckle over my "tale" of the quarry murder?'

Clifford's face remained impassive. 'No, my lady, that would have been entirely inappropriate considering…'

She frowned. 'Considering what, Clifford?'

'That I am certain of the events you saw at the quarry, my lady.'

Eleanor blinked. 'What? You mean you believe me about the murder at the quarry? Because if you do, you're the only dashed one who does!'

Clifford nodded. 'That may be true, my lady, but I for one certainly believe your version of events.'

To find that someone took her seriously, and that it was Clifford of all people, touched her. 'Look here, if you believe me, then why have you been dashedly stiff and silent about it until now?'

'I am a butler, my lady,' Clifford answered, as if that clarified everything.

Eleanor laughed. 'Well, all credit to you. But when it's just the two of us, you really can let it slip just a little if you wish.'

'Thank you, my lady, I'll bear that in mind.'

'Right, now that's sorted, let's get back to the all-important matter. When the world is treating me like a liar and a lunatic, what has led you to be so certain that I am in my right mind?'

'If I could ask your indulgence, my lady, there are a great many things on which we might confer but I fear the hour is growing late. A supper tray and a bath may be the best course of action, if you'll forgive my proposal.'

Eleanor considered rebuking him for his 'bath' comment and his obvious dig at yet another missed mealtime. Then she remembered she'd given him permission not to hold his tongue. She might regret that decision, she thought ruefully.

Clifford continued. 'We could reconvene tomorrow after a hearty plate of Mrs Trotman's fine breakfast fayre, with a full stomach, and an open mind.'

Tired after her epic cycle ride and the emotion of the last hour, she conceded. 'Whatever you say, Clifford, you're the boss!'

CHAPTER 12

'So, Clifford, I must say you surprised me.'

'How is that, my lady?' Clifford replaced the salver lid on the few remaining sausages.

'Oh, this home-made onion relish is simply divine!' Eleanor took another mouthful.

Clifford waited patiently.

Eventually she paused in her single-handed demolition of Mrs Trotman's delectable fayre.

'You surprised me, Clifford, by believing that I saw someone shot that night in the quarry, and that that someone was poor Mr Atkins.'

Clifford offered her a salver from which she speared a large forkful of braised mushrooms. 'There is a predominant reason, my lady, why I am in agreement with your version of events.'

Eleanor stopped waving her fork around. 'Go on.'

He placed the salver back onto the side table and stood next to her. 'Mr Sandford, the butler at Langham Manor, whom I believe you'll meet when you go to luncheon with Lord and Lady Fenwick-Langham tomorrow, has a niece, Miss Abigail, who works as a typist at Chipstone Police Station. She is a delightful young lady and quite… observant.'

Eleanor grinned. 'So, you have a mole at the police station. I say, that might be jolly handy, given that I've my suspicions about Sergeant Wilby, but we'll come to that presently. Do continue.'

Clifford half-bowed. 'Thank you, my lady. You see, I too thought it a strange coincidence that you should report seeing a man shot over at the quarry, and a body should turn up the following day shot, not half a mile away.'

Eleanor started. 'I didn't know he lived so near.'

'Indeed. Mr Atkins' property backs onto the north of Mr Cartwright's land as Henley Estate does the south. It would be a relatively easy task to transfer the body from the quarry to Mr Atkins' house. It's half a mile at best.'

'And under the cover of darkness, very unlikely anyone would see?'

'Indeed, there are very few other properties around that area.'

Eleanor frowned. 'But what's Abigail got to do with all this?'

'Miss Abigail types up the reports as none of the policemen themselves can type with more than one finger. Subsequently, she typed up the report on Mr Atkins' "accidental" death.' He coughed, which Eleanor assumed was a butler's version of a dramatic pause. 'Mr Atkins was found holding a bottle of gun oil in his right hand.'

Eleanor blinked. 'So?'

'I had the opportunity on many occasions when Mr Atkins visited the Hall to note that he was a left-handed gentleman.'

Eleanor slapped the table, upending her mushroom-laden fork and sending it flying across the room. She saw Clifford wince. 'By Jove, good work! If Atkins were to have tried oiling the pin holes wrong-handedly as it were…'

'Quite so. Even a poor shot understands the dangers of trying to fire an incorrectly oiled firearm. I believe the killer made a mistake. He was arrogant enough to believe that Mr Atkins' reputation for being less than a crack shot would lead to a verdict of "accidental death". Id est, that a man who couldn't handle his gun in the field would indubitably mishandle it whilst cleaning the powder residue from the barrels. However, he placed the gun oil in the wrong hand.'

Eleanor nodded, letting the 'id est' wash over her. She could look it up later. For the moment, she saw that, with Clifford's encyclopaedic knowledge, unwavering logic and keen observation, he could be a huge aid in solving her quarry murder. Assuming, of course, he wasn't the murderer.

'Hmm.' She drummed her fingers on the table. 'Clifford, I can see you possess skills beyond those of a... er, regulation butler, as it were.'

'If that is a compliment, thank you, my lady.'

She grinned. 'Of course it is! Now, let's get together and solve the questions around poor Atkins' last moments. What do you say?'

She saw the hesitation in his face, but was clueless as to what was behind it. Had she stepped too far across the Lady of the House and butler divide? Was he still mourning the loss of his relationship with her uncle? Or was it something else?

'Yes, my lady.'

'What?' She jerked out of supposing and surmising. 'Sorry... oh, yes?'

Clifford took a long breath and adjusted the cuffs of his gloves. 'Shall we begin with the event itself, perhaps?'

'The event?'

'The murder.' There was that 'obviously' tone again. She let it go.

'Absolutely. So, we both agree Atkins was shot in the quarry and his death arranged to look like an accident. The question that now arises, Clifford, is... why?'

'Indeed, there is the conundrum: what reason can we deduce for the murderer moving the body to the victim's home?'

'The straightforward answer is glaringly obvious – to make it seem like an accident.'

'Then why did the murderer not complete his terrible act in the house?'

She scratched the back of her head. 'Erm... Ah! Too risky. Someone might have heard the gunshot.'

'My lady, this is the country. Everyone has access to a shotgun in areas like Little Buckford, hence the county's fondness for pigeon pie. Mr Atkins' land is bordered by Poddington Woods to the east and Cartwright's land to the south. No one takes any notice of the sound of a shotgun.'

'But Atkins' staff would have jolly well taken notice at a shot ringing through the house, for goodness' sake!'

'Normally that would be the case, but Mrs Campbell, the housekeeper, was the only staff, and she was away visiting her sick sister that evening.'

'But how would the killer have known that? Unless they are local, I suppose.'

'So, our list of suspects at this juncture runs to anyone local with access to a shotgun. I would suggest that is almost the entire local population, my lady.'

He had a point. 'We'll come back to that. Besides, I already have a list of suspects, thank you. First though, one question keeps rattling round and round my brain: how did the murderer lure Atkins to the quarry? Knowing him as you did, it must have been a frightfully convincing ruse, wouldn't you say?'

Clifford nodded slowly. 'That too has been dominating my thoughts. He was not a gentleman fond of evening excursions. Thus, to agree to a rendezvous in a disused quarry seems most uncharacteristic. Then again, men do the oddest things when pressed.'

'I suppose he may have known his murderer, so, while you kindly load me up with some more eggs, perhaps you could also tell me more about Atkins?'

'Mr Atkins was an upright and honest man. Your uncle held him in the highest regard.'

'So he wouldn't have had many enemies?'

'Not necessarily. A man of honour cannot be bought or swayed. Such a man can make as many, if not more, enemies, than one willing to waive his morals for money and power.'

'True, Clifford, too true. And were any of them known to you?'

For a moment she swore he hesitated before replying. 'Unfortunately, no, my lady.'

'Was he married?'

'No. He lived a resigned bachelor's life following a disappointment in love. A certain young lady, an acquaintance of your uncle's. In the event it seemed there was some incompatibility as she married another gentleman and moved to Devon, I understand.'

She frowned. 'We need to find out more about his movements that night.'

Clifford refilled her cup again. 'His housekeeper, Mrs Campbell, was most informative. She told me that Mr Atkins was out from late afternoon and returned just before six. It would appear she made him supper and then left at seven thirty to spend the evening and night at her ill sister's side. She returned at seven the following morning and discovered the body. Miss Abigail mentioned that the report she typed noted there had been no sign of a break-in.'

Eleanor finished her mouthful before replying. 'Honestly, the police really are more inept than is conceivable! I should think the criminals of Buckinghamshire are doing spectacularly well as a result. Even the bluntest brick of a man in uniform could have worked out Atkins would have had his house key on him.'

'Indeed. And that may have been how his murderer guessed his housekeeper was away.'

'Good sleuthing, Clifford.'

'Thank you, my lady. I rather imagine, however, that I am merely postulating at this point.'

Eleanor wrinkled her nose. 'What else has Abigail been able to pass on?'

'Only that there were no fingerprints other than Mr Atkins' on the gun found next to the deceased.'

'And the gun itself? Have they checked it with a firearms Johnny who knows what he's talking about?'

'A ballistics expert, I believe you mean, my lady. And the answer is no, I believe they are assuming the gun found next to the deceased was the murder weapon. In any case, it is notoriously difficult with shotguns and cartridges to tell one from the other. More sausages? Eggs? Bac—?'

Eleanor held up her hand. 'Absolutely not! I fear I will burst if I eat any more.' She stared at her stomach. 'I shall have to take up some strenuous exercise if Mrs Trotman is going to keep up her splendid efforts.'

As Clifford busied himself clearing her place setting, he suggested they switch their attention to the suspects she had identified, taking each in turn. 'That way I might be able to supply a motive or two as I knew Mr Atkins better than yourself.'

'Okay, Clifford, but let's do it with a coffee in the morning room. I need a change of scene to get the cogs working.'

He nodded. 'Certainly, my lady. Perhaps you should take the long way round, out through the garden and back in via the kitchen, to aid your overburdened digestive system?'

She rolled her eyes. 'Out through the garden and back via London might just do it!'

CHAPTER 13

It was a good twenty minutes later that Eleanor finished her brisk walk around the grounds. Confident she would now be able to sit up, rather than needing to lay full stretch to let her breakfast go down, she located Clifford in the morning room. He handed her a coffee as she ruffled Gladstone's ears.

'Perhaps I should instruct cook to prepare lighter meals and smaller portions thereof in future?'

'Don't you dare! I shall simply work it all off running after our suspects.'

She was impressed that he managed to look disbelieving and disapproving at the same time. That was no mean feat.

He interrupted her thoughts. 'On the note of suspects, shall we reconvene our discussion?'

'Definitely. We need to discuss Sergeant Wilby, that oaf Cartwright and, er… Lancelot.' She cleared her throat. 'Let's kick off with that idiot Wilby.'

'Is that because you have stronger suspicions about him than the others?'

'No, it's because I dislike him the most. Until I'm in front of Cartwright, then I waver between the two.'

'In which case, my lady, might I suggest that we start with another suspect, to bring our thoughts round to a more, shall we say, objective frame of mind?'

She managed to resist the urge to stick her tongue out at him. 'Oh alright, let's start with Cartwright. As I say, he's just as objectionable.'

He let out a small groan, which she ignored.

'Now, he has not only been obstructive, he also lied about the quarry gates always being locked. And he owns the land, and certainly he'll own a shotgun, he's a farmer. He also owns a motorbike, or at least I saw him carrying out some dubious dealings with a man who owns a motorbike similar to the one that almost ran me down. Oh, and Mr Penry, the butcher doesn't seem to like him at all.'

'I am not sure a judge would be swayed by those points alone, my lady. Especially Mr Cartwright being unpopular with individual members of the village. He is,' he adjusted the cuffs of his white gloves, 'not the kind of man to be universally liked.'

She flapped her hand. 'Oh, for heaven's sake, even you can't be that polite about him. He's the type of man who would pick a fight with his own shadow!'

'I couldn't comment, my lady, but even if that is the case, it doesn't make him a murderer. When you spoke with him, did he furnish an alibi?'

'Yes, but a mighty flimflam one, to say the least. He said he was indoors at the time of the murder, sharpening tools by the fire. And the best he could come up with as proof was to say that his good lady wife would vouch for him.'

'Hmm, without slighting Mrs Cartwright, it is de rigueur in the rural communities for a wife to back up her husband's word whether it is true or not. We need to establish Mr Cartwright's exact movements that night. For the moment, perhaps we should concentrate on possible motives?'

Eleanor nodded as she sipped her coffee. 'But that's where you need to come in, Clifford. I can only stab in the dark about what might have got Cartwright's goat sufficiently to resort to murder. Are you aware of any conflict between Atkins and Cartwright?'

'Regrettably yes, theirs was not the best of neighbourly relationships.'

'Ooh, another coffee please and then spill all the juicy gossip.'

'I will relay the matters that I am aware of but abstain from labelling them "juicy" or "gossip".'

She grinned and took her refilled cup when he returned from the serving table. Patting the chair next to her for Gladstone to join her, she listened to Clifford. A few minutes later, she let out a long low whistle. 'So, Cartwright was pumping his livestock's slurry onto Atkins' land?'

Clifford nodded. 'He denied it was done knowingly. I recall he blamed a split drainage system.'

'What three times over the course of seven months? Nonsense!'

'Equally though, Mr Cartwright caught Mr Atkins shooting on his land without permission on more than one occasion. A further point of conflict between them was the boundary fence. Mr Cartwright's more adventurous livestock often strayed onto Mr Atkins' land due to, in Mr Atkins' opinion, Mr Cartwright leaving the aforementioned fence in disrepair on purpose.'

'Swings and roundabouts, you might say. But did any of these incidents happen recently?'

'The previous month I believe was the last occasion. But, of course, there may have been others that I am not aware of. On one occasion I believe the police were called when the two gentlemen actually came to blows. For a man as mild-mannered as Mr Atkins, he must have felt provoked in the extreme.'

She frowned. 'And do you think any of these instances were a strong enough motive for murder though?'

'Men have killed over much less, my lady, as I'm sure you are aware. Combined, it is certainly a possibility.'

'Well then Cartwright definitely has a motive which could have smouldered and then been easily ignited into violence. He had the means, being a shotgun owner for sure.'

'And with the quarry being on his land, also the opportunity. However, as I said, my lady, we need to re-interview Mr Cartwright and establish more precisely his movements between the hours of ten and eleven thirty the evening of the murder at least.'

'Until we do, you have to admit his alibi is weak to say the least, and he's even got the key to the gate that was unlocked that night. He might have nudged that idiot Wilby down to number two, dash it!'

'I didn't enquire the exact number on your suspect list, my lady?'

'Er, three.' She looked down at her hands. 'We could consider Lancelot next. Hopefully he'll be quicker to rule out, or at least move to the bottom of the list.'

'As you wish. Might I ask what has led you to include young Lord Fenwick-Langham in the line-up?'

'First, he has a motorbike. Second, consequently he has goggles and a helmet the same as, or too similar to distinguish from, those worn by the chap who almost ran me and Gladstone down that night. Third, he keeps his plane in the field very near the quarry. Fourth, he didn't seem very surprised when I told him there had been a murder.' A thought struck her. 'Oh, I'm such a ninny for having forgotten until now. The Sand Gang! Lancelot suggested it might be the work of a local gang, but maybe he was just trying to throw suspicion off himself?'

Clifford coughed again. Eleanor gave a mock cough in return. 'That's another habit we need to work on, Clifford, that cough. If we are alone and you wish to disagree, you have my permission to offer a contrary view without pretending you are suddenly afflicted by laryngitis.'

'Thank you, my lady. I fear that young Lord Fenwick-Langham may have been making a joke with his reference to the Sand Gang.'

'Sand? Gang? I don't get… oh no.' She groaned. Sometimes she could be so obtuse, especially when it involved a handsome man. 'Sand, as in *quarry*. Oh snap, he must think me such a fool for swallowing that.'

'It takes courage to make a fool of yourself.'

'Shakespeare?'

'Chaplin.'

Eleanor looked confused.

'Charlie Chaplin, my lady.'

'Did you and my late uncle spend the bulk of your days engrossed in the exploits of heroic cowboys and silent comics of the silver screen?'

'To a certain extent, yes.'

Curious though she was to learn more about her late uncle's eccentricities, she dragged her attention back to the case. 'So, perhaps Lancelot was just ribbing me with this Sand Gang nonsense? Or maybe he *was* trying to throw me off the scent?'

'Are you aware of his alibi for the night in question?'

'Yes, he told me he was at a masked ball and that some of his chums could vouch for him.'

'It would be a simple matter to find out which ball he attended and to verify his story.'

'Excellent. I have to say, though, I'm clueless on a possible motive for Lancelot, unless he was mixed up in something very rummy and Atkins found out somehow?'

'Well, my lady, I am obviously not intimately acquainted with young Lord Fenwick-Langham but, as I said, I am acquainted with Mr Sandford, the butler at Langham Manor. Your late uncle was good friends with Lord and Lady Fenwick-Langham. Without wishing to be indiscreet, Mr Sandford mentioned her ladyship's perturbation at her son's involvement with an *actual* gang.'

'A gang! What a criminal gang? Mafia? Or Chinese triads, do you suppose?'

Clifford raised an eyebrow. 'I believe Lady Fenwick-Langham was referring to something more akin to a *social* gang. Other young people of titled parents, though some of them are artists and bohemians.'

'And does this gang have a name?'

'No, but I believe they model themselves on the so-called "Bright Young Things".'

'Ah, so over-privileged and over-monied wastrels rebelling against their parents and running around shocking the general population and delighting the press?'

'That is one interpretation, my lady, although I shouldn't wish to put my name to such a definition.'

'Maybe I should join them, this gang of Lancelot's? I have the opportunity to play the spoilt little rich kid if I want to now.' She waved off his polite face of dissent. 'No, don't bother to reject that confession. I am acutely aware of the immense good fortune life has bestowed on me.'

'Which, with all due respect, is precisely why I suspect that young Lord Fenwick-Langham's gang would not suit you. Not at all.'

'But you don't know me *at all*, Clifford.' Eleanor realised her voice had wobbled, which surprised her.

'Indeed, my lady, we haven't been much acquainted… until your recent arrival. When you were younger, we didn't see enough of you at the Hall and then you went abroad…' He broke off.

'And then my uncle passed away…'

He took a deep breath. 'If I might be permitted, your uncle regretted not seeing more of you.'

A flame of anger surged up inside her. She found her voice, but not her composure. 'Really, that surprises me, because he packed me off to boarding school and failed to play any meaningful part in my life. Where was he all those years when I was growing up without parents?'

She could see from his stiff demeanour that he wished he'd held his tongue.

'Perhaps another time, my lady.'

'Whatever.' She took a swig from her water glass, hoping to dowse her anger before it spilled out any further into the discussion. 'Now, we are here to solve a murder.'

'Yes, my lady.' He took his cue and retreated to safer ground. 'Shall we turn our attention to Sergeant Wilby? What suspicions do you harbour that have led to him being on your list?'

'In short, when I reported witnessing a murder, he refused to investigate until the following day, leaving him plenty of time to remove any evidence of the crime. Surely, that is enough in itself? There are, however, two more good reasons to suspect him. One, when he did finally turn up the next day, he did nothing but fob me off and refused to take down most of my account for his report. Then when Inspector Seldon turned up here, he told me that Wilby hadn't passed my eyewitness account on to any higher authority.'

'Far from ideal, my lady, although I fear his actions could equally be a result of his incompetence, general laziness and boorish attitude to women as reliable witnesses.'

Eleanor glowered at the memory. 'Possibly.'

'As he answered the phone at Chipstone Police Station when you rang, we can place him there at…?'

Eleanor thought. 'He was obviously there when I rang that night, but that must have been hours after it happened. As I've said, I checked my watch about five to ten minutes before I saw Atkins shot, which would have put the murder around ten fifteen to ten twenty. I was rather… erm, lost, I confess, so it took forever to find a route back to the Hall. Gladstone was thoroughly fed up and straggled all the way. Then trying to get through to the police took an absolute age.'

His brow creased. 'Regrettably, I did not note the precise time of your return home, my lady. I was out looking for you and only returned shortly before you arrived. However, I was aware of you using the telephone, so we can be sure therefore that Sergeant Wilby was at Chipstone Police Station manning the phones at around twelve thirty. What we really need to know, however, is if he was at the station the hours preceding the murder. We might, however, have trouble verifying his alibi, assuming we can find out what it is. Discretion may be needed.'

'No need to get too hung up on discretion, Clifford. I usually find the direct approach to work best.'

'If I might suggest we ask Miss Abigail to uncover what she can without arousing suspicion. It would, after all, be a shame to alert the possible murderer to the fact that we have him on our list of suspects.'

'Oh, very well.' She sighed. 'What about a motive for Wilby? Anything in your vast insider knowledge?'

'Only the tenuous information through the village grapevine that Mr Atkins met with Sergeant Wilby a week ago. And apparently it was not a cordial meeting.'

Eleanor's ears pricked up. This is what she was looking for! 'Do you have any idea what the meeting was about?'

'Unfortunately, no. I have heard, however, that Mr Atkins has met with a number of high- and low-ranking members of the constabulary and council over the last few weeks.'

'Maybe his remit from Whitehall is to weed out incompetence and laziness and Wilby was read the riot act. That would give him a motive – to save his sorry backside before Atkins could act.'

'Possibly, my lady, but this is all conjecture at the moment.'

'Agreed. I think the only course of action then is to interview Wilby, Cartwright and Lancelot again. But this time together we should be able to crowbar some decent clues out of them.'

She looked across at Clifford's pained expression.

'Okay, Clifford, discreetly pry some clues out of them. Agreed?'

He nodded and went to leave but stopped at her raised hand.

'Clifford, what a chump I've been. What with all the novelty of being at the Hall and this murder investigation, I've quite overlooked the loss you have suffered in my uncle's passing.'

Clifford swallowed. 'If I may be so bold as to say your uncle considered me not just a trusted servant, but also a trusted friend, despite the difference in our social status.'

Eleanor gave a soft smile, borne of genuine warmth. Trying to ease his discomfort she said, 'Can I help the transition to your new situation, less familiar though it is? Maybe you'd like me to foster a love of watching cowboy films or indulging in some comedies to help keep my uncle's memory alive?'

Clifford didn't flinch. 'It is kind of your ladyship, but perhaps I could suggest a more suitable way to honour your uncle's memory?'

'Suggest away. Anything to help.'

'If we might work on your timing for dinner? Your uncle was always most punctual for meals, which was greatly appreciated by the staff. Perhaps you would like to continue in his footsteps?'

Eleanor grinned. 'That's quite enough, Clifford. It's one thing to honour someone's memory and quite another to ape it!'

CHAPTER 14

By the afternoon Clifford had vanished once again. Eleanor resolved to learn more about her enigmatic butler and his mysterious absences.

Upstairs, she pulled on her new flannel cycling britches, a hip-length sweater in a not too incompatible tone of sage, and a patterned silk scarf from the wardrobe. Opening her bedroom door, she looked for her boots.

'Gladstone!' There was no reply. She'd have to see Mrs Trotman in stockinged feet.

Padding downstairs, she stuck her head round the kitchen door. 'Good afternoon, Mrs Trotman.'

'Good afternoon, my lady. Is there something I can get you?' The cook paused in flouring a long wooden board.

'Mrs Trotman, am I interrupting you?'

'Why, no, my lady, of course not.'

Eleanor realised the cook was still standing, with hands over the board. 'Please don't let me stop you. I fear Mr Clifford might start blowing smoke from his ears if I upset the meal schedule again.'

Mrs Trotman laughed. 'Mr Clifford has a most particular internal clock for routine, my lady. I think if all the clocks stopped, he'd still know when it was time to serve tiffin.'

Eleanor was grateful for her cook's warm personality. She was like everyone's favourite granny.

'Do you know where Mr Clifford is, Mrs Trotman?'

Mrs Trotman shook her head. 'It's your uncle, m'lady. Even though he was brought up a gentleman, he never liked a lot of servants. Said it made him feel as if he couldn't tie his own shoelaces without help. The Henleys have always been very self-sufficient, m'lady.'

'Of course, Mrs Trotman, but what has this got to do with Mr Clifford's frequent absences?'

'Well, in a household of this size you'd normally have other servants, footmen and the like, to run errands and so forth, but if Mrs Butters or me is tied up with laundry and cooking and such like, it's down to Mr Clifford.'

'But what about Polly?'

The cook giggled. 'Polly is… well, Polly. You can send her on an errand, but whether she ever comes back, and whether she comes back with anything you sent her to get…' She held her hands up in the air.

'But doesn't Mr Clifford find running errands, well…' She thought of Clifford's sniffy demeanour. '… beneath him?'

Mrs Trotman gave her a quizzical look. 'If I may, without speaking out of turn, my lady, perhaps you don't know Mr Clifford all that well yet.'

Eleanor cast around for something to break the slightly awkward silence.

'Gosh, something smells amazing.'

Mrs Trotman looked relieved to be back on safe ground.

'Ah, that'll be the bacon and onions. I'm making your late uncle's favourite, bacon badger pie.'

'Bacon badger pie? I've never heard of that, it sounds delicious.'

'It's an old Buckinghamshire recipe, looks a little like a giant sausage roll with crimped ends when it's finished, my lady. It takes three hours to prepare, but the result is worth it. Well, that's what your late uncle, God rest his soul, used to say.' She looked wistfully out of the window.

Eleanor was struck again at how much love and respect the staff and villagers showed when talking about her late uncle.

Mrs Trotman turned back to Eleanor. 'Mind you, I warrant you've eaten quite a few strange things on your travels, my lady.'

Eleanor laughed. 'Well, let's see… I've eaten goat, buffalo, kangaroo, alligator… and yak.'

'What on earth is a yak, my lady?'

'Oh, it's a kind of giant Himalayan cow. They make yak tea as well.'

'Tea from a cow! I never heard the like. Some folk are partial to a bit of squirrel round these parts, but I've never heard of no one making squirrel tea.'

Eleanor decided not to tell Mrs Trotman about the even more exotic items she'd eaten on her travels and switched subject. 'Please do continue cooking, I'm fascinated. I hope I'm not crowding your workspace?'

'Not at all, my lady, 'tis very nice to have the company.' The cook deftly shook the pan of sizzling bacon and onions on the stove, sending a delicious odour to Eleanor's nose. Back at the table, she arranged a cloth-wrapped parcel, another wooden board and a large knife.

Unwrapping the parcel, she took out four huge potatoes and sliced them into equally sized thin batons. A wisp of steam twirled up with each cut. Through the open pantry door, she reached for a jug of milk. After splashing a generous amount into a smaller jug she filled a small glass and set it at Eleanor's side with a smile.

Eleanor took a sip as the cook shuffled round and lifted down two of the most enormous mixing bowls she had ever seen. In a trice, flour, cubes of butter and the milk were transformed into a crafted ball of dough in the first bowl.

Transfixed by the activity, Eleanor looked up. 'What happens next?'

'Now we make the badger.'

Make a badger? How on earth did one make a badger?

As if she'd read Eleanor's mind, the cook continued. 'But that needs the flour to be sifted just right.'

'May I?' Eleanor said the words without thinking.

The cook smiled as she handed her an apron and a sieve before pushing a small sack of flour across the table.

Eleanor struggled to lift it. 'Perhaps, I should take up cooking for the sake of the exercise.'

The cook laughed and came to Eleanor's side. 'The trick, my lady, is to hook it in the crook of your arm and tilt it forward, guiding the neck of the bag with your other hand.'

Eleanor was enjoying Mrs Trotman's company and from the way the cook was bustling around her, gently explaining, Eleanor thought the feeling must be mutual.

The 'badger' element proved more complicated than Eleanor had expected. After sifting the flour and cleaning up the extra that had spilt, the cook showed her how to add shredded suet and water in exact proportions.

'I fear precision is not my strong suit, Mrs Trotman.' Eleanor peered into the bowl.

'There's always a rescue remedy for too much water, don't fret, my lady. But it isn't simply flour as some folk think.' She took what looked like a giant saltshaker and sprinkled a fine dusting of rusk into Eleanor's bowl. She then added a generous handful of finely chopped herbs.

'I'm reminded of the ballad of "Scarborough Fair"!' Eleanor exclaimed.

'Very close, my lady. Only there's no rosemary in bacon badger pie, only parsley, sage and thyme.'

Eleanor finished the milk in her glass. 'And the herbs are from the garden?'

'Gracious, yes. Mr Clifford made sure Joseph brought them up first thing before he left.'

Clifford! She'd come to grill Mrs Trotman about Clifford, not to learn how to bake four and twenty badgers in a pie.

'Did Clifford say where he was going, I wonder?'

'Mr Clifford did say he had some errands outside of the village but that he would be back in good time to serve dinner, should her ladyship be at home.' The cook gave Eleanor a wink as she rolled out the pastry that had finished resting in the bowl.

'He's an intriguing fellow,' said Eleanor. 'I know he has been with my uncle for, well, longer than I've been alive I suppose. And you're right, I don't really know him. I was, well, only a child when I used to stay here.'

'Mr Clifford is the epitome of loyalty. Your uncle, bless his soul, was most fortunate to have him in service all those years.'

'Indeed. Does Clifford have any friends in the village?'

'Friends? Well, everyone knows him. He does like to keep himself rather private, although him and Mr Sandford enjoy a tipple together sometimes, as is appropriate.'

'Clifford seemed awfully cross that I turned up unannounced that first day.'

'He was a little agitated under his starched collar, alright. But only on account of him having wanted to meet you properly at the station in the manner befitting the new lady of the house.' The cook looked down at the spoon in her mixing bowl for a minute.

Eleanor thought Mrs Trotman seemed embarrassed. *Oh dear, you've no idea about the proper boundaries between employer and staff, Ellie.* She looked at her food-covered hands and her empty milk glass. Whatever those lines were, it was obvious even to her that she'd seriously crossed them this afternoon.

Deciding the staff would just have to get used to her ways, she asked a question that had been niggling her for a while.

'The night of the storm, when I returned to the house a little…'

'Dishevelled, my lady?'

The women smiled at each other. The cook continued adroitly wrapping the neat pastry parcel with a fine web of hand-cut strings.

'Yes. Where was Clifford? Was he at home while I was out?'

'Initially, my lady, but not for long because the wind and rain got right up. So he went out to start the Rolls and then returned to find Mrs Butters.'

'Why did he need to find Mrs Butters?'

'Well, Mr Clifford worried that you might get lost, my lady, seeing as how you'd only just arrived. Mrs Butters came down with the message to keep lots of water boiling and to have tea and hot soup ready at a moment's notice. Then I saw Mr Clifford driving past.'

'And when did he return?'

'Oh, much about the time you yourself did, my lady, maybe a few minutes before.'

'That was most kind of you all. I fear I may have put you all to rather a lot of trouble after only a few hours of having arrived.'

'Oh, it was no trouble, my lady. That's what we're all here for, after all.'

'Yes, I suppose it is.' Eleanor untied her apron.

'Oh, leave that there. I'm nearly finished stringing up the pie. I'll be all cleared up in a jiffy and then I'll start in on the stewed apples.'

'Thank you, Mrs Trotman. This has been most enlightening, and enjoyable. What time will the bacon badger pie be appearing?'

'Seeing as he's to be the star of the dinner table, eight o'clock if that would suit you, my lady? Truth is, badger pie works at any time of the day so he'll be happy to fit right around your schedule.'

'Eight o'clock it is. I shall wait with tingling taste buds until then. Thank you again, Mrs Trotman.'

'A true pleasure, my lady.'

For the first time since arriving at Henley Hall, Eleanor decided it might, just might, one day feel like home.

CHAPTER 15

The following morning, Eleanor thought a gentle stroll with her trusty sidekick through the woods behind the Hall would quell her nerves about the upcoming invitation to Langham Manor, but it was futile.

'Oh stuff it, Gladstone. Why did I agree to go for this hideous luncheon? It will be a nightmare of etiquette and formalities.'

Brought up abroad by bohemian parents, she was more at home at a Uyghur wedding parade or a Zulu reed dance than a stuffy English society ball. Her uncle had been aware of that, so, after her parents' mysterious disappearance, he had sent her to that expensive girls boarding school where they'd tried to instil strict social etiquette into her. But by then she was an inveterate free spirit and all their Victorian teaching had been like water off a rather independent duck's back.

Gladstone picked up a stick that would have been better described as a tree and dropped it at her feet.

'I can't throw that, silly. I'd probably knock you out with it.'

Having thus vetoed the game of 'fetch', she fell into a comfortable pace, while the bulldog charged left and right after squirrels. Eleanor needed to talk her thoughts through with someone and, seeing as Clifford had disappeared again this morning, she settled for Gladstone.

'I don't feel I've got very far with the case, Gladstone. I mean, who have I got as suspects? Cartwright acted most unhelpfully and his story with the gate always being locked doesn't add up at all.

Not to mention his mysterious "transaction" with our mystery man. And there was a motorbike in his outbuilding, although I couldn't hear whether our mystery man rode off on it or not as Lancelot's plane was overhead. Maybe it's still in the outbuilding? Either way, Cartwright is suspect one. Then there's our rather dashing pilot, Lancelot. He hangs around near the quarry and has a motorbike and goggles. So, I suppose that makes him suspect number two.'

Gladstone had found a murky pool of water at the base of a tree. He looked up at her with algae green jowls.

'Yucky, boy! Okay, I'll bring some water next time.' She carried on pondering as they took the left-hand path. 'And Sergeant Wilby is definitely suspect number three.' She sighed. So, her total tally of suspects was the grand sum of… three. And she'd yet to establish a motive, even a tenuous one, for any of them.

Her hand flew to her mouth. Oh golly! Clifford! How had she not thought of him before? He knew Atkins, and had been peculiarly absent since the man died. Another thought struck her: Mrs Trotman had told her that on the night of the murder he had gone out in the Rolls after she'd left the house. *Think, Ellie, think!* Clifford had returned just before her and for him, he was positively flustered. He would have had time to drive round to the quarry entrance and… She looked behind her before turning back to Gladstone and whispering, '… and commit the murder!'

She gathered her thoughts at this unexpected twist. Clifford may have had the means and opportunity, but, like the others, what possible motive could he have had? Her uncle had trusted him all these years. Could he have been that bad a judge of character?

'Then again, Gladstone, I never really knew my uncle.' She bent down and tickled the dog's ear. 'The truth is, I have no idea who to trust. Except you, boy.' Pulling out her uncle's fob watch she groaned. *Time to get ready, Ellie. No chance of wriggling out of it now!* She blinked and shook her head. *Listen to yourself. Wriggle out of it? That's not the Ellie we know!*

As she set off back to the Hall with Gladstone trotting by her side, she wondered what had happened to the bold, fun-loving Ellie who would have taken whatever shenanigans lay ahead in her stride?

Later, up in her room, no matter how hard she tried to hurry, it seemed her body was as unwilling as her mind to get ready for the Langham Manor lunch.

She stared at the three dresses she'd thrown on the bed. 'Hmm, none of those are "the thing", I'm sure. What do you think, Gladstone?' A snore was his only reply.

Pulling on the fanciest, she looked in the full-length mirror. She twisted left and right, staring at her rear view. What was the point? It was wrong in every conceivable way. The black-and-white, dotted dress had been designed for a lady to interview tradesmen or deliver chicken broth to an aged relative, not attend a society function.

Ever the optimist, she threw on the crepe silk dress with a generous collar and asymmetrical wide ribbon placket on the outer hem, running from the neck to the waist. Stepping into her comfortable brown Oxfords, she was re-tying the laces when there was a knock at the door.

'Your car, my lady.' Clifford's eyes swept up and down Eleanor. 'May I enquire how long you would like me to ask Jenkins, the Langham Manor chauffeur, to wait?'

'Wait, Clifford?'

'In order that you can dress for the event.'

'I am dressed for the event.' She smoothed the front of her dress and pointed one foot out to the side. 'This is it.'

'If I may be permitted, my lady, you may want to reconsider.' He pulled open the door of the armoire.

Eleanor gasped. Beautifully sequinned, silk and feathered dresses filled the hanging space. 'Clifford, those are…'

'Your mother's. Yes, my lady.'

The lump in her throat stopped her from saying another word. With teary eyes, she stumbled over and ran her hand along the row of sleeves.

Clifford cleared his throat gently. 'My apologies for the shock. I had hoped you would find these for yourself.'

She nodded, still staring forward at the precious slice of her childhood that hung in front of her.

'I'll tell Jenkins that you will be twenty minutes.' Clifford closed the door and she was alone, with a melting pot of emotions and questions.

Mother's dresses? How had they got here? Her mind reeled. She reached out and touched the closest one – it was so familiar, so soft, and it was bringing back so many snippets of memories she'd buried. Her heart ached and skipped at the same time. Those sleeves had held the arms that had hugged her, the ones that had tickled her and picked her up when she'd fallen.

She pictured her mother. That loving smile and those piercing green eyes that always seemed to know what Eleanor was thinking. Brushing a hand across her cheek, she remembered how her mother had done the same before kissing her. 'Good night, God bless, sweet dreams.'

And then one morning, she had been gone.

Eleanor realised she was swaying. She held a finger under each eye to hold back her tears and reached for her mother's favourite grey silk gown. Her fingers ran over the bluebirds that were embroidered on the bustier and the delicate peonies set amongst an exquisite pattern of grasses swirling up from the skirt's base. She peeled off the poor cousin of an outfit she'd been wearing and slid into the dress, holding her breath. The fine lace sleeves stopped just above her elbows, and the waist hugged her perfectly.

In front of the mirror she gave in and allowed her tears to stream down her face, feeling a strange mix of grief and comfort as she stood seeing every inch of her mother in her own reflection. She wrapped her arms around an imaginary figure in front of her, hearing her mother's strong and comforting voice, *Ellie, this won't do. Come on, darling.*

Her mother was right, as always. She could unleash those emotions later, but it couldn't happen now. She had a murderer to catch.

Placing the matching shawl on her shoulders, she scrubbed at her face with a handkerchief. After hastily reapplying a little kohl to her eyes and a dash of rouge to her cheeks, she took a deep breath and opened the door.

Polly and Mrs Butters peeped over the bannisters as Eleanor made her way downstairs. 'So beautiful!' she heard Polly mutter before being silenced with a hasty, 'Shhh, girl!'

At the bottom of the stairs, Clifford stood waiting. He nodded without a word and turned. With her heart pounding, she followed him out to the waiting car.

CHAPTER 16

'Welcome to Langham Manor, Lady Swift.' The butler's hazel eyes twinkled.

'Ah, Sandford, I presume.'

He gave a perfect butlery half-bow that Clifford would have been proud of. As he bent, Eleanor held back a giggle. She stood over him by several inches, enough to note the shiny bald crown of his head and his remaining hair slicked into a neat parting.

'Lord and Lady Fenwick-Langham are receiving the luncheon guests in the rose garden, my lady. If you would be so kind as to follow me?'

Sandford led her through the grand hall to the terrace. Eleanor looked out over the garden, with each bed marked out by geometric lines of cut box hedges. She closed her eyes and drank in the heavy scent of the blooms as they continued along the central path to a circular, narrow moat, filled with flowering lilies. In the centre was a scrolling ironwork pagoda, large enough to seat a party of thirty.

'Lady Swift,' Sandford announced from the terrace to the group under the shade of the cream silk awning.

Carrying the elegance of her title with impeccable grace, a tall lady in her late fifties bustled down the path, her arms outstretched, with her tight, greying curls and deep-blue eyes creating a striking combination. Lady Fenwick-Langham was obviously a force to be reckoned with.

'Lady Swift, welcome, my dear. We've been so looking forward to making your acquaintance.'

'Lady Fenwick-Langham, such a pleasure.' Eleanor smiled. 'I have to congratulate you on your beautiful rose garden, I have never seen anything so exquisite.'

The lady of the house puffed up with pride. 'Thank you, my dear. It is my own little project, my haven. And you must forgive me. It was very remiss not to have asked you to Langham Hall earlier.'

Turning to the stout man who had appeared at her elbow, Eleanor held out a hand and tried hard not to stare at the monstrous handlebar moustache that met each ear in an unruly curl of grey whiskers. 'Lord Fenwick-Langham, I presume?'

'It's Harold, my dear, and the pleasure is all ours. Fancy the wife not having asked you up before, quite shocking.' He winked and offered his arm. 'Shall we introduce our new guest to the rest of the gang, or is there something else on the social agenda first?'

Eleanor giggled. Lady Fenwick-Langham gave him a mock slap on the shoulder. 'Ignore him, my dear. I think the champagne has begun to leak into his boots already. Shall we?' She pointed towards the others.

Under the awning, coloured silk sashes decorated a handful of chairs suggesting it was an intimate gathering. Lady Fenwick-Langham clapped her hands. 'Everyone, this is Lady Swift, our latest and most welcome addition to the area. Lady Swift has taken over Henley Hall after the tragic death of Lord Henley.' She turned to Eleanor. 'We all extend our deepest sympathies.'

Eleanor turned to the assembled company. 'Thank you, you are so kind.'

'Champers, my dear?' Lord Fenwick-Langham waved to the drinks waiter. 'Personally, I'd take two. Oils the tongue superbly if polite chatter isn't quite your thing.' He gave her elbow a gentle nudge and tootled off, calling 'Pudders, you reprobate, your glass is empty, what!'

His wife shook her head at his retreating form. 'I should have banished him to roam the fields with his favourite hunting gun, rather than pouring him into a morning suit and inflicting him on our guests,' she whispered to Eleanor.

Lady Fenwick-Langham took her arm. 'Now then, introductions. Lady Swift, Viscount and Viscountess Littleton.' She lowered her voice. 'His *American* wife. From Boston.' Her lips twitched. Eleanor held out her hand to the immaculately suited gentleman who started to rise at their arrival. His wife was swathed from head to toe in the latest Parisian fashion of violet silk pleats.

'Delighted.' As Viscount Littleton rose, he knocked the stiffened lace brim of his wife's hat.

'Let it alone!' she hissed, adjusting it back to the *mode de societé* angle and fiddling with her matching parasol in embarrassment. 'I already told you to keep your mitts to yourself!' The Viscountess' pronunciation of 'you' as 'yuh' seemed to offend her host, who winced visibly.

'Forgive me, my dears, I must continue with the introductions.' Lady Fenwick-Langham steered Eleanor to the next guests.

'Lady Swift, Dowager Countess Goldsworthy and her delightful niece, Miss Cora Wynne,' she announced with a flourish.

'Good afternoon.' Eleanor smiled at the elderly lady, marvelling at how tightly her ivory hair had been pulled into a bun beneath a neat tartan fantasia with half-length lace veil.

'Delighted to meet you, Lady Swift,' the dowager countess replied with a strong Scottish burr.

Before she could reply, a bellowing voice cut in. 'So, you must be Lady Wift?'

'Swift, with an "s". Really, Colonel.' Lady Fenwick-Langham tutted at the uniformed figure who had bowled into their conversation.

'Can always count on Pudders to stuff it up,' Lord Fenwick-Langham said with a laugh on his way past in search of more champagne.

'Colonel Puddifoot-Barton, at your service.' The military man saluted.

'Delighted, Colonel.' Eleanor saluted back.

'Dear, dear, whatever next,' he muttered and stood staring at her.

Lady Fenwick-Langham squeezed Eleanor's arm and tactfully steered her away.

'Is this the full group for luncheon, Lady Fenwick-Langham?' Eleanor asked as they set off down the path on their left.

'Yes, unless we are to be graced by the presence of my errant son. Oh, my dear Eleanor, I'm at quite my wit's end to know how to turn him into anything useful.'

Eleanor smiled and patted Lady Fenwick-Langham's hand, looped as it was through her arm. 'All boys grow up one day, I'm told.'

'Well, let us pray for that day to come sooner rather than later. Let us talk of the roses instead, my dear, it will calm my nerves.' She paused and sniffed delicately at a crimson bloom. 'The history of these glorious flowers fascinates me. There's so much romance in their stories. This one'– she cupped the bloom – '*Rosa gallica Officinalis*, more commonly known as The Apothecary's Rose or *Versicolour*. Can you believe that the crusaders fought to bring this exquisite bloom all the way from the Middle East to France?'

Eleanor nodded, distracted as a voice yelled across the garden.

'What ho, Sherlock!'

Lady Fenwick-Langham raised her eyebrows. 'When exactly did you say boys grow up, my dear?'

Eleanor smiled with a shrug as she watched Lancelot sliding down the stone balustrade of the staircase with his arms outstretched instead of using the steps. Jumping off deftly at the end, he gave his mother a peck on the cheek.

'Afternoon, Mater.'

Lady Fenwick-Langham sighed. 'Lady Swift, this is my son, Lancelot Germaine Benedict Fenwick-Langham.'

He ran his fingers through his hair and gave a boyish grin. 'Lady Swift and I have already met. She's been pursuing me in a most unladylike fashion.' Seeing his mother's red cheeks, he gave her a squeeze.

'Lancelot!' his mother shrieked in a hushed voice. 'Where are your manners? Dear Eleanor, I am so sorry.'

Eleanor laughed. 'Please don't apologise, we have already met, though I can't say there was any kind of pursuit.'

'Nonsense, first you scramble halfway across Cartwright's field…'

'He prefers Thomas,' Eleanor said.

'Then you hang on to me like a leech riding pillion on my bike to Chipstone.'

Lady Fenwick-Langham stared at Lancelot, her mouth agape, then at Eleanor.

Eleanor stuttered. 'Well, you see what happened was… I needed to get to the town hall… and Lancelot happened to be going.'

'Harold, where's that champagne?' The hostess turned. 'If you'll both excuse me a moment.'

Once they were alone, Eleanor dug Lancelot in the ribs. 'You total ape! How am I supposed to impress your mother if you go telling her tall tales about me? Especially saying I'm chasing after you and riding around on whatever silly name you've given your motorbike.'

Lancelot chuckled. 'Be honest, Sherlock, you've been looking forward to seeing me ever since the invitation arrived.' He cocked an eyebrow and stroked his chin waiting for her response.

Eleanor pushed him playfully. 'Actually, you weren't the highlight of the invitation.'

'Fibber!' He took her arm as the gong sounded for luncheon. 'Now, your job is to keep me free from the clutches of the delightful Miss Cora Wynne. Her aunt has got me in her sights as a wealthy suitor, the parsimonious old kilt.'

'Lancelot! That's no way to talk about a widow in her, what seventies or eighties? And Cora seemed sweet.'

'Wet as lettuce, old fruit. I like my girls with spirit.' He looked her up and down. 'And with a peculiar fashion sense and a penchant for bicycles. Let's eat, I'm famished.' Grabbing her hand he pulled her down the path.

'Stop, stop! Someone will see.' She giggled, holding onto her hat. Despite her desire to behave correctly at this real society event, her competitive streak kicked in and she raced Lancelot to the dining room, easily outpacing him.

At the entrance, Lancelot gave Eleanor's arm a gentle squeeze and then disappeared without explanation.

She snorted. *Men!* The minute you really need them, they disappear.

Sighing, she slapped on a smile and marched into the dining room.

CHAPTER 17

'Eleanor dear,' Lady Fenwick-Langham said. 'You are seated on the right, next to the dowager countess.' She pointed down the impossibly long table dressed with ivory linen and flawless floral arrangements. 'Delia dear, you are on the left beside the colonel. Hector dear, you are to the left of the countess.'

Predictably, Lancelot was still nowhere to be seen. Even his father had made it to the table and stood as he waited for the ladies to finish seating themselves. He gave a ding on his champagne glass with his fish knife and in a commanding tone announced, 'I declare this wonderful luncheon open. All sit.'

'Harold, where do you suppose Lancelot is?' Lady Fenwick-Langham looked at her husband with imploring eyes.

'No clue, light of my life. Want me to send the dogs out to find him?'

Eleanor snuck a peak at Sandford who stared forward, the corners of his mouth curling slightly.

Lady Fenwick-Langham sighed. 'Ladies and gentlemen, thank you all for coming. It is such a delight to see you all together. Let us enjoy a splendid luncheon in friendship.'

Cora stole a look at Lancelot's empty seat. This pulled Eleanor up short. She had been enjoying Lancelot's attention. In fact, she realised she had been staring at the door waiting for him to arrive too. There was something about the way he made her feel… She pulled herself together. *Until you've ruled him out as a suspect in your murder investigation, keep him at arm's length, Ellie!*

The dowager countess leaned past Eleanor to the hostess. 'A long stint in service, my dear Augusta, that's what he needs. You've pampered the boy terribly.'

'Here, here,' the colonel jumped in. 'Youngsters without direction or leadership turn into a menace all too easily. I'd soon stamp that errant behaviour out of him.'

Lady Fenwick-Langham raised her hand. 'Countess, Colonel, thank you for your thoughtful opinions. However, Lancelot is a fine young man, and it may have gone unnoticed that he is our son, so we will be the judges of—'

Just then the dining-room doors crashed open as Lancelot wobbled in on a bicycle and started a haphazard lap of the table. Eleanor covered her mouth with her napkin to hide her laughter. On his second lap, he produced a handful of small parcels from the handlebar basket and tossed one at each place setting.

'Fortune tea cakes!' Lancelot cheered with glee as he finished his final lap. 'Pal of mine has just come back from San Francisco, these tea cake things are all the rage. Thought it a great wheeze to kick off the luncheon travel tales with a bang.'

Lord Fenwick-Langham saved the moment by splitting the awkward silence with a roar of laughter. 'Enterprising initiative, son! What are they? Fortune cakes, you say?'

'They're to be taken at the conclusion of the meal, Harold,' his wife said from the head of the table, with her mouth set in a thin line. 'Thank you, Lancelot. A surprising addition to luncheon but we appreciate the thought.'

The colonel let out a contemptuous snort.

'Pudders!' Lord Fenwick-Langham cautioned. 'Wind your neck in, man!'

Eleanor kept her gaze away from Lancelot's, knowing she would lose her fragile composure if she caught his eye.

Viscountess Littleton spoke up with nervous excitement. 'Lancelot is right, Lady Augusta, these fortune cookie fellows really are the ultimate. They are served in Golden Gate Park in a Japanese tea ceremony. When Hector finally takes me back to The Hub, that's what we Bostonites call home of course, we're going to make the trip across the centre to visit. It is very firmly on our list of "must-dos", isn't it, Hector?'

Viscount Littleton gave a weak smile and looked across at Lancelot. 'Love the entertainment, old man, but I'm confused. Why the bicycle?'

His wife tutted and folded her arms. Eleanor groaned and wished Lancelot was close enough to kick under the table.

'In honour of our guest of honour, silly!' Lancelot pointed at Eleanor and grinned. 'You must have heard about her intrepid two-wheeled travels?'

Fearing the hostess' luncheon plans would soon be in ruins, Eleanor looked to Lady Fenwick-Langham for guidance. The lady of the house patted her hand and smiled. 'Dear guests, perhaps we should begin the meal, now that we have had the cabaret.' She glared at Lancelot. 'Let's allow Lady Swift the chance to fortify herself before she regales us with her travel stories. Sandford, please.' She nodded to the butler.

During the preliminary bouillon and sherry Viscount Littleton turned to his host. 'I say, I heard one of the fellows we were on last week's shoot with met with a rather nasty accident.'

Viscountess Littleton slapped her husband's hand and hissed, 'I told you not to bring up such matters at luncheon, it's uncouth!'

The viscount smiled at his wife coldly. 'Not at all, my dear, I merely wished to pass on my condolences.'

Before she could stop herself, Eleanor blurted out, 'Did you know him well, Lord Fenwick-Langham?'

Lord Fenwick-Langham grunted. 'Atkins? Only through your uncle. Atkins came to the estate to join the shoot a few times. Rotten shot.'

Lancelot laughed. 'There isn't a poohbah this side of Scotland who hasn't joined Pater's shoots. Every pompous old suit with a titled job and a stuffy, oak office has to be seen on at least one. You do know that Pater is one of the lead shots in the country, surely?'

Feeling as though she had just crawled out of a cave, Eleanor tried to wave his comment off. 'Of course, silly.' She frowned, trying to work out how to ask more about Atkins without arousing suspicion. Unable to, she asked anyway. 'What did Mr Atkins do? I remember meeting him as a child at Henley Hall, but I never really knew much about him.'

Lord Fenwick-Langham drained his sherry. 'He was some bigwig in Whitehall or some such, I believe. No idea what those johnnies do in those dreary offices all day.'

Viscount Littleton looked around the table. 'I recall asking him the same question on the shoot. I think he said he was some sort of investigator, as it were.'

'And what sort of investigator would that be?' the dowager countess asked drily.

The viscount wrinkled his brow. 'I don't remember his exact reply. Something quite hush-hush, I think.'

Lord Fenwick-Langham grunted again. 'Those Whitehall johnnies are always trying to justify their jobs and make out they're more than they are. I imagine he was just another pen-pusher who thought he could handle a gun.'

Lancelot laughed. 'I wonder if he was trying to fill his gun with ink when it went off! Probably couldn't tell the difference.'

'Lancelot!' Lady Fenwick-Langham glared at her son. 'The poor man's dead. Have some respect. Now, I agree with Viscountess Littleton, I think that's enough of that topic at the luncheon table.'

She turned to the dowager countess. 'Countess, how was your journey down from the Highlands?'

The dowager countess finished her spoonful of bouillon. 'Fiercely uncomfortable and tediously long. I fear this will be the last year I make the dreadful trip.'

'What rot!' Lord Fenwick-Langham waved his glass in her direction. 'Daffers, old fruit, you've been saying this will be your last year of travelling down for the past fifteen years!'

'Travelling does so improve a person we're told,' Viscountess Littleton said. 'Especially abroad.'

'Savages out there. A proper rabble and no mistake.' The colonel ran his cuff over the medals hanging on his chest. 'No place for women!'

'And where would you say was "a place for women"?' Lady Fenwick-Langham asked, looking coldly at the colonel.

'At home. They only get themselves into trouble abroad. No idea how to behave around Johnny Foreigner.'

Lady Fenwick-Langham flushed with anger and looked to her guest of honour. 'Tell me, dear Lady Swift, did you ever need a man to "escort" you abroad?'

The dowager countess turned to Eleanor. 'Your husband, perhaps?'

Eleanor held the countess' eye. 'Actually, I'm a widow. My husband was killed during the war.'

The dowager countess nodded. 'Aye, many were. Were you married long?'

'No, only four months.' And that was a few too many, she wanted to add. She'd met him in South Africa, a few months before war broke out. She'd been swept off her feet by the dashing officer. Until, that is, he disappeared two months later pursued by the South African authorities. She never found out for what, but the last she'd heard of him, he'd been shot by his own side for selling arms to the enemy.

Before the dowager countess could continue her interrogation, Lady Fenwick-Langham intervened. 'I'm sure Eleanor doesn't want to talk about such matters, perhaps she can be allowed to answer my original question?'

Eleanor smiled gratefully at her hostess. 'Thank you, Lady Fenwick-Langham. And to answer your question, I can't say that I ever did need a man to escort me abroad, even when married. I feel that the point of travel is to see what one is made of when difficult circumstances arise. To rely on one's own mettle, as it were.'

'Bravo!' Lancelot cheered. 'Score one to Mater and Eleanor. You going to take that lying down, Colonel?'

The colonel obviously wasn't. 'Of course, there's travelling and then there's *travelling*. It's all very well floating elegantly round the nadirs of tourism in a few capital cities, taking in a painting and a ruin. I, however, was referring to navigating the wilds beyond civilised Europe.'

Viscount Littleton had clearly had enough of the colonel's pompous attitude and innocently asked, 'Forgive me, Lady Swift, but I thought I had heard that you had been abroad in the deserts and jungles? Have I mis-imagined your tour *à la bicyclette*? I pictured you far past the border posts of civilised Europe.'

Eleanor beamed back at him, ignoring his wife's angry hiss. 'Really, I'd hate to bore you all with any of my inconsequential travel tales.'

'Oh, please do!' Cora said.

Lord Fenwick-Langham and Lancelot banged their soup spoons on the table, shouting, 'Speech, speech!' Viscount Littleton clapped along, ignoring his wife's death glare. The colonel just sat back in his chair and stroked his moustache. Only the dowager countess shook her head.

'Lady Swift, please consider the impressionable mind of my niece. I do not wish to spend my summer fending off her requests to embark on some caper with a carpetbag and a bundle of banknotes.'

'Aunt Daphne.' Cora clucked her tongue. 'I don't think Lady Swift's travels resemble Phileas Fogg's fictional adventure in *Around the World in Eighty Days*.'

'Too right,' Lancelot blurted out. 'Sherlock never had a Passepartout. You didn't, did you?'

Keen to avoid awkward questions about the origin of Lancelot's nickname for her, Eleanor hurried to answer him. 'Well, in truth, there were many occasions when the company of a valet would have been helpful. Cycling solo can be quite a lonely pursuit, if I'm honest. But no, I almost always travelled on my own, whether in Europe or beyond.'

'Almost always?' Lancelot's voice was quieter now. Cora frowned and leaned forward to be more in his line of sight.

The colonel couldn't contain himself. 'Dash it, do you mean to tell us that you, a woman, cycled around the subcontinent?'

Eleanor laughed. 'Of course not, Colonel. I only cycled part of the subcontinent… on my way around the world.'

There was a brief hush and then the table erupted, the colonel's voice cutting across the din. 'Around the world! A woman? On a bicycle? Impossible!'

The table quietened down to listen to Eleanor's reply. 'Actually, Colonel, I can take no credit. I was only following in the footsteps of the indefatigable Mrs Londonderry, who was the first woman to cycle around the world in 1894. Although I believe I may have pedalled quite a lot further than Mrs Londonderry.'

Despite her annoyance that Eleanor was taking centre stage, the viscountess couldn't help herself. 'Do tell us more, Lady Swift. Might one ask exactly what you were doing on your travels?'

Lady Fenwick-Langham answered for her. 'Delia dear, Lady Eleanor was Thomas Walker's Trailblazer. She mapped out and organised many of the routes of his travel company's inaugural tours of India and more. It is a remarkable achievement, my dear.'

Her praise touched Eleanor. 'That is kind of you. I did indeed meet Mr Walker but not until the end of my world trip. He offered me a job scouting out new routes. I was exploring a possible safari route in South Africa, the company's latest travel destination, when I received the news of my uncle's passing.'

'Oh, I see, you were working,' said the dowager countess, emphasising the word 'working' with disdain.

'Wasn't that frightfully dangerous?' Cora whispered, her eyes open wide.

'Thankfully never to the point that I felt compelled to call in her majesty's cavalry.' Eleanor smiled and met the colonel's gaze.

'I can't wait to hear how you pedalled through the deserts,' the colonel sneered.

'If you insist,' Eleanor said. 'Where would you like to hear about? Following the Silk Road through Turkey, Persia and China? Crossing the Himalayas? Travelling in Egypt through the Valley of the Kings? Seeking out new safari locations in South Africa?'

'Oh, Africa!' Miss Wynne cooed.

'China, for sure,' the viscountess offered. 'The silks are to die for.'

'Persia!' Viscount Littleton called out. 'I want to hear the desert stories.'

'No, I vote for Turkey,' Lady Fenwick-Langham countered, 'the home of the rose. I want to hear all about where my beautiful blooms originated. Did you know that royalty considered rose water to be currency three hundred years ago, so highly prized was it?'

'The Silk Road!' Lord Fenwick-Langham waved enthusiastically to the footman to refill everyone's glasses.

Lancelot sat back with a grin and winked at Eleanor.

Lady Fenwick-Langham nodded for Sandford to serve the entrées while Eleanor enthralled the table with her adventures.

*

The viscountess dabbed her napkin at the corners of her mouth. 'Lady Fenwick-Langham, the lobster was quite sublime. One must congratulate the chef.'

'Thank you, Delia, they were the finest of yesterday's Isle of Tiree catch, shipped overnight by train.'

This stirred the dowager countess from her doze. 'They'll have left Hynish Pier at eight o'clock on the dot, mind ye. Aye, our Scots fishermen are the finest in the world.'

The conversation was interrupted by the arrival of beef Wellington vol-au-vents served with caramelised onions and Madeira port relish, and the pouring of glasses of claret.

Lord Fenwick-Langham smacked his lips. 'Let the feasting and storytelling recommence. Where are you whisking us to now, my dear Eleanor?'

Out of deference to the hostess, Eleanor proposed, 'Turkey, the land of the rose and of the magnificent Ottomans, such a fiercely proud and dynamic group of people.'

'Come on, spill the beans, old girl, what scrapes did you get into… and out of?' Lancelot muttered.

Eleanor took a breath and looked around at the expectant faces. 'Well, perhaps I could tell you about my stay with the eminent Sultan, Mehmed the Fifth. You see, he needed a little help in solving a small problem.'

'And you helped solve it?' Cora lay across her plate in her excitement.

'It was merely a matter of miscommunication.'

The colonel snorted. 'Are we to believe you were an ambassador for His Majesty's government?'

'Gracious, no. I simply thought it a tragedy that lives should be lost over such a misunderstanding. You see, the sultan had inadvertently angered a powerful leader in the south of the country. They are a fearsomely proud race, the Turks. The sultan, however, was a very kind and gentle man, more suited to learning than fighting. After consulting his advisors, all of whom informed him that bloodshed was inevitable, he asked me, as an outsider, what I thought he should do.

'I asked him what was his most-prized possession, to which he replied without hesitation, "Muhteşeml". I must explain, the Turks are extraordinary horsemen and love their horses, and Muhteşeml was the sultan's favourite. A Turkoman stud, the father of no less than three champions, his incredible coat shone like gold in sunlight. I suggested that the only answer was to offer Muhteşeml to his adversary as a gift, which, even though it tore at his heart, he did.

'His adversary was so humbled that the sultan was willing to part with his most-prized possession to maintain their friendship, that he immediately ceased all hostilities. In fact, the gift of Muhteşeml not only reunited the two regions again, but went on to inspire an annual interstate horse race they've run every year since.'

Her audience devoured every word throughout the main course of roast pheasant and garden vegetables roasted in honey from the manor's hives. Among other exploits, she recounted the tale of her run-in with the Persian army in the Dasht-e Lut salt flats and the Hunza tribesmen befriending her in the high Himalayas. Her exploits in South Africa entranced the assembled company through the entremêts of dressed vegetables, devilled sardines and savarin of peach with goat's cheese. But over the dessert course of cherry and pear tart they returned, fascinated, to her tales of the Silk Road.

'But you couldn't have pushed your bicycle across that desert for two whole days!' groaned the viscountess.

'I didn't really have a choice,' Eleanor said. 'It was either that or lie down in the sand and hope the buzzards were hungry.'

CHAPTER 18

There was a most peculiar huffing sound coming from the room the staff referred to as 'the snug'. Eleanor saw nothing snug or cosy about it save for the fact it was a tenth the size of every other room. She peered round the door. Inside, Mrs Butters had a hand either side of Gladstone's chest and was attempting to dislodge him from the sofa.

She grunted and gave him an extra hard yank, but succeeded only in falling backwards at Eleanor's feet.

'I'm afraid Gladstone is becoming more wilful in his old age, my lady. And with his paws all over the leather Polly put her best elbow grease into buffing up only the other week.'

Eleanor laughed and offered Mrs Butters a hand up.

'Perhaps we could let him rest. To save Polly wasting her efforts in future, there is a red-and-blue blanket in my valise. It's a quirky combination of twill and plaid but it would cover the sofa perfectly. And it would protect the leather from Gladstone's scrabbling claws when he dreams of chasing rabbits.'

Mrs Butters laughed. 'But we probably have something less precious than your travelling blanket in the linen store that we could use.'

'Really, it is a well-used old thing. I only brought it along out of habit… and maybe a little sentimentality. It was a present from a delightful family that helped me out in a tiny mountain village in Chinese Turkestan. I did so often get lost trying to follow that elusive Silk Road.' She beamed at the housekeeper. 'I can't think of a more fitting end for a beautiful gift that kept me warm… well, mostly warm, on many a freezing night.'

'I'll go and fetch it now, my lady. Gladstone will think he's already up and gone to heaven. It's kind of you to think of Polly not wasting her time too.' Mrs Butters bobbed a half-curtsey and left the room.

Eleanor leaned over and rubbed the bulldog's soft, warm tummy. 'Sleep well, old friend. I'll see you later.'

'All aboard!' Eleanor closed the passenger door with considerable force.

'Did you find your coffee a little strong, my lady?'

Eleanor ignored Clifford. Even though she now had him pegged loosely as suspect number four, she saw no choice but to work with him. After all, he was the only one who believed her and besides, she'd yet to come up with anything remotely resembling a motive for him wanting to kill her uncle's old friend, so he was largely on her list to make it seem less lacking in suspects. 'Now, I'm going to watch your every move so I can learn how to drive this infernal machine.'

'Very good.' Clifford remained expressionless but Eleanor suspected she had seen a tiny shudder.

'Excellent idea of yours, this, Clifford, two chaps out on field ops, rooting out the killer. He's as good as caught!' She rubbed her hands together.

'Or her.'

'Or her?' Eleanor considered the idea. 'You think it might be a her? I'd never thought of that!'

'I have no reason to think so in this particular case, my lady, I was merely giving the fairer sex their due. After all, "Destruction often lurks in women's eyes" as Edward Counsel noted in his famous

Maxims. And in these times of increasing equality, it would be churlish having given women the right to vote, not to give them the right to murder. Or at least the equal chance to be considered as a suspect in a murder.'

'Well said, Clifford, how very Victorian of me, even though I'm reasonably sure that isn't what the noble ladies Pankhurst and Fawcett necessarily have at the centre of their suffragette vision.' She frowned. 'But we know the murderer was a man, I saw him.'

The car rumbled into life. 'True, my lady. Then again, as you proved yourself, it is a fairly simple matter for a woman to pass herself off as a man. Especially on a dark, stormy night.'

'Yes, you're quite right, Clifford, that does…' she trailed off as she digested his words. 'What the…! Clifford, how did you know about that?'

'About what, my lady?'

'About me passing myself off as a man? That was in Isfahan.'

The Rolls pulled away, forcing Eleanor back in her seat. How could Clifford have known? Unless…

'Clifford, did my uncle keep tabs on me after I left England?'

The car picked up speed and Clifford changed gear, his expression enigmatic. 'I really couldn't say, my lady.'

Eleanor went to speak and then stopped. If Clifford wanted to tell her at his own pace, then she would let him. She glanced at her uncle's butler, former batman and, she realised, friend. There was so much she didn't know about him and her uncle. But, it seemed, there was plenty they had both known about her.

Before going to the quarry, they stopped off in the village for an errand for Mrs Butters. Eleanor was out of the car before Clifford could react.

'I'll get the items on Mrs Butters' list while you wait here, Clifford. I can meet some more of the villagers, as I'm supposed to be the Lady of the Manor.'

Before he could respond, she crossed the pavement and entered the bakery they'd parked next to. The doorbell pinged as Eleanor stepped inside. The delicious smell of fresh bread and hot cinnamon instantly seduced her senses.

Feeling like an orphan clutching a precious penny she had found on the pavement, she tried to take in the full array of goodies on display. The counter was crammed with tray after tray of tempting sultana slices, cherry sponge cakes and mixed fruit pies, each with a perfect crust. Behind it, spotless wooden racking with loaves of every shape and size filled the rest of the shop. Glazed wheatsheafs decorated the walls, complete with wheaten harvest mice nestled amongst the sheaves.

'Why, Lady Swift, what an honour!' A radish-cheeked man wiped his floured hands on his apron.

Eleanor was accustomed to being the latest news now. 'Good morning, Mr…?'

'Morace Shackley. Welcome to our wonderful village. Little Buckford is in mourning for the death of your uncle. My sincere condolences, m'lady.'

'Thank you, Mr Shackley. You're very kind. Mrs Butters has… er, sent me with a most comprehensive list.'

'Sent you! Oh dear. 'Tis most uncommon, m'lady.' Shackley's face turned red. 'But… but most welcome.' Taking the proffered list, he peered at it. 'I see, the usual and summat a bit extra. I won't keep you a moment.'

'No hurry at all, Mr Shackley. Perhaps you'd be good enough to tell me a little about the village whilst you pack up Mrs Butters' order.'

'With pleasure.'

'I've just come from Mr Penry's fine establishment' – another little white lie – 'and I rather think I might have put my foot in it. You see, I mentioned Mr Cartwright of Pike's Farm.'

Shackley sighed. 'Oh, that would be an awkward conversation alright, m'lady.'

'Dear, dear, are they fighting over something particular?'

'Oh, they's not fighting. No, no. You got to be near enough to take a swing if you're going to fight. Penry wouldn't stand for being within thirty yards of Cartwright, I'd bet my bakery on that. Unless that is, it's for one of the local amateur dramatic society plays we put on twice a year. They're both members, same as me, but they have to be kept apart even then.'

'Just so I know what to avoid, what is Mr Penry's difficulty with Mr Cartwright?'

Shackley wiped his hands distractedly. 'Well, thing is, Dylan Penry is a cornerstone of the village so I wouldn't want to spread gossip.'

Eleanor rested her wicker pannier on the counter. 'Quite the opposite, Mr Shackley. You are simply sparing me some unladylike blushes.'

'Yes, of course, quite a different thing altogether.' Shackley leaned towards her conspiratorially. 'Truth is, m'lady, some folk would say stealing was wrong, whether it was you who stole it or you who are merely profiting by another man stealing it.' He paused. 'But then Mr Cartwright isn't "some folk", if you get my drift. And Mr Penry is a man of strong moral principles.'

The shop bell jangled. Two old ladies shuffled in, greeting Mr Shackley and Eleanor as they did so. It was obvious that Shackley had no intention of saying any more with the ladies present.

'Thank you, Mr Shackley.' Eleanor added the white-paper parcels to her shopping pannier. 'You've been most illuminating. And, you've definitely spared a lady's blushes.'

Shackley nodded. 'Delighted to have been of help, Lady Swift.'

*

Eleanor drummed her fingers on the walnut dashboard of the Rolls as a vista of hedgerows passed unheeded.

'Well, that wasn't very illuminating, except now we know Cartwright is definitely mixed up in something crooked. But what exactly?'

Clifford nodded. 'In a close-knit village like Little Buckford, my lady, everyone may know everyone else's business, but it does not mean they want to impart that knowledge to…' He hesitated.

'A stranger? An offcomer?' She shrugged. 'Anyway, to the quarry!'

The quarry gates were eight-foot high and barred with a row of uncapped prongs protruding from the top. She lifted the heavy padlock, which felt surprisingly cold given the warmth of the sun.

'Well, Cartwright's story of the gates always being locked seems to be true,' she called to Clifford as he walked round to the rear of the car. 'At least, it is this morning.'

Leaning back, she scanned the run of the fence. Clifford came to join her.

'Clifford, I'd say the easiest route is up and over the right-hand gate. Do you see that tall pile of… whatever that is by the gatepost? We simply scramble over, using the post to balance ourselves. Then drop down the other side landing neatly on that other pile of…' she peered through the bars, hands holding the upright metal struts '… of, well, it looks like gravel, wouldn't you say?'

The voice that answered wasn't Clifford's.

'Gravel it be. Just right for turning an ankle on.'

Eleanor and Clifford spun in unison.

'Even in stout boots.' Cartwright nodded at Eleanor's feet and lifted the front of his cap the barest half an inch in greeting.

'Mr Clifford.'

Clifford nodded back.

Cartwright looked across to Eleanor. 'Perhaps I shouldn't be surprised, Lady Swift, that you appear to have taken up a keen interest in the business of quarrying. 'Tis a bit unusual for a lady, mind.'

'Oh, I'm quite the student, Mr Cartwright. One must expand the mind to save it from stagnating like a rotten cabbage.'

Cartwright smiled as he pushed himself off the wall he was leaning on and rocked on his heels. 'So, 'tis flint and sand you're interested in now, is it?'

It sounded more like a threat than a question.

'Less so than murder, Mr Cartwright. But I think you know that already.'

'Seems I do know that. And what I'm more interested in is two people, lurking about trespassing somewhere they've no business.'

'Quite the model citizen, aren't you, Mr Cartwright? Well, you can rest assured, there's simply no trespassing going on, none that I can see from where I'm standing, anyway.'

Cartwright looked unconvinced.

Clifford gestured towards a substantial beech tree that lay where it had fallen on the opposite side of the road. 'Not a good time for that storm last week, Mr Cartwright.'

Eleanor smiled to herself. Clifford had all the subtlety she lacked. The night of the storm had also been the night of the murder! Now they could find out if Cartwright's alibi held water or not.

Cartwright nodded. 'Yep, bad timing alright. Could have been worse, I suppose. I didn't lose any lambs, but the flock was in a heck of a state. And then blow me if the wind didn't get under the roof of the barn with the nursing pens in. Ripped it half off. I had a job hanging on to the beams and trying to stop the tin top from sailing off over the copse altogether. Nailing roofs in high winds ain't my favourite.'

'Well, at least your tools would have been ready at hand, Mr Cartwright,' Eleanor chimed in.

Cartwright shot her a look that made her pleased Clifford was standing between them.

'Is you suggesting something, Lady Swift?'

'Good gosh, not at all. I was merely saying that you omitted to mention the barn roof coming unpinned in your previous conversation with me. After all, the night of the storm was also the night of the murder I witnessed in the quarry, and you told me you were sharpening your tools at home all evening.'

Clifford stepped in. 'Would that have been around ten o'clock you left the farmhouse to mend the roof, Mr Cartwright?'

'As it happens, yes. Took me almost two hours in the end to fix that darned roof.'

Clifford and Eleanor exchanged a glance. *Just long enough to get to the quarry, shoot Atkins, take the body to his house, arrange it to look like an accident, get back and clean up!*

She decided to go for a different tack. 'I believe we have a mutual acquaintance, Mr Cartwright.'

The farmer's bushy brow furrowed, but he said nothing.

'When we last met I thought I saw you with someone I… recognised,' she lied. 'He seemed to be handing you some sort of package.'

Cartwright folded his arms and stared at her coldly. 'My business is my business, Lady Swift, and I'll thank you to keep yourself out of it!'

Eleanor smiled sweetly. 'I absolutely agree, Mr Cartwright. It's just that some people, Mr Penry, for instance, might disagree.'

Cartwright's eyes flashed. 'That damned sanctimonious Welsh fool! He's a fine one to talk! You ask him where he really gets his meat from and see how high and mighty he is!'

'From our mutual friend, perhaps?' It was a stab in the dark, but it seemed to hit home. Cartwright's eyes narrowed, but he stayed silent. Unabashed Eleanor tried again. 'It's just that I could swear I knew the gentleman from somewhere. Is he a quarry worker, perhaps?'

Cartwright took a step forward. A cough interrupted his reply.

'Perhaps we should be getting along to your other appointment, my lady?' said Clifford.

Reluctantly, Eleanor could see that they weren't going to get anything more out of Cartwright. 'I suppose so. Goodbye, Mr Cartwright.'

Clifford nodded at the farmer. 'Mr Cartwright.'

'Mr Clifford. Lady Swift.' Cartwright leaned back against the wall watching until they were both aboard and Clifford had eased the Rolls back out onto the road.

CHAPTER 19

'What an obstructive fellow,' said Eleanor.

'Farming stock have their way.' Clifford slowed to take a long left-hand bend. 'And we were contemplating trespass.'

Eleanor harrumphed. 'But he was being deliberately obtuse.'

'Forgive the directness of my observations but I rather fear he felt the same way about us.'

'Point taken, Clifford. However, for some reason that man riles me. He's definitely hiding something. And did you see how he reacted when I mentioned the man on the motorbike supplying meat to Penry?' She frowned. 'Do you think that Cartwright is involved in some illegal farming activity? Maybe he's supplying sub-standard meat or similar?'

'Perhaps, my lady. Possibly Mr Atkins stumbled upon it?'

Clifford pulled the stop brake on the car and watched the small biplane that had circled the field dip below the hedge as its engine puttered to a halt.

'Lancelot!' Eleanor muttered. She instinctively patted her curls and straightened her hat.

'Shall we see if young Lord Fenwick-Langham can back up the alibi he gave you on your last visit? We can discuss Mr Cartwright's veracity back at the Hall, if that would suit?'

'Absolutely.' Eleanor stared forward. 'And I could look more closely at his motorbike to see if it resembles the one from the quarry road. I didn't think to look when I rode into Chipstone with him.'

'I suspect your mind was on other matters.'

She spun round. 'Clifford?'

His face remained expressionless. 'Such as hanging on, my lady. Young Lord Fenwick-Langham has a reputation for riding his motorcycle with great… gusto.' He adjusted his driving gloves and gestured towards the gate. 'Shall we?'

Clifford suggested they wait until Lancelot was on his way to his motorbike. That way they could pretend to be admiring the machine while surreptitiously checking it for similarities with the one from the quarry road. However, the sight of Lancelot waving as he strolled across the field scuppered their plan.

'Hey, Sherlock!' he called.

'Hey, Goggles!' she shot back.

'Goggles! I love it.' He swung them on his wrist. 'They are quite the image, aren't they?' Standing close to her, he ruffled his hair. 'Ah, Mr Clifford. Good day.' He gave Clifford a mock salute.

'Good day, Lord Fenwick-Langham.'

The wind rippled Lancelot's loosely tucked white shirt across his chest. He grinned at Eleanor. 'So how's it going? Are the delights of Little Buckford keeping you up at all hours?'

She laughed. 'Well, for what should win sleepy village of the year award, there has been a lot to occupy my time.'

'Oh, what have I missed? Have you dreamed up the ultimate wheeze and not invited me in as your accomplice? Shame on you!' He waggled a leather-clad finger close enough to brush her nose, which she couldn't help giggling at.

'No, you fatuous thing. I mean the murder I saw.'

'Oh, that old chestnut. You still up to that amateur detective lark? And dragging poor Clifford round the county interviewing suspects, I suppose.' He paused for a second. 'Hold on a tick, isn't this a social call?' His voice showed a hint of vexation.

Eleanor wondered if it was disappointment. 'It is, and it isn't.'

He patted the top of her head and grinned. 'Well, start with the non-social bit and get the dull stuff out of the way pronto.'

'Right, so tell us again where you were the night the murder happened in the quarry.'

He looked at Eleanor with his steel-grey eyes. 'Oh my! So now I get it. You're accusing *me* of the murder.'

'Gosh no, Lancelot! But you rent the field next to the quarry where I saw the murder. I am merely trying to establish those who might have seen anything.'

'Well, that's something of a shame. I wouldn't mind the notoriety.' He chuckled. 'Was that the night before you scandalously pursued me across a muddy field and then accosted me in the cockpit?'

'Well, if one were to remove the words "scandalously", "pursued" and "accosted", yes.'

'Sorry to disappoint, old fruit, but, as I told you before, I was at a masked ball in Oxford.'

'Where in Oxford exactly?'

'The Goat Club. It's quite fabulous.'

'What time were you there?'

'I don't usually keep track of these things, you know.' He thought for moment. 'I suppose I arrived around nine, but I've no idea what time I left. I was far too pickled.'

'Can anyone else vouch for that?'

'Probably a fair percentage of the hundred or so of us who were there.' He smiled and folded his arms.

'But weren't you in a mask?'

He tutted and put a gentle arm around her shoulder so he could whisper conspiratorially into her ear. 'That's kind of the point of a masked ball. The clue really is in the name.' Standing straight he laughed. 'I'd say you might want to work on the easier aspects of sleuthing first. Perhaps you've jumped in too deep, too soon?'

His patronising tone provoked Eleanor but the feel of his arm around her shoulder did so even more strongly. She groaned. *This wasn't supposed to happen…*

'So, were you with your "Bright Young Things" crowd? I suppose they can vouch for you?'

'Sherlock, you're hilarious! "Bright Young Things" is just some sensationalist moniker, dreamt up by an embittered newspaper hack in a back office somewhere dreadfully dreary. It has caught on though.'

'Yes, it has. I gathered it was your sort of thing.'

'Ah! Perhaps you're better at this snooping lark than I realised.' He leaned in sideways. 'Or, you just can't stop talking about me.'

Eleanor ignored his comment. 'But were you with whatever you would call the gang you hang out with or not?'

'Of course, some of my friends were there. The usual lot.'

'I'd like to meet them sometime. None of them were at the lunch yesterday, were they?'

'No, the parentals aren't that keen on my "Bright Young Things Gang", as I shall call them from now on. They don't mind them in small doses at the balls and suchlike, but not at more intimate social gatherings.'

'The parentals?'

Lancelot laughed. 'Mater and Pater. They've got very set ideas about what I should be doing and who I should be seeing. It's all for my own good and blah, blah, blah…' He shook his head. 'You know what I mean.'

Eleanor laughed and swallowed hard at the same time. 'I don't think I was ever really old enough to get up to anything my parents disapproved of while they were around.'

'What a pity. But to answer your question, none of my friends are murderers. Mind, there are a couple of them who might not be above that kind of thing if the opportunity arose. Anything to enliven a dull evening.' He grinned at her shocked look. 'Now, spill the beans, old girl. Who bought it in the quarry?'

'Spencer Atkins,' she blurted out before she could stop herself.

Lancelot whistled. 'Really? No wonder you were asking all those questions about him at luncheon. Now, are we done with the interrogation stuff? Because I have to be off. Got to see a man about a duck.'

'A duck?' She glanced at Clifford who raised an eyebrow, signifying Lancelot was teasing her again. Despite her irritation at Lancelot's mockery, Eleanor was disappointed he had to go. 'Absolutely, yes, quite done. I'm running late myself,' she said.

Turning to leave, Lancelot squeezed her wrist. 'How about more of the social stuff instead, next time? Make it soon, okay?'

'I haven't forgotten your promise of a flight,' Eleanor called after him.

With a cheery, 'Happy sleuthing,' he roared off, leaving the gate swinging on its hinges.

As they walked back to the Rolls, Eleanor felt rather lost. Had that conversation come to anything? What had they learned? More importantly, was Lancelot just teasing or did he like her too?

Clifford held the passenger door open for her as she climbed in. 'Do you think the conversation moved us on in our investigation, Clifford?'

'Well, my lady, we can at least now check out young Lord Fenwick-Langham's alibi for the evening of the murder. I am acquainted with the doorman of The Goat Club, so if it suits you, I will make some enquiries.'

Eleanor climbed into the Rolls. 'Of course, Clifford, that would be splendid.'

As Clifford eased the car out on the lane, he turned and coughed. 'But if I may say so, I'm not sure it was entirely prudent to mention your theory about Mr Atkins to young Lord Fenwick-Langham.'

Eleanor gasped. 'You really do suspect Lancelot, don't you?'

'At this stage, my lady, I fear everyone must remain a suspect. Everyone.'

'Including you?' Eleanor prickled.

'I would fall in the collective of "everyone", so in that respect, yes.'

'Well, if your theory holds water, I must be a suspect too. Maybe I killed the man and then made up the story? How fiendish of me! We should both hand ourselves over to the authorities.'

Clifford seemed to consider the suggestion. 'It would save his majesty's overstretched police force a lot of time and trouble.'

Eleanor smiled. 'I think we can rule ourselves out of the list of suspects.' But she did have a twinge of doubt. *Except I'm not absolutely sure about you, Clifford.*

CHAPTER 20

As the Rolls rolled on through the lanes, Eleanor turned to Clifford. 'You know it was a dashed shame we couldn't check Lancelot's motorcycle more closely.'

'Indeed. Although…'

'STOP!' She pulled at the passenger door handle. 'Grab him!' Eleanor was out of the car before it stopped.

'Hey! I say, you there!' She ran across the road.

A van emblazoned with the slogan *Chiltern Provisions. Delivering the Best* screeched to a halt only feet from her. The van itself looked as if its best was well behind it. A concerned face stared out of the driver's window. 'What the… oh, goodness, excuse me, madam.' The man glanced across at the Rolls and grinned. 'Are you in trouble? Is this gentleman bothering you?' He winked across at Clifford still sitting in the Rolls.

'Not at this precise moment, but I'm sure the time will come. I do apologise though for my rather dramatic way of accosting you.'

'That was a little close for comfort, madam, do excuse me. The van's brakes, well they don't get tested like that too often, thank goodness.'

'No, it is for me to be excused. I startled you and now I'm going to cap it all by asking for a favour.'

'A favour? Have… have we met?'

'Not at all,' she replied breezily. 'Lady Swift, pleased to meet you.'

'Good afternoon… m'lady. I'm Pete.' He hesitated. 'And… I'm sorry about your uncle.'

Eleanor started. 'You knew my uncle?'

'Not personally, of course. Highly respected throughout the area, without a doubt.'

'Thank you.' Once more she was surprised at the level of respect her late uncle seemed to have aroused, even in the tradesmen of Chipstone.

Clifford walked up, having found a spot where the car wouldn't become stuck in the mud left by the passing tractors.

'Clifford, this is Pete. But wait, you probably both know each other already?'

'Of course we do. Morning, Mr Clifford.' Pete nodded as he touched his cap.

'Good morning, Mr Sturgess.'

Pete looked back to Eleanor. 'So has your fancy car broken down? Is it a lift you're after?'

'Not today, thank you, Pete. I flagged you down to pick your brain.'

'Well, I'd have to wish you good luck with that, m'lady, not sure my brain's going to do you much good. I've never been much of a thinker. Most I do is try and stick to the delivery schedule and offload the right boxes at the right place.'

'Nonsense, Pete, I have learned the world over that delivery drivers are the ears and eyes of the road.'

'We are, m'lady?'

'Indeed, you know your routes inside and out. If anything is out of place, it strikes you immediately.'

Pete nodded but his brow was furrowed.

Clifford took half a step forward. 'I believe Lady Swift is asking if you have seen anything unusual in the last few days while making your deliveries in the Little Buckford area.'

'Ah, thanks, Mr Clifford. That's plenty clearer.' The delivery driver scratched the front of his shirt. 'Well, now you come to say, there's one of them guests up at Langham Manor as has got a terrific appetite for canned shrimps. I've taken I don't know how many trays of them up there.' He paused. 'Can't think of much else unusual.'

'What about on the evening of the storm? Did you, perhaps, see a motorcyclist around say ten and eleven thirty anywhere in the vicinity?'

Pete rubbed his chin. 'That was a real blind-man's holiday, that was!'

'A dark night, my lady,' Clifford translated.

Pete nodded and grinned. 'Come to think of it, there was something. Not a motorcyclist but—'

Eleanor leaned forward eagerly. 'What?'

Pete instinctively stepped back. 'It's probably nothing, but a car drove clean off the road from Chipstone to Radington that evening and got well stuck. Them verges were well soft that night what with the storm and all the rain we've been having. Took some heaving with Cartwright's tractor the next morning to pull it out.'

'Where exactly? Before the turning to the old quarry, or after?' Clifford asked.

Pete thought for a moment. 'Funny you should say that, 'cos it was on the junction with the quarry road itself.'

Clifford raised an eyebrow. 'Strange it should get stuck there. Unless it was coming from the quarry road onto the main road at speed and misjudged the turn in the dark.'

Pete shrugged. 'Could be, but what would anyone be doing up that road on a night like that? Don't lead anywhere except to the quarry and there haven't been any workings going on there for a while.'

'Do you have any idea when it got stuck?'

Pete frowned. 'Not really. I saw Cartwright dragging it back on to the road in the morning and he told me it got stuck the night before, but I never asked him when.'

Eleanor jumped in. 'Did you by any chance see the driver? Or ask Cartwright who owned the car?'

Pete grinned. 'I only saw old Cartwright there. Never thought to ask about the driver. If I'd known a lady would be interested, I'd have asked.'

Eleanor digested this information. 'No matter, you have been most helpful, Pete.'

'Really? Why, thank you, m'lady. Now, if it's all the same to you, I'd better be getting along. I've a full list of deliveries today.'

'Absolutely, I am sorry we've detained you for so long.'

'No problem.' Pete pulled his cap back on and swung himself up into the van.

'Oh, one last thing.' Eleanor couldn't restrain her natural directness. 'Maybe you could ask your colleagues if they saw anyone with… a body, a dead person that is, perhaps being loaded into a van?'

Pete frowned. 'None of us could carry a body, m'lady, not in with foodstuffs. 'Tis against regulations. Most folk use a horse and cart round here for funerals. Old Clackett did once use his lorry when one of his horses went lame in coffin season.'

'The undertaker, my lady,' Clifford said.

Pete crunched his van into gear and leaned out of the window. 'I hear that in London, fancy folk use a Rolls for funerals, Mr Clifford. City folk!' He waved and lurched away.

Clifford and Eleanor walked back to the car.

'You know, Clifford, we need to find out more about the car that got stuck the night of the murder. And why Cartwright never mentioned it.' She stopped by the Rolls and stared at it for a moment. 'You know though, I'm not sure I agree with Pete. The Rolls would make a great vehicle for a funeral.'

Clifford bent down on the other side and spoke through the window. 'Is that how you would like to go, my lady, "lying in state" in the Rolls?'

Eleanor laughed, still peering into the rear of the car, imagining the looks on the faces of the villagers as the unorthodox funeral procession passed. 'Sadly not. I shall be cremated.'

'Cremated, my lady?'

'Of course.' Eleanor tapped her chin. 'However, I fancy it might still be illegal here.'

'On the contrary, the Cremation Act was passed a good while ago. Her Royal Highness, The Duchess of Connaught and Strathearn, Princess Louise Margaret, was cremated last year and interred less than thirty miles away in the grounds of Windsor Castle.'

'Fascinating, Clifford, thank you. What a simply splendid mine of information you are. A simple cremation for me then. But what of my uncle, was he cremated?'

'Heavens no, my lady, your late uncle was firmly against such a practice.'

'Did he say why he was so set against it?'

'Indeed, he always insisted that if he were to be cremated, it would significantly hinder his plan.'

'Which was…?'

'To come back from the dead, my lady.'

CHAPTER 21

They were greeted by the ding of the doorbell, the genteel murmur of voices and the clinking of fine bone china. Eleanor looked around. Soft wall lights complemented the tasteful chandeliers and helped illuminate the silver thistle relief of the vanilla damask wallpaper. Below each light a framed farming scene had been hung: gleaming cows munching emerald grass, and spotless farm maids bearing baskets of wholesome vegetables.

After their encounter with Pete, Clifford had suggested they stop for sustenance given, as he had pointedly put it, 'Luncheon has been missed, *again*.'

She'd agreed immediately, never being one to turn down food, especially when, according to Clifford, there was not five minutes from there an excellent tea shop whose fruitcake had won several awards.

Before Eleanor could pick out a place to sit, a waitress approached and bobbed a curtsey. 'Welcome, miss, sir, a table for two?'

The doorbell dinged again.

'Why, Inspector, good afternoon.'

'Good afternoon, Lady Swift, Mr Clifford.' DCI Seldon removed his bowler hat and balanced it against a large notebook he held to his chest. He shook her hand, then Clifford's.

Eleanor smiled. 'How wonderful to run into you. Are you taking a break or has there been murder and mayhem in these delightful tea rooms?'

The waitress gave her a brief glance of horror. DCI Seldon shook his head at the young woman. 'Rest assured I am here for nothing more dangerous than the fruitcake.'

'A man after my own heart,' Eleanor said. 'Inspector, would you care to join us? Only don't feel the need to be polite if you'd planned for this to be a working break.' She nodded at the notebook. 'I shan't be at all offended if you decline.'

DCI Seldon's brown eyes twinkled, in a way that belied his gruff exterior. 'That is a kind offer, thank you.'

'That's sorted then.'

Clifford turned to the waitress. 'A table for three. In the gallery, please.'

From her apron pocket the waitress produced a tiny notepad and a perfectly sharpened pencil. She smiled nervously. 'What would you like today?'

Eleanor cocked an eyebrow at the inspector. 'How much time do you have? Shall we do justice to this fine establishment's reputation and take three full afternoon teas?'

'If that suits you, Lady Swift, that would be most welcome. I have to confess that luncheon passed me by, a hazard of the job.'

'Three set afternoon teas, with warmed cups, and extra preserves.' Clifford nodded to the waitress who wrote out the order with care and then led them to a short, raised section at the far end of the building. A highly polished handrail led them up the five steps to a generous, rectangular table, flanked by cream button-backed chairs. It promised a degree of privacy, since anyone approaching would be readily spotted.

Clifford took her coat and hung it on the hat stand at the top of the short staircase, along with his hat. DCI Seldon shrugged out of his substantial blue wool overcoat and hooked the small chain loop over the peg alongside. He added his hat to the stand and ran a hand through his wavy brown hair. The gentlemen waited for Eleanor to sit down, then took their places.

DCI Seldon appeared distracted as he still held onto his note-book. 'Actually, Lady Swift, there is a matter I wished to discuss with you. I had planned to call at Henley Hall. Perhaps you would prefer me to do so rather than be so coarse as to mention police matters over tea?'

'Not at all. You are welcome to call at the Hall anytime. However, I'm caught up in a rather pressing matter myself, and you are unlikely to find me at home. Besides, my stomach is not at all squeamish, so now is a fine time to discuss whatever it is. Ask away.'

Just then the waitress appeared with an even more nervous assistant in tow, both weighed down with an impressive array of tea and food.

'Splendid!' Eleanor beamed as they placed tiered stands of delicately cut sandwiches, fruit scones and cakes on the table. An enormous china teapot followed with three perfectly warmed cups.

'Will that be all?' the waitress asked.

'For now, thank you.' Eleanor stared at the quantity of food. It seemed that beneath their fine airs and manners, the clientele were proper country folk with robust appetites. 'Golly, I hadn't realised how famished I was.'

'Shall I pour the tea, my lady?' asked Clifford.

'Rather!' Eleanor sat back in her seat and put her hands together on the table. She smiled. 'So, Inspector, are you now more inclined to believe my report of the murder at the quarry?'

DCI Seldon grunted. 'Lady Swift, there was never a question as to my believing, or disbelieving, your account. There are simply not enough facts to pursue an investigation.'

Eleanor took the steaming teacup Clifford held out. 'Thank you, Clifford.' She sipped her tea. 'By jingo, that is hot!' She fanned her lips and clattered the cup and saucer down on to the table.

'Are you alright, Lady Swift?' DCI Seldon looked genuinely concerned, which surprised her, given his gruff manner.

'Quite alright, thank you,' she lied, taking a big gulp of iced lemon water.

'Right.' The inspector rearranged the finger sandwiches on his plate and picked up a salmon sandwich, looked at it with suspicion and took a bite. 'I am sorry, but my investigations simply do not point to any other conclusion than that Mr Atkins met with an unfortunate accident.'

Eleanor paused in the unladylike pose of having half a cucumber sandwich in her mouth, and half very much not. Setting the sandwich back on her plate, she stared at him. 'I fail to see how you can make such a sweeping statement, Inspector. Surely, it must strike you as odd that only the day after I reported the quarry murder, Mr Atkins' body turns up? Both men shot?' Eleanor hesitated between the second and third tiers of delicacies. 'Shall I start in on the fine-looking fancies or dive straight into the fruitcake? It's a dilemma. What do you think, Inspector?'

DCI Seldon sighed. 'Lady Swift, I understand your belief that the missing body from the quarry was that of Mr Atkins, but there are no facts to back this up. And from the impression I have formed of the gentleman so far, the thought of Mr Atkins stumbling about in the gloom in a muddy quarry is not an image that comes easily to mind.'

'And yet you did not bat an eye when I told you I had done exactly that!'

DCI Seldon failed to hide a smile. 'First impressions can be so unreliable… although not always.'

An awkward silence pervaded the table.

'More tea, my lady?'

'Thank you, Clifford.'

'Inspector?'

'No, thank you, I fear I must be getting along.' DCI Seldon rose to go.

Eleanor tutted. 'Inspector, you've only just sat down. And you haven't eaten a thing.'

DCI Seldon shrugged. 'A consequence of the job.' He pocketed his notebook and pen. 'May I ring you this evening, Lady Swift?'

This time it was Eleanor who raised an eyebrow. 'Ring me, Inspector?'

He coughed. 'If there are any further developments. I feel I owe you the courtesy.'

'No, Inspector.'

'No?'

Eleanor laughed. 'Not until you have devoured your share of the fruitcake.' She held a slice out to him.

He sighed but sat back down. 'Thank you. Then, Mr Clifford, it seems I will require another cup of tea after all.'

CHAPTER 22

From the Rolls Eleanor watched as the rows of flint houses gave way to hawthorn hedges and sheep scattered fields. Kites wheeled above in the cloudless sky. This was rural England at its finest.

It was the morning following their meeting with DCI Seldon and he had, as promised, called the previous evening. However, the conversation hadn't gone the way Eleanor had hoped.

'Firstly, all facts considered, there is insufficient evidence to warrant any further investigation into the "quarry murder",' he had said. 'I simply cannot justify the man-hours that would entail to my superiors, given the paucity of evidence. And secondly, Lady Swift, it is my duty to officially caution you against interfering in the investigation of Mr Atkins' death. I must insist…'

But she had replaced the receiver, and he was talking to himself.

In the Rolls, Eleanor sighed. 'It was a good idea of yours, Clifford, this drive after breakfast. I'm already feeling in a brighter mood.'

Clifford slowed for a sharp corner. 'I thought we could discuss the case and if you would permit me, my lady, I can show you the sites you never had a chance to get to know on your previous visits.'

She leaned back in her seat. 'That would be lovely, Clifford.'

'And I have some information from Mr Sandford that corroborates one of our suspect's alibi.'

Eleanor sat upright. Trying to sound casual, she asked, 'Oh, really, which suspect would that be?'

'Young Lord Fenwick-Langham, my lady. It seems he did indeed attend a masked ball at The Goat Club.'

'So someone recognised him? Even in a mask?'

'Whether or not he was recognised in his mask, I do not know. I was informed by Mr Sandford, however, that the doorman of The Goat Club recognised our young lord when he and his fellow "Bright Young Things" removed their masks.' Clifford coughed. 'And much else besides and went, I believe the expression is, "skinny-dipping" in the ornamental fountain.'

Eleanor suddenly found the scenery passing outside of great interest. She'd seen plenty of naked men in her time, you could hardly travel the world and not, but the thought of that particular gentleman in his birthday suit…

Pulling herself together, she turned her attention back to Clifford. 'Well, that takes him off our suspect list! But how did Sandford get to hear about all this?'

'The doorman at The Goat Club telephoned Mr Sandford to request Mr Jenkins, the Langham Manor chauffeur, you may recall, pick up young Lord Fenwick-Langham as he was not in a fit state to drive. As it turned out, none of his companions were either, so Jenkins did the rounds dropping them off before returning to Langham Manor with our young lord.'

'And the times tally?'

'Indeed, my lady. Our young friends arrived in a rather intoxicated state to start with around nine o'clock, so it seems they were cavorting in the fountain by the time you saw Mr Atkins shot. Jenkins picked up his lordship and his friends from the club at two a.m. and had to drop them off before finally arriving at the Manor with his young lordship around three thirty, well after the events at the quarry.'

A slow smile crept onto Eleanor's face despite her best efforts. *Don't even think about it, Ellie! He may no longer be a suspect, but he's still a complete clown!*

As the Rolls negotiated the corner, Eleanor switched her attention from the sheep-dotted fields outside to the dog sprawled on the rear seat.

'I say, Gladstone doesn't look the full ticket. Does he get car sick, Clifford?'

'Only if he rides in the back, my lady.'

Eleanor looked at the sulky bulldog again. 'Well, he can sit upfront with me. Anything to lose that hangdog expression.'

'Very good.' Clifford pulled to a careful stop on the grass verge. The bulldog almost broke Eleanor's arm in his enthusiasm to ride with her.

'Happy now, oh spoilt Prince of Pooches?' Eleanor teased as Clifford pulled away. The bulldog leaned against her, his chin resting on the window frame, relishing the wind flapping through his jowls.

'And why *Gladstone*? I've been meaning to ask since I first arrived. Was my uncle a Liberal? A fan of our famous ex-prime minister?'

'Not as such, my lady. Master Gladstone was named for another reason. On the day of his arrival at the Hall, he tumbled from the crate the courier set down in the hallway. The courier offered his unsympathetic view that the puppy was an unattractive, rigid fellow. He described it as a stiff creature, deeper in chest than he was long, and implied this was a most unfortunate purchase of your uncle's.'

'And how did my uncle respond?'

'He graciously thanked the man for his observations. Then he picked up the puppy and named him after his Gladstone bag, robust and sturdy.'

Eleanor chuckled. 'What a wonderful story.' She turned to Clifford. 'And did my uncle enjoy driving?'

'Your uncle enjoyed many long drives, my lady, even as far as Gwel an Mor House on the Western edge of Cornwall to visit his good friend Mr Cunliffe. Gwel an Mor is Cornish for sea view.'

'That's quite a trek.'

'Your late uncle found the sea air most rejuvenating.'

'And the brandy and card games most jovial, I'm sure.' Eleanor smiled.

Clifford studied the road ahead. 'I couldn't possibly comment, my lady.'

'Who was this Mr Cunliffe? I know so little of my uncle's life.'

Clifford took a sharp left-hand bend adroitly, easing back on the car's speed. 'Mr Cunliffe was an eminent financier, my lady. He retired from his noteworthy position at Cunliffe Brothers early in September 1912 and relocated to Cornwall to pursue his passion for collecting fine works of art. A loyal associate of your uncle's, he was partners with him in several… endeavours.'

'What a shame I didn't have the chance to meet him. He might have been able to share some wonderful anecdotes of their time together.'

'That can probably be arranged, my lady. Mr Cunliffe is still with us and was always most interested to hear your uncle's accounts of your foreign adventures.'

Oh heck, there was that lump in her throat again. She switched topic. 'What's that monument with the gold bauble on the hill?'

'The Wildmoor family mausoleum. And that is Wildmoor House on the left.'

Eleanor glanced at the bleak mausoleum and then switched her attention to the sprawling mansion. 'It looks quite new.'

'Despite its modern looks it was constructed around 1751. At the time the incumbent was Sir Cuthbert, third baronet.' Clifford honked the horn as a pheasant threatened to commit hara-kiri under the Rolls' wheels. 'Around this time there were three consecutive years of bad harvests, or "Devil-walked fields", as is the common expression in this area. This led to much hardship and unemployment in the area. To alleviate this, Sir Cuthbert took it upon himself to offer labouring positions to local villagers. The four-mile run of road that we have just driven had fallen into such disrepair that carriages frequently overturned. So he had the locals repair it from the centre of Radington to the entrance to Wildmoor House.'

'What a fine fellow!' Eleanor said.

'Quite so. Of course, there was the other business which somewhat marred his good deeds in the eyes of some.'

Her ears pricked up. 'Go on.'

'Sir Cuthbert was a colourful character who had, among other extravagances, a full-sized galleon brought to the grounds of the house and moored in the lake.'

'Whatever for?'

'During parties Sir Cuthbert would divide the guests into two teams. One team would try to storm the galleon while Sir Cuthbert defended it with the other.'

'What fun! Did the opposing sides throw rotten fruit and vegetables at each other?'

'No, my lady. Sir Cuthbert was very much the "eccentric". He insisted they used real weapons loaded with wooden bullets. Even the galleon's cannons fired wooden cannon balls. On one occasion a stray cannon ball set fire to the west wing.'

'But surely guests would have been injured?'

'Frequently, my lady, but Sir Cuthbert was something of a throwback to earlier, more primitive times. He also instigated the notorious Order of the Friars of Wildmoor, later known as the Wildmoor Club. They held their secret meetings in the West Radington Caves.' He pointed up the hill to the right as they entered the small village of West Radington itself.

Eleanor looked thoughtful. 'And now many ancient families like the Wildmoors are struggling just to pay the taxes from that beastly war!'

'Indeed, my lady, a lot has changed in terms of money and power. Whereas Lord Wildmoor would have been the most powerful man in the area, now the head of police or the mayor could rightly claim that title.'

Eleanor nodded slowly. 'I bet Lancelot wishes the Order of the Friars of Wildmoor was still in operation, that sounds just his sort of thing.'

'Indeed. On one occasion a member of the club impersonated the King of Sweden at a royal gala.'

Eleanor giggled. 'I can imagine him doing just that! What happened?'

'When the real king turned up, the imposter ridiculed him in front of the Royal Court and had him arrested before fleeing the Palace. Despite young Lord Fenwick-Langham's natural… exuberance, I fear even he would have struggled to match such hijinks.'

Eleanor wasn't so sure. She felt certain that Lancelot had hidden talents that she was looking forward to discovering. Now, that is, she knew they weren't for murder.

CHAPTER 23

'All rise.'

Eleanor looked around the post office from the doorway. 'What the dickens?'

A lugubrious rendition of 'God Save The Queen' wailed from an unseen gramophone.

She stepped back out onto the road and looked up at the sign reading West Radington Post Office. Returning, she called out, 'Hello?'

'Long live our noble queen…' The wobbling voice failed to hit anything other than one excruciating note. 'Happy and glorious. Long to reign over us. God save the Queen.'

'Mother!' The gramophone cut off. 'Mother, we've been over this.' A gaunt woman in her early fifties stepped in from the adjoining room. 'Our noble Queen Victoria is long departed. It's Long Live the King, King George V, please catch up.'

'Oh, you'll swing for treason, my girl. Play it again and stop your treacherous talk. Next it'll be that we're having acorns for tea again. I told you they give me the gripes.'

There was a scuffle and then the graunch of a needle being wrenched across the shellac surface.

On her previous errand for Mrs Butters, Eleanor had forgotten the last items on the list: two envelopes and the accompanying stamps. However, having asked Clifford to pause on their sightseeing trip so she could correct this oversight, she was now wondering if it had been a bad idea.

The voices continued from the back room.

'Mother, it's time for your nap. Please go on upstairs.'

'Tsk, a nap indeed, I have to practise. Let me alone.'

'Mother' appeared, followed by her daughter, and began a procession of the shop, knees high as she stepped, making a trumpeting noise along the way.

The daughter saw Eleanor and her hand flew to her mouth. Then a sly look crossed her face. 'Mother, you'll see the parade far better from the upstairs bedroom window.'

With the elderly woman dispatched, the daughter turned to Eleanor. 'Madam, what must you think of us? How may I help?'

Eleanor walked up to the counter. 'Good morning, Mrs…?'

'Oh my, how rude of me. It's Miss Green, sub-postmistress and owner of this convenience store.'

Eleanor looked around, noting for the first time the cigarette machine on the wall and the rack of shelves laden with an extraordinary number of random items. 'Good morning, Miss Green. Perhaps you would be so good as to provide me with the items on this list.' She handed over the crumpled piece of paper.

Miss Green looked at the list and then at Eleanor. 'You know, Doctor Browning popped in here only the other day.' She paused. 'But maybe you haven't met Doctor Browning?'

Eleanor shook her head.

'Ah, well he's attended royalty, has our Doctor Browning. Well, almost royalty.'

Eleanor tried to take part in the conversation. 'I'm not from around here. Well, I am sort of now.' She realised she wasn't sounding any more coherent than Miss Green. 'I come from Little Buckford, over the way. I'm Lady Swift of Henley Hall.'

Miss Green's jaw dropped. 'Lady Swift? Then you must know Mr Stoker.'

Eleanor was tiring of this nonsense. 'Mr Stoker?'

'Everyone knows Mr Stoker. Well travelled, he is. He's got a fair collection alright, put it on display in The Badger he did.'

Eleanor blinked. 'On display *in a badger*?'

The postmistress looked at Eleanor as if she was the one behaving oddly. 'Not *a* badger, *the* Badger. The local public house.'

Eleanor smiled weakly. 'Oh, of course, *that* Badger.' She blinked again. 'Collection of what though?' She regretted asking immediately, but it was too late.

'Well, mosses, fungi and algae, of course. There's not much Mr Stoker doesn't know about that kind of thing.'

Eleanor fixed the postmistress with a wan smile. 'Perhaps, Miss Green, you could get me my stamps and…' Eleanor stopped. After all, the quarry wasn't far from here and this woman, however unhinged, obviously knew everyone in the local area. Ever the opportunist, she changed tack. 'Actually, Miss Green, I wonder if you can help me in a most important matter?'

Miss Green swelled with pride. 'Of course, Lady Swit.'

Eleanor let it go. 'I witnessed a most unfortunate accident just down the road from here. A poor chap fell from his motorbike by a disued quarry.' *Well, it's only a small lie in a good cause, Ellie!* 'He was in such a fearful rush he dashed away before I could check if he needed assistance. I feel bad about the whole affair.'

Miss Green interrupted her. 'All vehicles in the surrounding area have to be registered each year and the authorities have deemed my post office as an outer fringe point for accepting registration paperwork.' Eleanor couldn't believe her luck as Miss Green continued. 'There's only four who ride one of those death traps around here.' She picked up a large, dog-eared notebook and rummaged through the pages, reading out four names: 'A Mr Jonas Trundle, a Mr Jack Cornell, a Mr Bartholemew Blount and a Mr Lancelot Germaine Benedict Fenwick-Langham.' She gave Eleanor a knowing look. 'He's the son of a lord, you know.'

She did indeed know and with the names secured in her memory, she thanked Miss Green for her expert knowledge. 'One last question,' Eleanor called from the doorway. 'Has anyone sent any unusual telegrams lately? Anything about a murder or moving a body?'

Well, it was worth a shot.

Further on, the lane wound up a steep climb. The Rolls had run out of gears early and was crawling upwards with its engine labouring. A hand-painted sign on a piece of scrap metal attached to a gatepost caught her eye: 'STEEP DOWNHILL'.

Eleanor pointed, shouting to Clifford. 'Sort of obvious, what?'

'Cyclists,' Clifford said. 'Local touring clubs erect their own danger boards. They are lobbying Parliament for signs to be erected nationwide.'

'That's going to look dashed untidy.' She pictured every road festooned with warning signs of steep gradients, wayward sheep and drunken villagers.

The Rolls ground over the crest. The engine noise subsided.

'What a beautiful view.' She was entranced, but Clifford seemed less interested in the view and more interested in his feet. A few yards over the rise, the verges started to shoot past her window at an alarming rate. Eleanor grabbed the doorframe with one hand and Gladstone with the other. The car slewed around the first corner, barely keeping to the road.

'Clifford, slow down!' she admonished.

'I can't… my… lady.' Clifford wrestled with the steering wheel, his feet pressed hard to the floor. 'I fear the… brakes… are defective.'

The back end of the car spun round, the front wheels fighting for grip. It seemed inevitable they would plunge over the edge and down into the valley. Clifford wrenched the wheel desperately. The rear wheels caught, and the car spun away from the steep drop.

Before Eleanor had time to feel relieved, she realised that they were about to hit a very large oak tree. *This is going to hurt, Ellie!* She held Gladstone tightly.

'My lady,' Clifford's voice was loud but calm. 'Brace!'

CHAPTER 24

That flapping was making her wince. Eleanor struggled to brush it away. Something soft and wet…

'Gladstone!' Mrs Butters whispered. 'Stop licking her ladyship. The mistress is sleeping.' Eleanor stirred and opened her eyes.

The housekeeper tutted. 'My lady, you're awake. I am so sorry about Gladstone. I tried to keep him out, but he must have barged the door open.'

'No matter. How long have I been… unconscious?'

'Since the accident, my lady. About midday they brought you here.'

Eleanor groaned. 'Really? Well, I need to be up now anyway.'

'Oh no, full bed rest was the doctor's orders. That was a very nasty knock to your head. And the cut as well.'

Eleanor reached up and felt her head. 'It seems I am bandaged up. Most inelegant, I'm sure.' Eleanor's hand flew to her mouth. 'Clifford! How is he?'

Mrs Butters smiled. 'Mr Clifford is just fine, my lady. You know what he's like, wouldn't say if his leg was hanging off. But he's walking alright, carrying on with his duties and getting the car sorted.'

Eleanor patted the exuberant bulldog. 'And amazingly Gladstone seems to have survived unscratched. He's built like a tank, this one!'

'He is indeed.' The housekeeper straightened Eleanor's eiderdown and plumped her pillow.

'Anything important I need to know about?'

'Nothing urgent, my lady. The Reverend called again, but Mr Clifford told him to come back in a few days when you're better. You rest, my lady. I'll check on you later.'

Eleanor winced. 'Perhaps you're right, Mrs Butters. A short nap will shift this bothersome headache.' She snuggled down in the bed.

The housekeeper closed the door softly behind her.

Four hours and several most peculiar dreams later, Eleanor woke in an unladylike sweat.

'What! Oh, Gladstone. This won't do, boy. Come on.' She clambered out of bed, then washed and dressed slowly due to her pounding head and throbbing shoulder. Gently she made it down the stairs to the hall and bumped into her maid.

Polly squeaked then curtsied and scurried back to the kitchen. Mrs Butters and Mrs Trotman appeared before Eleanor had reached the morning room.

'My lady!' they chorused.

'I'm fine, ladies.' Eleanor smiled with a wince. 'Thank you for your concern. Is Clifford around?'

'Apologies, my lady. He has popped out. He should be back within the hour.' Mrs Butters frowned at Eleanor's pale complexion and tired eyes.

'Good. Then he won't hear me asking for a spot of lunch at the obscene hour of four o'clock in the afternoon.'

'Perhaps you'd like to take your lunch in the kitchen, my lady? The range is lit and it's nice and toasty in there.'

'Absolutely!' Eleanor wished with all her heart this kind housekeeper had been around for those lonely visits when she was a child. *Why is it against the rules to hug one's staff?*

*

'There you are! No, do please carry on.' Eleanor waved Clifford back onto the bench he was starting to rise from as she entered. Having finished her late lunch, she had set out to see if her fellow invalid had returned. 'So, this is the boot room?'

'Indeed, my lady.'

Clifford sat back down, with a shoe slipped over one hand, and a brush in the other. He dipped his head and peered at her over a pair of spectacles. He cleared his throat. 'Can I get you something, my lady? Perhaps some tea in the drawing room?'

'I'm swimming in tea, thank you. And I'm done with lying about. Honestly, how do women do it in those romance novels? All that lounging about. It's ghastly!'

'I couldn't say, my lady, not being an admirer of the romance genre.'

'No, I imagine not.' Eleanor thought about the countless hundreds of them that she had devoured with intense and secret delight.

'My lady, forgive my presumption, but perhaps you have risen rather earlier than the doctor thought prudent?' He put down the shoe and brush and made to undo his apron.

'Tosh! I merely have a headache.' She raised her hand to her head to illustrate and winced for the hundredth time. 'Okay, and a slightly painful shoulder. But enough about me. What of you, Clifford? Did we hit a tree? I don't remember much after we spun round.'

Clifford looked at his feet for a second. 'My lady, with deep regret I was unable to stop the car meeting a most solid and unforgiving oak tree. Fortunately, the Rolls survived the impact intact. In fact, I was able to drive straight to Doctor Browning, who attended to you.'

So now I have met Doctor Browning.

'Then I returned with you to the Hall, my lady, and dropped the Rolls off at Johnson's, the coachbuilders. It should be back in service within a few days.'

'Oh, for goodness' sake, Clifford! I don't care about the Rolls, I'm asking if you're alright?'

'Thank you, my lady. I emerged in one piece.'

'Yes, and if your leg was hanging off, you wouldn't say, as Mrs Butters rightly pointed out. Now, you have my permission to take as much rest as you need to recover.'

He nodded. 'Most kind.'

She sat down on the bench opposite him. 'But tell me, what on earth happened?'

Clifford removed his spectacles and set them on the table. 'It would appear that someone tampered with the brakes.'

She digested the information. Now her headache had receded a little, she was able to think more clearly, and for the first time it struck her. 'Do you think they were trying to kill us?'

'It is a distinct possibility.'

She was furious. It wasn't the first time someone had tried to kill her but that had been abroad. This was England. And rural England at that!

Clifford continued. 'Or it might be that it was merely a warning.'

Eleanor snorted. 'Well, they are going to have to work a lot harder than that!'

Clifford nodded at Eleanor's bandaged head and shoulder. 'I have noted you are rather hard to kill, my lady, but perhaps they won't need to work an awful lot harder?'

'I didn't have you pegged as a scaredy-cat, Clifford.'

Clifford almost looked annoyed. 'My concern was with your safety, my lady, not my own. Your uncle…' He paused.

'Go on.'

He hesitated. 'I think, my lady, that that is perhaps for some other time.'

Eleanor decided her head hurt too much to argue.

'Okay, Clifford.'

He laid down the brush. 'There is another more pressing matter. Miss Abigail, who works at Chipstone Police Station…'

Eleanor forgot her headache. 'Yes, yes, I recall, my memory hasn't been affected. And…?'

'It seems she overheard two policemen discussing the news that a body has been found.'

Eleanor threw her hands up. 'Another body!'

'Indeed. The body was found around twelve fifteen today by the postman, who informed the police. And next to the body the police found a suicide note, in which…' Clifford paused. '… the deceased confessed to having killed Mr Atkins.'

Eleanor gasped. 'So Mr Atkins *was* murdered just as we thought?'

'It seems so, but Miss Abigail was unable to ascertain if the suicide note gave a reason for the murder.'

'But now at least we know who the murderer is. Did she get a name?'

Clifford shook his head. 'Miss Abigail has not been able to establish the deceased's identity yet, but she will no doubt know soon enough, or else the tabloids will publish it.'

Eleanor sat back on the hard, wooden bench and tried to think. 'Wonderful though it is to have our theory validated, a great many things don't add up, but in particular two are screaming at me.' She raised one finger. 'It seems rather convenient that this person was indecent enough to commit murder but decent enough to confess to it. Makes for a nice open-and-shut case for the police, wouldn't you say?'

Clifford nodded. 'Very perceptive, my lady. And the second point?'

She raised a second finger. 'If this chap was behind the affair, why would he have tried to kill or scare us off just before he took his own life?'

Clifford nodded. 'Agreed. There is a third point, similar to your first that puzzles me also. If the deceased did murder Mr Atkins, why would he have gone to all the trouble of making it look like an accident, only to confess to the murder a week later?'

Eleanor thumped the bench and regretted it as her head swam and a sharp pain shot across her shoulders. She waited a moment to recover. 'Clifford, it seems to me that we have been reading this case all wrong.'

Clifford raised an eyebrow a fraction. 'How so, my lady?'

'Do you remember when you told me about Lord Wildmoor? And we talked about how power has changed hands from the nobility in these rural areas? Well, up till now we've been looking at Mr Atkins' death as a personal matter. A feud that got out of hand with Cartwright perhaps, or Wilby. Obviously not Lancelot.' She blushed lightly and hurried on, 'As we've ruled him out as a suspect.'

Clifford nodded thoughtfully. 'Indeed, my lady, I can see where your train of thought is going. This affair seems to be much more than a merely personal matter if our current suspicions are correct – and they are only that at the moment, suspicions. But if we are right, then the newly deceased was also murdered, and again the murder disguised as something else, in this case, suicide. But did the murderer fake a suicide note to persuade the police to treat it as an open-and-shut case or—'

Eleanor jumped in. 'Or did our Sergeant Wilby conveniently arrange it?'

Clifford nodded. 'Indeed. Whoever is orchestrating this has a certain amount of power. There have long been rumours of corruption in the local constabulary or council, but nothing has ever been proven. Some say it is just the usual thing, the police and councillors taking backhanders to turn a blind eye.'

Eleanor slapped the bench, wincing only slightly. 'We need to break into Mr Atkins' house and find some *real* evidence. Evidence those idiot police have overlooked, or are hiding.'

Clifford smiled. 'Once again, my lady, I see your uncle in you. But, with respect, perhaps allowing Miss Abigail another day to uncover more details might be a safer plan?'

Eleanor sighed. 'I suppose so.'

The door into the hallway opened and Mrs Butters bustled in. She stopped, seeing Eleanor. 'Oh, my lady, I do apologise. I had no idea you were here.'

Eleanor smiled. 'No trouble, Mrs Butters.'

The housekeeper blushed and turned to Clifford. 'Mr Clifford, Doctor Browning is waiting in the hall.'

Clifford rose, folded his apron on the table, then held the door 'My lady…'

CHAPTER 25

The following morning, Gladstone was keeping Eleanor company at the breakfast table. Truth be told, he was more interested in keeping the breakfast company as he preferred human food to his normal dog food. Eleanor had been trying to wean him onto plain toast as his sausage habit was clearly not a healthy one. Clifford made his usual silent entrance and refilled her teacup. 'Might I enquire if you are feeling brighter this morning, my lady?'

'You may, and the answer is yes. Doctor Browning attended to me most thoroughly. He asked how my head felt, enquired as to my shoulder pain and then asked how many fingers he was holding up.'

Clifford turned back from checking the sausage salver. 'And did you guess correctly, my lady?'

Before Eleanor could answer, Clifford placed a heartily filled plate in front of her. 'Yum! See, nothing wrong with my appetite,' she said, adding salt and pepper to her eggs. 'What news from Miss Abigail?'

'None yet, but the next snippet of information is already out and widely about.'

'How so?'

Clifford retrieved a newspaper from the occasional table by the door and passed it to her. 'Page two, my lady.'

Eleanor read the headline. 'Accidental Death of Whitehall Minister Now Known to be Murder.' She scanned the first few paragraphs. 'The killer, Jack Cornell… Is that a name you know?'

'Indeed, my lady, it is one I am familiar with. He is an ex-con. He was a… guest here at one time. Your uncle helped him onto the straight and narrow. I would have found it hard to believe that he would have fallen back into his old ways, but even if he had, he was no killer. And to kill such an upstanding man as Mr Atkins, why?'

Polly knocked and popped her head around the door. 'Excuse me interrupting, your ladyship. Mrs Butters said Mr Clifford is wanted on the telephone.' With a flick of her apron she disappeared like a jittery sprite.

Clifford left Eleanor to devour more egg and toast and returned, soundlessly, a few minutes later, making her jump and crack an egg.

'Was it about the Rolls?' Eleanor was in the middle of restocking her plate from the salvers. She definitely needed to put a bell on Clifford.

'No, my lady, it was Mr Sandford. Miss Abigail has sent word to her uncle of further developments.'

Eleanor reluctantly lowered her fork.

'It seems the suicide note contained further details. And it reveals more than the newspaper. Jack Cornell did indeed give a reason for the murder.'

Eleanor nodded for Clifford to continue.

'It seems Mr Atkins was… blackmailing him.'

Eleanor picked her fork back up. 'And you believe that?'

'Categorically, no. I believe Mr Atkins was incapable of using such underhand tactics.'

'As I thought.' She paused in spearing another mushroom. 'I am sorry, Clifford, I do appreciate this is difficult for you. Whilst Mr Atkins was a friend of my uncle's and I have fond memories of him from my childhood, you were clearly fond of him too.'

'Thank you, my lady. He was, as I have said, an upstanding gentleman and was a familiar part of your uncle's life for many years.'

'Then he was obviously a very fine fellow and we must defend his name, albeit posthumously. And Jack Cornell's, of course. I am sure my uncle would have moved heaven and earth to see justice done for both men, and so shall we. Agreed?'

Clifford nodded. 'Agreed, my lady.'

Eleanor studied the photograph in the newspaper. 'You know I simply didn't see the man on the motorcycle clearly enough. It could be him, but then again…' She shrugged, then drew her breath in sharply. 'Wait a moment. Cornell was one of the motorcyclists' names that the sub-postmistress in West Radington gave to me. Oh gosh, Clifford! I forgot to mention them to you at the time. And then we had the crash and I've only just remembered.'

'Can you still recall them, my lady?'

'I think so, unless that bump on the head has knocked them out. One was Lancelot, I remember that, but we knew that already seeing as I've actually ridden pillion on his motorbike. One was this Jack Cornell character. Who else was there? Ah, yes! Mr Jonas T-Tr-Trundle and Mr… Mr? It began with a B? Blount! Mr something Blount, that's it. Do you know either of those two?'

'Mr Trundle is known to everyone, my lady. He was the captain of the Chipstone cricket team for almost thirty years and only retired when he reached the admirable age of seventy-five. I don't believe he's actually ridden his motorbike for many years.'

'Well, he's definitely not the motorcyclist from the quarry then. And Mr Blount, is he someone you are familiar with?'

Clifford nodded slowly. 'Yes, but I fear that is another dead end, my lady. Mr Bartholemew Blount is a younger gentleman, but he would never have been able to drive a motorbike in such a wild fashion without crashing.'

'Why ever not? Is he grotesquely overweight or something?'

A slight frown crossed Clifford's brow. 'No, my lady, he is somewhat deficient in the leg department having lost one in an accident several years ago.'

'Poor chap! How on earth does he ride a motorbike then?'

'Considerably more carefully than the night he rode into the old oak tree by the vicarage and consequentially lost his aforementioned limb.'

'Fair enough, we'll rule him out as well. You know, I definitely saw a motorbike in Cartwright's outhouse, but Miss Green never mentioned his name.'

'Perhaps it is an old motorcycle and not currently licensed? However, there is an element we may have overlooked altogether. The motorbike may have been a stolen machine.'

'True, or… the person I saw at Cartwright's was Jack Cornell and it was his motorcycle?'

He nodded slowly. 'Possibly. There is another potentially tricky point. Alibis might be hard to find, and test this time.'

'Why particularly this time?'

'Miss Abigail passed on the information that, given the state of the body, the police believe Mr Cornell died somewhere between eleven thirty in the evening, when a neighbour saw him returning home to his flat on Old Kiln Lane, and eight the following morning, four hours or so before his body was discovered by the postman at twelve fifteen. As rigor mortis had set in, he must have been dead at least four hours before the police examined him. There is little way to narrow down the time of death any further at the moment. In the case of Mr Atkins, you saw him shot, so we can pinpoint that.'

Eleanor sighed. 'It's not going to be easy to verify anyone's alibi for that time, is it? I imagine they'll all say they were in bed. It could all be a wild goose chase.' She shivered at the word 'goose'. She thought about this new twist in the case. 'You know, if Mr Atkins wasn't blackmailing Jack Cornell, and Jack Cornell didn't kill him, then we are dealing with a monster!'

'Certainly a very calculating individual.'

'With the morals of a jackal!'

'I should say that the jackal has been much maligned as a species. They are actually—'

'Not now, Clifford. Monster or not, it seems this man – or woman – has killed twice, and may again. What could be their motive?' Eleanor drummed her fingers on the table. 'I do think it is more likely this latest setup was to provide an open-and-shut case for the police. Or the police were in on it.'

'Indeed, person one murders person two who is blackmailing him and then kills himself. Case closed, as you say, my lady.' Clifford picked up the empty teapot. 'As I said, it takes a brilliant mind to conceive and execute such a plan.'

'And as I said, a ruthless, cold-blooded one.'

'However…' Clifford turned back from refilling the teapot '… the killer did not allow for the intervention of a thoroughly modern woman.'

Eleanor laughed. 'You know, Clifford, if you pay me any more compliments, I might think you are actually an old softie under that gruff exterior.'

Clifford merely bowed. 'Whatever you say, my lady.'

CHAPTER 26

The news next day that the Rolls was not yet back from the repair shop did little to ease Eleanor's sore head.

'I have been informed it should be returned before lunch,' Clifford offered by way of consolation. Eleanor gritted her teeth. 'All this waiting is infuriating. I really can't eat any more or I shall explode. We're wasting time while the murderer is running around free!'

'Sir Isaac Newton would disagree, my lady.'

Eleanor scowled.

'He once said, "If I have ever made any valuable discoveries, it has been owing more to patient attention, than to any other talent."'

'Why is it that all this talk of patience makes me want to scream?'

'Perhaps it might be a good moment to review where we are with the case and where we need to go next, as it were?'

Eleanor huffed. 'Okay, I suppose you're right. You start, Clifford.'

Clifford cleared his throat. 'Well, my lady, you saw a man, as yet unidentified, shoot Mr Atkins at around ten fifteen in the evening at the disused quarry on Saturday, the night of the storm. The following day Mr Atkins' body was discovered by his housekeeper at his house half a mile away. Mr Atkins' murder had been made to look like an accident. As the police agreed with this, it seemed the murderer had got away with the crime.'

Eleanor nodded. 'And then, confusingly, Jack Cornell's body is discovered the following Saturday morning in his flat on Old Kiln Lane. By his dead body is a suicide note confessing to killing Atkins, his reason for killing Atkins being that Atkins had been blackmailing him.'

It was Clifford's turn to nod. 'Exactly, my lady. Our remaining suspects for Mr Atkins' murder, as we don't believe Mr Cornell did in fact kill him, are Mr Cartwright and Sergeant Wilby, young Lord Fenwick-Langham's alibi having been confirmed and him eliminated as a suspect.'

'So now all we have to do is find out which one of them hasn't got a verifiable alibi for the time of Jack Cornell's death, find some incontrovertible evidence that they committed both murders, and have them arrested. Easy.' She rose. 'Unless, of course, Atkins' and Cornell's murderer isn't actually one of our two suspects.' She headed out of the drawing room, saying over her shoulder, 'Please call me the moment the Rolls is returned. I'll be in the garden.'

Two hours later Clifford finally announced the car was back and waiting by the front steps.

At that moment, Mrs Butters hurried out and informed Clifford that she needed some items from the village. Never one to miss an opportunity, Eleanor jumped up from the stone bench, whipped the list out of the housekeeper's surprised fingers and headed for the Rolls.

Eleanor paused at the door of Brenchley Stores, marvelling at the multitude of items neatly displayed on shelves, racks and hanging rails. Stepping inside, she was struck by the heady mix of wax polish and coal tar soap. She peeped round the trays of miscellaneous fixings and canned provisions expecting Aladdin to jump out and ask what on earth she was doing mooching about his cave.

Huddled by a rack of tinned goods were two felt-hatted ladies twittering like sparrows.

'You know, he was here again. I heard him asking questions.'

'Who, dear?'

'That detective fellow.'

'That broad-shouldered young man in the blue wool overcoat? There's a spectacle that would brighten the rainiest December day.'

The women giggled like schoolgirls but froze on seeing Eleanor.

'Good afternoon, ladies.' She nodded politely.

'Good afternoon, Lady Swift,' they chorused.

Eleanor sized up the square-shouldered man in the tan work coat behind the counter. She took in the greying strands at his temples and the crease in his forehead and decided he was a man who took his business seriously. His smile on seeing her, however, carried on up to his warm brown eyes.

'Lady Swift, welcome to Little Buckford. And my heartfelt condolences on the loss of your uncle. I am Arthur Brenchley, owner of Brenchley Stores.'

'Thank you, Mr Brenchley. Delighted to meet you. What a capital store you have here. You must be quite the centre of the village.'

'Thank you, m'lady. And how may I help you?'

'Mrs Butters has dispatched me with a list of errands.' *Well, it was only a small white lie.*

The two women clutched their hats and looked at each other, clearly horrified.

'Dispatched, you say? By Mrs Butters?' Brenchley rubbed his forehead. 'I must be getting old, things aren't quite as I expect some days.'

A young man in a matching apron appeared behind him.

'Your son, Mr Brenchley?' Eleanor ventured.

'A shrewd guess. Yes, this is John, my eldest and only son. Heir to the Brenchley emporium fortune.'

They all laughed at this.

'It's a pleasure to meet you, Lady Swift.' John hopped from foot to foot.

'Likewise, John. Tell me, what do you do when you're not busy working on building your fine inheritance here?'

John looked at his father, seemingly tongue-tied.

'John here's got his head in a bicycle every hour he's not working.' Brenchley senior explained.

Eleanor's ears pricked up. 'A fellow cyclist indeed! I have just purchased a bicycle of my own. Perhaps I might call on your expertise in the future?'

John's face lit up. 'Why, I'd be most pleased to help you in any way I can, m'lady.'

'Excellent! So, as a keen cyclist you must also know the best routes in the area. I saw a simply splendid road out past Henley Hall and then on to what looked to be a quarry near, I believe, Mr Cartwright's farm?'

Brenchley clucked his tongue. 'John knows that road alright. Don't you, son?'

'Dad!' John dipped his head.

Brenchley leaned towards Eleanor. 'He's got a girl, up yonder of Cartwright's.'

'Dad!' John blushed as Eleanor jumped in.

'John, perhaps you would be kind enough to act as my cycling guide? It would save me from getting lost on unfamiliar back roads.'

'I… I usually cycle with the Chipstone Club, m'lady.' John squirmed.

Eleanor smiled. 'Then I'll join.'

John's eyes popped. 'I… I don't think they allow women, I mean… ladies.'

'Nonsense, I'm sure Chipstone is a more progressive town than that,' she lied.

'Mrs Butters' list, m'lady?' Brenchley senior reminded her while laughing at his son's obvious discomfort.

She handed it over and while he rounded up the items casually asked, 'Tell me, Mr Brenchley, has Mr Cartwright been in recently?'

Brenchley looked at her oddly. 'Cartwright? He was in here a few days back buying some more cartridges. Like most farmers round these parts he gets through a fair few what with shooting pigeons, rabbits and the like.'

'And he bought some new overalls, Dad, remember?' John added. 'Normally never get farmers like him buying new work clothes, they just wear them till they fall apart.'

Eleanor's imagination raced. *Perhaps he burned his old ones? Perhaps they were covered in blood!* She tried to keep her voice casual. 'Has he made any other… unusual purchases lately?'

Brenchley looked amused. 'Well, that depends what you'd call "unusual"?'

Eleanor shrugged. 'Oh, you know, a shovel? Or a bag of lime, perhaps?'

'Where are we exactly, Clifford?'

Eleanor rather fancied she knew the way to Chipstone by now, and this was definitely not it. 'I distinctly told you to head for Chipstone.'

'Forgive my use of initiative, my lady, but an opportunity has presented itself this afternoon.'

She clucked her tongue with irritation. 'We've already been held up running errands for Mrs Butters and I wanted one more tilt at that buffoon, Sergeant Wilby.'

Clifford raised an eyebrow. 'Really, my lady, I fear this is not a jousting tournament.'

'Shame! I would love to see him wriggling on the business end of a sharpened lance!' A brief image of her former husband wriggling on the same lance popped into her head but she charitably shook it out. 'Chipstone Police Station it is! And after Brenchley's revelation about Cartwright's purchases recently, I fancied another go with him as well. So, what is this unmissable opportunity we're driving to first?'

'We will be there shortly. It is but a quick detour.'

Eleanor's miniscule supply of patience gave out. 'Oh, for goodness' sake! Whilst I appreciate your solicitude, Clifford, I have no intention of following Doctor Browning's laborious orders for rest and recuperation. So, any ideas for restoratives such as watching the newborn lambs gambolling on the hills or dying of tedium reading Coleridge poems by the babbling brook can go hang!'

'Perhaps reading Alfred Lord Tennyson, my lady?'

'What?'

'Since there is no babbling brook in Little Buckford, or Chipstone for that matter, I rather thought you were referring to the poem "The Brook" penned by the eminent Mr Tennyson.'

Eleanor slapped the dashboard of the Rolls in frustration. 'Clifford, are you immune to sarcasm or does it merely sharpen your needle-like wit?'

'I really couldn't say, my lady.' Clifford stared straight ahead. 'But to answer your question, our detour will indeed be quite the restorative for you, perhaps not one Doctor Browning would condone, however.'

At this point they passed the entrance to Cartwright's farm. The car rumbled on down the lane, up the rise and round a sweeping right-hand bend before Clifford swung into a gravelled driveway. With a deft flick of the wheel, he manoeuvred the Rolls under an arch of box hedging and let it roll to a stop behind a large flint outbuilding, in front of which was parked an Austin motor car. It seemed strangely familiar to Eleanor.

'Where the dickens…?' Eleanor started but then followed Clifford's gloved finger, pointing to a distant row of now familiar ornate chimney towers. 'That's… Henley Hall on the hill. So this must be…'

'Mr Atkins' house, my lady.'

'Top-notch initiative, Clifford!'

Eleanor got out of the car and stared up at the charming, three-storey Georgian house. How compact and homely it looked after the sprawling rooms and endless corridors of Henley Hall. Their feet crunched on the gravel as they stole round to the back of the house, which overlooked a small orchard.

A moment later she stepped tentatively inside through the door Clifford now held open. She looked around at the brightly decorated kitchen, well equipped with a long rack of pans for every possible culinary purpose. A row of potted herbs filled the windowsill. On the nearest counter, a floral tray stood with a ready-plated supper of cold cuts under a cloth cover. She pulled her jacket tighter round her shoulders. 'It certainly feels chilly. And rather forlorn. Let's not hang around now that you've broken in… hang on though, you didn't?'

Clifford drew out a large steel key from one of his pockets. 'Understandably, Mrs Campbell was unwilling to stay here since the discovery of Mr Atkins' body. She contacted me to ask if Silas might be available to keep an extra eye on the property. Word will have travelled fast that the house is standing empty.'

'Gracious yes, it's the least we could do. Where is Silas?'

'Around and about.'

'Come on then.' Eleanor shivered. 'It does feel odd creeping around a dead man's house.'

Clifford nodded. 'I agree, my lady, but "Justice is a certain rectitude of mind whereby a man does what he ought to do in the circumstances confronting him."'

'Charlie Chaplin again?'

'Thomas Aquinas, my lady. But one could say they were in the same business of putting life in perspective. Shall we?'

CHAPTER 27

He led her out into the hallway, the noise of their footsteps muffled by the full-length Wilton runner carpet. Halfway along, they turned into a room filled with leather Chesterfields and huge oak bookcases. Eleanor caught her breath at the sight of one of the silver photograph frames acting as a bookend on the shelves. Set inside was a picture of her and Atkins playing bowls on the lawn at Henley Hall. Her uncle sat clapping and smiling in a lawn chair. Clifford coughed gently. 'I remember that day too, my lady. It was a fun afternoon that taught us all you were better at winning than losing.'

She gave a weak smile and picked up the photograph frame. 'Looking at a photo of someone who has passed away feels like they've just walked out of your life that very minute. What an unwelcome rush of emotions. Poor uncle, poor Mr Atkins.' She fought the lump in her throat. The eerie stillness made her shiver as she accepted the pristinely starched handkerchief Clifford held out.

Pulling herself together, she crossed the floor and peered into the empty gun case mounted on the wall. Rectangular stains of oil dotted the base of the cabinet, but there was no tin of gun oil, only a sheepskin mop and a chamber brush. The police must have taken it, she guessed, along with the shotgun.

But it was the enormous carved wooden desk that caught Eleanor's attention next. She moved the deep-buttoned, green leather chair aside easily with her knee. 'I've never seen a gentleman's desk so empty. No files, notebooks or tray of correspondence. No papers anywhere. Have the police removed everything for evidence, do you suppose?'

'Given their hasty acceptance that Mr Atkins died by his own "careless hand", I fear not. Indeed, no one has even thought to remove the meal Mrs Campbell had prepared earlier on the day in question. Someone, however, has stripped his desk of any papers.'

Eleanor scratched her cheek thoughtfully. 'So... perhaps whoever killed Atkins truly believed Atkins was blackmailing him?'

'Possibly.' He tapped the ends of his fingers together pensively. 'It is possible the theft of papers was intended to ensure the police would draw the same conclusion, that Mr Atkins was blackmailing the killer.' He folded his hands together. 'I have another theory, one that has bounced from your initial thoughts.'

'Go on.'

'That the killer did indeed believe there was something incriminating here amongst Mr Atkins' papers and he was anxious to remove all and any possible evidence.'

'And he would have just scooped up everything in his haste to get out quickly. I don't suppose Sergeant Wilby even noticed the desk was cleared. Unless of course, he's our man and he was the one who cleared it.' She cocked an eyebrow. 'Are the drawers empty too?'

Clifford pulled the top drawer open. 'Empty, save for a lid-less ink pen and a handkerchief.'

The other drawers were much the same, just a few incidental items floating in a wooden sea of emptiness: a paper fastener torn from its charge of papers, a magnifying glass and a roll of red government ribbon for sealing authenticated documents.

She looked around the room for inspiration. A dark stain on the backrest of the leather desk chair caught her eye. 'You know, Clifford, our killer would surely have been in quite a state after moving the body from the quarry to here. And the dead are notoriously uncooperative. It must have been a struggle to even get the body from the car into the house.'

Clifford nodded slowly. 'I wonder…' He dropped to his knees by the chair.

Not knowing what else to do, she followed suit. 'How odd, it's got five legs but… whatever are you… the wheels, you clever bean! The killer pushed this to the door and then wheeled poor Mr Atkins through into here, didn't he?'

'I very much suspect so, my lady. And as it would be less conspicuous, I imagine he used the back door, just as we have.'

They took a different side of the desk each and shuffled on their haunches as they examined the floor.

'Clifford, Atkins' magnifying glass!' Eleanor shouted and then clapped her hands over her mouth as her voice echoed out into the hallway.

'Good idea, my lady,' Clifford replied at half her volume. A few minutes later, he let out an uncharacteristic whistle over by the door. 'Bingo!'

'What have you found?' She dropped to his side again and took the magnifying glass. 'I say, bingo indeed! Wheel marks. You can see a definite indent. Let's follow them out to the back door.'

It didn't take long to find the trail left by the wheels of the chair. Aside from the wooden sections of the floor, the indent was quite clear once they knew what to search for.

'But look here, Clifford.' Eleanor knelt carefully away from where she was pointing. 'There's a white powder caught in the tracks in some places, but not all of them. And an awful lot of muddy boot prints that have stamped across our evidence trail, quite literally.'

'Those will be the police, I suspect, my lady. There will be even more by the front door. Whilst we feel they may have been hasty in their conclusions as to the circumstances of Mr Atkins' demise, I am sure they would have arrived in good number.'

'Oh absolutely! The more dim-witted buffoons you have at the scene, the more you can stuff up working out what happened.'

'And the more separate reports you can guarantee will be filed all backing up the original conclusion of accidental death.'

'Clifford! You're right. If it is Wilby, he probably marched about the place pointing at all the obvious clues he left to make the whole thing look like an accident.'

He stood up. 'Whoever moved Mr Atkins on the chair was at the quarry. In fact, I would stake my reputation on it.'

'What have you found?'

He held up his gloved finger. 'Chalk and sand. Denser patches up by the back door, diminishing as the wheel tracks move towards the room in which Mr Atkins was found.'

Eleanor shook her head. 'I know being shot isn't a very elegant way to go, but to then be manhandled in one's own house really isn't cricket.' She wrinkled her nose. 'So, we need to find out if Wilby has an alibi for the time I saw Atkins shot in the quarry.'

Clifford nodded. 'If he has a watertight alibi, then it couldn't have been him who pulled the trigger.'

'If, being quite the operative word. But how on earth could we find out? It's not the kind of information he's likely to impart to me, or you.'

'Agreed, my lady. I can make enquiries, and there is always Abigail, but…' He shrugged.

'Well.' Eleanor held the door open. 'Whoever the killer was, he was either scared out of his wits by what he'd done or the most cold-blooded murderer imaginable.'

'How so?'

She stepped across to the supper tray on the worktop. 'Everything is untouched as we know Atkins never made it home alive from the quarry to eat. Except…' She pointed to the cut-glass brandy decanter. It was open, with the decanter's stopper lying next to an unused brandy glass. 'Except it looks like someone helped themselves to a swig of Atkins' finest Napoleon Brandy.'

'And as no gentleman would leave the stopper off a decanter of fine brandy and nobody except the police have been in the house since his demise…'

'… and as I imagine even Chipstone's constabulary wouldn't contaminate a crime scene by swigging from the dead man's decanter…'

'… it must have been the killer.' Clifford shook his head slowly. 'It would seem our killer needed to steady his nerves. Nevertheless, a true monster, my lady.'

She nodded in agreement. 'I know. Drinking a dead man's liquor when you're the reason he is no more and standing over him whilst doing so. An unimaginable monster.'

Clifford coughed gently. 'No, my lady, I was referring to the murderer drinking directly from the decanter.' He shuddered. 'What sort of man would countenance such a thing!'

As Clifford locked the back door, Eleanor caught a movement behind the apple trees.

Cupping her hands in front of her mouth, she called out. 'Trespassing, Mr Cartwright?'

The farmer stepped out from the orchard and strolled towards them, a shotgun resting in the crook of his arm. 'Can't say that I am, Lady Swift.'

She folded her arms. 'Really? Well, from where I'm standing it looks very much like you are doing precisely what you accused Mr Clifford and myself of a few days ago at the quarry. What was it? Ah yes! "Lurking about trespassing somewhere you've no business".'

Cartwright pulled a toothpick from his pocket and tucked it into the corner of his mouth, letting the end poke out. 'Must be summat odd about where you're standing then, Lady Swift.'

'Oh, don't be so ridiculous! You have no right to be on Mr Atkins' property.'

'Ridiculous, am I? Folks call me many things, mostly Thomas as it happens to be my name, but not ridiculous. But then, most folks have manners.'

'Do they, Mr Cartwright? In that case, you won't mind explaining what you are doing here. Mr Clifford and I are being neighbourly and keeping a watchful eye on Mr Atkins' house whilst his estate is sorted out.' *Well, it was partly true.*

Cartwright shrugged. 'Maybe I am too.'

Eleanor scowled. 'Only you aren't. Perhaps I should go back inside and telephone Sergeant Wilby and ask him to come out here and ask you where you were when Mr Cornell died?'

Cartwright started at Cornell's name, but instantly regained his composure. He rolled the toothpick round his mouth. 'You do that, Lady Swift. Only leave the door ajar so I can hear you. 'Cos from where I was standing when you dragged Wilby out to the quarry, the sergeant didn't seem too impressed with anything you had to say. And I reckon him bellowing what he thought of you trying to report me for trespassing, or maybe… murder, would carry all the way out here.'

A discreet cough behind her shoulder interrupted her reply. She threw her hands up. 'Okay, Clifford, you try!'

He stepped forward and nodded to the farmer. 'Mr Cartwright.'

He nodded back. 'Mr Clifford.'

'Would you mind telling us where you were between the hours of eleven on Friday night and eight on Saturday morning? I realise we have no right to ask, but would be most obliged if you could furnish us with the information.'

The farmer smiled and glanced at Eleanor. 'You see, you just need to ask polite like. If you must know I had some sick lambing ewes and the vet came over from West Radington around five and ten to eleven. He stayed for half an hour and then I went back to my good lady wife in the farmhouse.'

'And did you stay in from then on, Mr Cartwright?'

'Happen I had to check on ewes again around one in morning. And before you ask, Jake Smiggins, my farmhand, can verify all of that as can Mr Beard, the West Radington vet.'

'Thank you, Mr Cartwright, you've been most helpful. One last question, you say you went to check on your ewes again around one?'

'That's right. I was there about an hour-ish and then went back to bed for the night. Well, what was left of it as I had to be up at five.' He glanced from Clifford to Eleanor and back. 'Seems mighty odd, you asking these questions seeing as Jack took his own life.'

Eleanor stepped in quickly. 'Possibly, Mr Cartwright, but the fact is you still haven't explained what you're doing on Mr Atkins' property.'

The farmer looked at her coldly. 'Mr Atkins' house, and land, backs onto mine. A farmer's got to protect his assets, same as all the moneymen do up London. Only I can't lock my fields up against gypsies and squatters, but I can scare the living daylights out of them so they leave sharpish.' He indicated the shotgun he had in the crook of his arm and winked at her. 'Good day, Lady Swift. Mr Clifford.' He touched his cap and wandered off back through into the apple orchard.

'So help me, I'll…' Eleanor looked around for something to throw at his retreating form. 'Clifford, that man is—'

'Immensely enjoying irritating you, my lady. It is worth remembering the words of Mrs Kenny, "He who angers you, conquers you."'

She stomped off, calling over her shoulder, 'He doesn't anger me, Clifford, he infuriates me!'

CHAPTER 28

Fifteen minutes later Clifford pulled into a parking space alongside Chipstone Police Station's steps.

'Bingo! That's a perfectly worked out plan,' Eleanor enthused.

'If you say so, my lady.'

'Now, you see, here we need to broach the topic of your delivery, Clifford. Like your facial expressions, you really only do have two: inscrutable or disapproving. You managed to make that statement sound both.'

'I am sorry, my lady,' Clifford deadpanned. 'I'll work on a third.'

'Thank you. Now, at least we managed to drag an alibi out of Cartwright for the time of Cornell's death. Well, you did.'

Clifford nodded. 'True, my lady, although even if Mr Beard, the vet, and young Jake, the farmhand, can vouch for its veracity, Mr Cartwright would still have had time to drive to Mr Cornell's house, kill him, plant the fake suicide note, and return between the hours of say, two and four Saturday morning.'

Eleanor shrugged. 'We'll see. In the meantime we've got another suspect to interrogate and distract while you perform a little sleight of hand. And I shall be the very essence of calm and convincing, just watch.' She got out of the car and slammed the door. She couldn't be sure, but was that a muttered, 'Oh, dear Lord,' she heard from the driver's seat?

In the lacklustre reception area the policeman behind the counter greeted Eleanor with a notable lack of enthusiasm. She crossed to the desk and announced herself. 'I am Lady Swift. I wish to speak with Sergeant Wilby on a most important matter.'

'Well, Lady Swift, if it's most important, you won't mind waiting.'

'Waiting?' Eleanor always minded waiting. It wasn't that she was innately impatient, it was just that any patience she had had as a small child had entirely evaporated by the time she was a young adult. 'I wish to see him now.'

'Then you are in the wrong place.' At the look on Eleanor's face the young constable hurried on. 'What I meant to say, m'lady, is Sergeant Wilby is over at the town hall.'

Eleanor gestured to the three wooden chairs against one wall. 'Is that your waiting room?'

The policeman nodded and added, 'Mr Clifford,' as Clifford joined her. Eleanor pursed her lips. 'Sit down, Clifford.'

He took the chair next to her, sitting poker upright.

Once the constable had returned to leaning on the counter, Eleanor turned to Clifford. 'How come *everybody* knows you, Clifford? If we were to venture four thousand miles to Timbuktu, we would still be shaking the sand from our boots when a turbaned gentleman would nod and say, 'Mr Clifford,' as he shuffled past with his donkey. Don't you tire of being so widely known?'

'My being recognised is just a reflection of your late uncle's reputation, my lady. And as to Timbuktu, it was always a pleasure to receive such a warm and cordial welcome, particularly given the local troubles. But forgive my correction, it is not a turban they wear in those parts but a tagelmust, really quite a different form of headwear.'

'Touché!' Eleanor muttered.

The wait for Sergeant Wilby seemed as interminable as one of Clifford's long-winded explanations. So when the sergeant returned, Eleanor almost tripped over her own feet as she jumped up to greet him.

'You have a visitor, Sarge,' the front desk officer pointed out needlessly.

'So I see. Lady Swift. Mr Clifford.'

Clifford acknowledged Wilby with a faint tilt of his head.

Turning to Eleanor, Wilby crossed his arms over his portly frame. 'Lady Swift, I am a busy man. I trust your call is important enough to warrant police time?'

'Unquestionably so.'

'It had better not be any more nonsense about Mayor Kingsley.'

'Indeed not, my visit does not concern Mayor Kingsley at all.'

Wilby leaned in, glowering. 'Just as well because I checked and he never sent you round here to ask questions.'

'Good gracious, Sergeant, I never said he had sent me to question you. You must have assumed something to that effect from our discourse.'

'But!' Wilby looked fit to blow. 'Lady Swift. Might I advise you that wasting police time is a prosecutable offence.'

'Trust me, Sergeant,' she said, 'you will definitely want to hear what we have to say.'

Wilby eyed her distrustfully. 'I haven't seen any evidence of that to date.'

'That's just it! You see, Clifford we were right about the sergeant all along.'

Wilby looked between the two of them. 'What exactly is it that you want?'

Clifford rose to the occasion. 'Want, Sergeant? We don't want anything. We have come to help you.'

Eleanor whispered in the sergeant's ear, 'To help you climb to the rank you were born to be, Sergeant Wilby.'

Wilby cocked his head, his interest at least mildly piqued. 'Go on.'

'But…' Eleanor pulled away and looked around. 'We couldn't possibly tell you here. Even in a police station the walls or… front desks have ears.'

The three of them turned their gaze towards the lone constable.

Feeling all eyes on him, the constable at the front desk jerked upright. 'Sarge?'

Wilby motioned him to be silent with a flap of his hand. 'Tea, Brice.' He gave the desk constable a glare. 'In scrubbed cups, mind.'

'On it, Sarge.' Brice disappeared through the door behind him.

'Three sugars, thank you,' Eleanor called after him.

'Now what is this about?'

Eleanor looked round again. 'Sergeant, I wonder if we should retire to a more… private place. Goodness, if what we have to tell you fell into the hands of…' – she feigned horror – '… a lesser man.'

'Which is not you, Sergeant Wilby,' Clifford clarified.

Eleanor shook her head vigorously. 'Heavens, no! A lesser man might use the information to pull that promotion from under your very feet.'

Wilby grimaced. 'That would never do. There are indeed some petty-minded individuals here who are jealous of my talents and like to nab the glory for themselves. Follow me.' He strode a few doors along the main corridor.

Eleanor followed but Clifford stayed where he was and called after them, 'I fear, my lady, you have left your handbag in the car. I'd best retrieve it.'

In the cramped interview room Wilby was lost. 'Let me get this right. If I solve this heinous crime here, I'll be promoted?'

Eleanor clapped her hands. 'Absolutely, Sergeant Wilby, your promotion will be in the bag! And not before time, either. National fame, just imagine.'

Clifford opened the door, nodded to Eleanor and stood aside as Constable Brice wobbled through with the tray.

'What crime?' Wilby was struggling to keep up.

Eleanor clapped her hands. 'Why, the murder of Jack Cornell, of course.'

'What!' Wilby exploded. 'There was no murder! He committed suicide. And left a note saying so.'

'Indeed, Sergeant. Were you the one who first examined the body?'

'As a matter of fact, I was, which is how I know it weren't no murder.'

'Then you won't mind telling me where you were between eleven Friday night and eight Saturday morning.'

Wilby somehow controlled his temper. 'As it happens I went off-duty at ten, which young Lowe can tell you, then I went home to bed – alone!'

'So no witnesses then?'

Wilby exploded. 'No, because I don't need no witness for a crime what ain't been committed!'

Eleanor straightened her hat. 'Well really, if that is how you thank us for trying to help your career, it's no wonder you are still a sergeant. I will suggest to Mayor Kingsley that your force employs women as some of the more progressive and successful forces are doing. A female sergeant is exactly what this station needs.' She stood. 'Clifford.' She indicated the door with a wave.

'My lady.' Clifford adjusted Constable Brice's tea tray with a gloved hand as he passed to stem the flow of tea pouring over the edge. 'Gentlemen.' Clifford touched his hat with one finger and caught up with Eleanor at the front door, which he opened for her.

As the Rolls pulled away, Clifford spoke. 'If I might offer a complimentary observation, my lady, that was indeed a most convincing performance.'

'Thank you, Clifford. It seems that Wilby has no alibi for the time of Cornell's death, so we'll have to work out where to go from there. But a hearty congratulations to you too. Tell me, on your side, was it as successful a plan as we hoped?'

'Better, my lady.'

Eleanor gasped. 'So at least one more of our theories is correct?'

'I would advance the status "theory" to "fact".'

'So Sergeant Wilby is covering up the goings on at the quarry! Please tell me all the details, I'm simply bursting to find out. Was my account of the murder mis-recorded?'

'Most definitely not, my lady.'

Eleanor was dumbfounded. 'What? But while I was with that idiot Wilby and the other policeman was making tea, didn't you check the recorded crimes register on the front desk? I'm confused, Clifford.'

Clifford cleared his throat. 'I was unable to assess the accuracy with which your account of the murderous events at the quarry were recorded because…' He paused dramatically. 'There was no record!'

Eleanor gasped. 'No record!' She let out a low whistle. 'Then it is worse than I feared. So that trip out to the quarry with Sergeant Wilby the following morning was all for nothing, just a sham. Probably in the hope that I would be satisfied and let the whole thing drop!'

'Your theory that Sergeant Wilby is corrupt is, I feel now, irrefutable. In the register, the pages for Saturday third April, the night your report of the murder at the quarry would have been recorded, and Sunday fourth April when you took the police to the quarry, have been deliberately removed.' He reached under the palm of his left-hand leather glove and pulled out a scrap of paper. 'I found only this.'

'Clifford! It's a definite cover-up. But not executed deftly enough to escape your sharp eyes, well done!'

'Thank you, my lady.'

'Now, Clifford, to the quarry!'

CHAPTER 29

It was the middle of the day and a sunny one at that. And without the hindering nuisances of that idiot Wilby or Cartwright…

'Oh, Clifford, we've forgotten about Cartwright!' Eleanor groaned. 'He'll be on us like a shot again, sticking his beak in, threatening to report us for trespassing. We'll have to evade him somehow.'

'Fortunately, Mr Cartwright is a creature of habit, my lady. As you saw, it is market day in Chipstone. Mr Cartwright always stays until the end, around five or six, and then retires to the Eagle bar.'

'A pie and a pint, no doubt?'

'Indeed, but "market pie". It is the Eagle's speciality, served only on Mondays. A hand-crafted, hot water crust pastry with gammon or steak and kidney options.'

'Hot water pastry? Yuk!'

'You would imagine so, but they are in fact distressingly moreish.'

'Well, when Cartwright has hung up his farmer's boots for good, I suggest you take me to sample this local delicacy. Until then, I fear his scowling face would sour even the tastiest meal.'

'Very good, my lady.'

A minute later, the quarry swung into view. Clifford drove a few hundred yards past the gates until he found a gap in the overgrown hawthorn hedge. The Rolls passed through with only minor scratching to its gleaming paintwork.

Clifford held the door open for her. Gladstone tumbled out first and started sniffing around.

In the car a thought struck Eleanor: here she was about to break into the very quarry where she witnessed a murder with a man she had loosely pegged as a suspect. Then again, he was still the only person who seemed to believe her about the quarry murder, although if he was the murderer he would do, wouldn't he?

She shook her head, what choice did she have? Besides, she'd still failed to come up with any further evidence of his involvement or any conceivable motive for killing Atkins. Or for that matter, Cornell, although she hadn't even thought about his possible involvement in that. She sighed. Having lived an adventurous life, she was used to uncertainty, but she wished now everything was black and white. Promising herself to be on her guard she stepped out of the Rolls.

Clifford strode forward, his eyes narrowing as he scoured the ground. Between the naturally occurring flints and gravel-filled potholes, the surface was still soft after the torrential storm, allowing Clifford to follow the faint imprint of tyre tracks.

'In my unprofessional estimation, my lady, I would deduce that there were two vehicles here, one more substantial than the other.'

'Hmm.' Eleanor had taken the thirty paces to the entrance and peeped out into the road. 'And you know, that is quite a trek from the other side of the gates along the three hundred yards or so of road to here. Especially with the dead weight of a corpse.'

'Then it would appear most unlikely that the murderer would have risked the body being carried out in the open.'

'And don't forget the gates were unlocked!' Eleanor exclaimed. 'Gladstone and I walked right through them, didn't we, boy?' She turned to Clifford. 'What a shame we can't pick Gladstone's memory. There might be a clue locked away in there.'

Gladstone stopped digging and looked up with a perfect pyramid of muddy sand on his snout.

'It does seem most unlikely that there would be much of use behind that grubby forehead,' Clifford offered.

Eleanor laughed and swished the dirt from the bulldog's nose. 'This is supposed to be a professional investigation, you rascal. Come on, let's get into the quarry while it's quiet. We can study the tracks in more detail later.'

'An admirable suggestion.' From the boot of the Rolls Clifford took out what appeared to be, with only two rungs, the world's shortest ladder.

'What on earth use is that, Clifford?'

'The gates are locked, my lady, so this will help us climb over. It's a ladder,' he added as if to a dim-witted child. 'This looks the best place.' He gestured to the right where unruly hedging engulfed the fence.

'I know it's a ladder, Clifford, but it's hardly going to help us get over a… oh!' Eleanor watched Clifford extend the two sides revealing hidden rungs, each tucked neatly inside the other. He continued on way past what she considered a necessary height, and with a deft twist of his wrists, clicked it in half, creating a giant stepladder. 'It belonged to your uncle, my lady. He was a most ingenious inventor.'

Eleanor was equally impressed and confused. 'Bravo! But why did my uncle design such an item and carry it around with him?'

'To assist him in climbing fences,' Clifford replied, again as if to a small child. With a slight struggle, he managed to place the feet of the first half of the ladder over the other side of the fence and then brought the second half to rest on their side, the apex just clearing the fence itself. He gestured up the rungs.

'But what about Gladstone? Don't tell me my uncle taught him to heave his lummocking frame up and down steps like this?'

'I'm sure Master Gladstone will find a way through, he is an excellent digger.'

'Here we go!' Eleanor bent forward and held the sides. She'd scaled plenty higher and more rickety obstacles. She was soon up and over and called to Gladstone. 'Come on, clever boy, find a hole!'

The bulldog sniffed along the fence before disappearing into the scrub along the bottom of the hedge. Clifford paused with his hands on the ladder until Gladstone appeared on Eleanor's side of the fence.

'Well done!' Eleanor bent down and patted Gladstone as Clifford quickly shimmied up and over with the ease of a man half his age.

'Shall we?' Clifford nodded across the scrub and haphazard piles of gravel to the dilapidated wooden workman's hut beyond the turning area for lorries. Eleanor felt a familiar frisson of excitement. She hadn't totally lost her appetite for adventure. She made her way through the weeds, skirting the muddier sections.

Standing by the hut, Clifford scanned the quarry. 'Tell me, again, my lady, exactly what you saw and heard.'

'Well, I can tell you that the wind made it hard to catch the details, but I heard snatches of shouting coming from inside. And I saw a man, Atkins, I'm sure, holding his hands up like he was surrendering.'

'And then?'

'Then I thought there was a flash of lightning, but I soon realised it was the shot from a gun as the man fell backwards.'

'How large would you say the flash was, my lady?'

'It's hard to say. It was just a flash.'

'Did it leave an image? Such as when you look quickly at the sun and then away again?'

'Yes, and no. I didn't have that blinding image you describe after the gun was fired. I believe it is called "after image" by the boffins,' she said smugly.

'Indeed it is, my lady. Of course, it would depend heavily on the density of your light-sensitive receptors and neuronal density. Professor Hering, the German physiologist, wrote most eloquently on the subject.'

They tried the door.

'Locked! Dash it. Stranger and stranger, Clifford. The quarry gates that, according to Cartwright, are always locked, were open the night of the murder, as was this hut, but the morning the police arrived with me, the gates were locked, but this hut still open. And now both are locked.'

Clifford nodded. 'Indeed, my lady, it certainly suggests someone has been here since the morning the police looked around with you.'

'The murderer?'

'A distinct possibility, my lady, but why would he return? When you were here with the police you said that all evidence of the murder was already removed.'

'Maybe the answer is inside?' She circled the building looking for another way in. Peering through the dusty windows she could see little inside… except Clifford.

She returned to the front of the hut and found the door open. 'How? What are you doing?'

'I believe the definition of breaking and entering is to enter a building or property by force so as to commit a crime of burglary. As you can see, I have not entered by force and have no intention of committing any crime, burglary or otherwise.'

'I know what breaking and entering is, Clifford.' She blushed, remembering how much it seemed Clifford and her uncle knew of her past. 'What I meant was, how did you get in? Do you have hat pins like they always use in penny dreadful novels?'

Clifford held up a slim set of keys. 'Universal skeleton keys, designed by your uncle.'

'Enough! Until you can tell me the whole story of your joint exploits, I fear I am forming a rather scandalous impression of you and my uncle.'

'Most unfortunate, my lady.'

Eleanor scoured the spot where she was convinced Atkins had fallen. 'I'm sure it was just here.' Together they peered hard, treading carefully so as not to disturb potential clues. 'The stain was right there.' Eleanor stared at the stubbornly stain-free sandy surface.

Clifford scrutinised the area. There was no discernible mark. 'The blood would have been quite easy to remove from the sand.'

He stretched his neck from side to side. Eleanor stared at him. He seemed to be lost in deep thought.

All this thinking and logicalising. *Was that even a word?* Her head hurt. She wanted to dive in, seize a solid piece of evidence and march into Chipstone Police Station and Wilby's office brandishing the answer. Although if Wilby was the murderer, that might not be such a good idea. She looked once more at Clifford, who was now stepping sideways around the area they had pinpointed as the site of the murder itself.

Clifford rubbed his chin. 'Why lure the victim here? There's our question.'

'We've gone over this. Because it is out of the way and pretty much disused, so a perfect place for a murder.' She wanted to add, 'Yawn!' to the end of that, but thought better of it.

'But what did the murderer possess, or know, that enticed a man of Mr Atkins' fastidiousness to wallow around in a murky quarry during a storm? And what did Mr Atkins possess, or know, that led to his murder in this remote place?'

'I see how you're thinking.' She looked around. 'Where's Gladstone?'

Not wanting to shout and draw attention to their presence, Eleanor held one hand over her eyes and scoured the undergrowth. A moment later a pheasant shot skywards with an anxious squawk. 'Ah, there he is.' Eleanor pointed.

Clifford pulled out a silver whistle from his waistcoat pocket and blew it once. There was no audible sound, but Gladstone appeared instantly in the hut with them.

'What a highly trained hound,' Eleanor marvelled, reaching for the bulldog's favourite treats, which she'd started keeping in her pockets. 'Good boy!' she murmured, removing a trailing piece of bramble from his ear. 'Now, Gladstone, use your doggie senses to tell us something about this dastardly murderer.'

Clifford looked on with mild amusement. The dog rolled on his back and wriggled his legs lazily.

'Hopeless!' Eleanor chided him. 'We'll have to do it ourselves. Right, getting into the mind of a murderer.'

She stood up and tried to focus. Suddenly Gladstone struggled onto his belly and heaved himself up with a grunt. He gambolled a short way behind Clifford and pawed under what looked like an old quarry engine on wood runners.

'There are no squirrels here, mutt brain,' Eleanor said.

The bulldog took no notice and continued scraping at the stones, ineffectually flicking small amounts of sand to the side.

'Probably the remains of a quarry worker's mouldy sandwich,' Eleanor said. 'Gladstone, you have no discernment!'

'I fear he may cut his paw on those flints, my lady. They can be extremely sharp,' Clifford noted.

They walked over to the dog, who was now partially lying down, scratching at the stones with both front feet.

'What are you doing, you stupid lump?' Eleanor bent down, then jumped up and spat the sand from her mouth as Gladstone showered her with his next pawful. 'Yuk!'

Clifford passed her a pristine handkerchief and squatted to get a clearer look at whatever it was that was so interesting to the bulldog.

'Good boy. Stand down, Gladstone,' he ordered. 'STAND. DOWN,' he commanded again.

Gladstone sat up and started whining, with sandy drool dripping from his jowls.

'Yuk again, Gladstone!' Eleanor wrinkled her nose and then tuned into the fact that Clifford was on his knees in the dirt! *Oh,*

for a box Brownie camera to snap his preposterously inelegant pose!
Eleanor giggled and then stopped short at Clifford's sideways glance.

'What is it?' she asked.

Clifford finally managed to move two huge flints from the compacted earth and reached into the dirt, which had been loosened up. He handed her an old boot.

Eleanor couldn't help laughing out loud. 'Oh, Gladstone, you and your shoes!'

Clifford stood up and brushed the dirt off his overcoat. 'It seems that I have burdened Mrs Butters with unnecessary laundry. I was hoping that Master Gladstone might have found something of interest.'

It was Eleanor's turn to squat and squint at the spot where Clifford had extracted the shoe. Something glinted at her.

'Your long-range vision may be superlative, Clifford, but you may need a trip to the optometrist for your short-range vision.'

She leaned forward and picked up a tiny, cut stone. Standing upright, she wiped the dust off it. 'Looks like a garnet. They don't mine garnets here, do they?'

'Ah, excellent. No, my lady, I—'

'Hang on!'

Eleanor dropped to her knees and then lay full-length on the dirt floor, despite Clifford's muttered comments about 'Mrs Butters' and 'more extra laundry'. She reached between the wooden runners with both hands and with a few pulls and grunts had her prize.

As she stood up, the state of her stockings and coat made Clifford wince. Ignoring him, she nodded to the metal box in her hands. 'I'd call that something of interest, wouldn't you?'

Placing it on the table, she brushed the dirt off it. She tried the lid.

'Locked!'

Without a word he stepped forward and took a rectangular metal object from his pocket. Extracting a slim, blade-like tool from the body, he slid it into the lock and after a few moments, stood back. She looked at him enquiringly.

'It's a *Schweizer Offiziersmesser,* my lady.'

Eleanor could speak German among a smattering of other languages. 'A Swiss Army Knife?'

'Yes, my lady, Mr Elsener, the founder of Victorinox, the makers of this ingenious little tool, and your uncle were mutual admirers. Your uncle asked Mr Elsener to make him a one-off Swiss Army Knife for his unique… requirements.'

'Well, we'll discuss what my uncle's "unique requirements" were at a later date. For the moment, let's see what we have here.' She opened the lid and tutted. 'Well, well, look at this.'

Inside were several bundles of money done up with rubber bands, two small red notebooks… and a Browning pistol.

CHAPTER 30

'Oh goodness, my lady, did you sleep badly?' Mrs Butters picked up the fallen pillows and placed them on the chair. She fussed about Eleanor, rescuing the eiderdown from a tangled heap at the bottom of the bed as her mistress frowned at the mirror.

'Can you claim to have slept badly if you haven't slept at all?' Eleanor grumbled. She tried to smile, but it came out more as a grimace. 'Ignore me being testy, Mrs Butters. I have lain awake all night, going back and forth over these wretched clues. I fear I will go mad if we don't have a breakthrough soon.'

'Mr Clifford is one for patient thinking. I can see how that would frustrate a lady like yourself.' Mrs Butters gave Eleanor a wink.

Eleanor laughed, her bad mood broken. 'You are very perceptive, Mrs Butters. Clifford has a fabulously analytical mind, but it drives me to absolute distraction! But you know, you always bring me a basket full of feel-good each morning.'

The housekeeper beamed and half-curtseyed. ''Tis my pleasure, my lady. No one wants a wet blanket in the face afore they've even eaten their breakfast. There's plenty of time later in the day for folk to pull clouds over the sunshine, after all.'

Eleanor chuckled and imitated Clifford's half-bow.

They both giggled and Eleanor went downstairs refreshed.

Clifford greeted her at the bottom of the stairs. 'Coffee in the morning room, my lady? I imagined you might wish to continue our discussion of yesterday before I leave?'

'Absolutely, but where are you going? We've got work to do, surely?'

'Quite so, my lady. Your coffee is ready.' He tilted his head towards the door, which she took to mean he wanted the other staff unaware of the details of his trip out.

With the door closed, Clifford spoke more freely. 'My lady, I have an uncomfortable feeling that someone may be aware of our discovery at the quarry.'

Eleanor sat bolt upright. 'But we left it where we found it. How can that be?'

'Last night I had the distinct impression we were being watched. I didn't mention it at the time as I couldn't be sure.'

Eleanor digested the information. 'So why mention it now?'

'This morning Silas reported that he found an intruder in the grounds. Unfortunately, the man made his getaway before Silas could detain him or get a good look at his face.'

'Silas, the gamekeeper?'

'Yes, my lady.'

'So, he probably disturbed a poacher?'

'Possibly, but it is well known in the area that there are no game birds on the estate.'

'Of course, you mentioned that. So Silas isn't really a gamekeeper, is he? He's more of a security guard?'

'Yes, my lady. Silas is our first line of defence, as it were, here at the Hall.'

Something was nagging at Eleanor's memory. 'Then, Clifford, where was he when an intruder broke into the garage and interfered with the Rolls?'

'Unfortunately he had other business to attend to that day.'

'Then maybe our murderer knew he was absent.'

'Exactly my thoughts. Which is why' – Clifford cleared his throat – 'I would ask you not to leave the Hall until I return. Silas will patrol the grounds.'

Eleanor fumed to herself. *The cheek! Men!* She fixed Clifford with her best steely stare. 'Sweet. Very sweet. But while you and my uncle were dressing up as cowboys, scaling fences and picking locks with your boys' toys, I was navigating my way around the world. And look, here I am, a grown, capable and independent woman.'

Clifford stepped back. 'I wonder if Mr Atkins might not have imagined himself capable? Mr Cornell too, perhaps he would have thought himself grown and independent? But the murderer has proven them both to be erroneous in their confidence.'

Eleanor felt a shiver run through her. She changed tack. 'Tell me, what is it that is taking you off out this morning?'

'With permission, I plan to talk to some contacts who, I hope, may be able to shine a light on our recent discoveries.'

Eleanor stood. 'I'll come with you. It's about time I met one of your mysterious contacts.'

Clifford shook his head. 'I'm sorry but this particular gentleman is of the nervous variety. Were I to turn up with a companion, he would most likely make a run for it.'

She wasn't very happy with his response, but again, what choice did she have?

'Okay, you have my permission. When will you return?'

'In good time to serve luncheon.' He turned to leave the room and paused. 'Your uncle would turn in his grave if I allowed the niece he cherished so much to come to harm.'

And with that he was gone.

Dash it! Why did Clifford have to keep mentioning how much her uncle cared for her? Where had he been when she'd needed him? And why hadn't he made himself a part of her life?

'Clearly too busy playing cowboys and Indians with Clifford,' she said aloud. 'I'll solve this case myself and without leaving the Hall.'

Ten minutes later, with Gladstone sprawled across the drawing-room sofa with her, she was ready, with an old notebook she'd found in her bedroom to hand. Eleanor frowned and chewed her pencil, trying to work out where to start. Eventually she decided to show Clifford that she too could be methodical by listing her and her chief suspects' movements around the time of the first murder. One of the detectives in a penny dreadful novel she'd once read under the bedclothes at her boarding school had done a similar thing and solved the murder there and then. She set to work, writing down all the details in two columns:

ATKINS	TIME
Atkins seen leaving his house by housekeeper	7.30 p.m. Sat 03 Apr
Lancelot seen by doorman arriving at The Goat Club	9.00 p.m.
I stomped out of the Hall needing some space (bad idea!)	9.30 p.m.
Mrs Butters said Clifford left to look for me	about 10 mins later
Abigail confirmed buffoon Wilby left police station	10.00 p.m.
Cartwright says he left farmhouse to mend barn roof	10.00 p.m. (wife only witness *Hmm!*)
I checked uncle's watch	10.10 p.m.
Gladstone and I saw man (Atkins) murdered (can a dog be a witness?)	about 10.15 p.m.
Whole club saw Lancelot skinny-dipping!!!	10.35 p.m.
Wilby arrived back at police station	11.10 p.m. (according to him!)
Clifford returned from looking for me	11.40 p.m. (guessing about then)

Cartwright said he returned to farmhouse	11.50 p.m. (wife only witness again!)
Gladstone and I finally got back to the Hall	11.55 p.m. (roughly)
I tried to report murder to idiot Wilby at police station	00.30 a.m. Sun 04 Apr
Lancelot picked up by chauffeur (drunk!)	02.00 a.m.
Atkins' body found at his house by housekeeper (poor woman)	07.00 a.m.

She tapped her notepad in frustration. This was horribly slow and laborious. Forcing herself to continue, she turned her focus to Jack Cornell.

CORNELL

Wilby went off duty	10.00 p.m.
Cartwright was with the vet	10.45 p.m.
Last sighting of Jack Cornell by neighbour	11.15 p.m.
Cartwright says he returned to farmhouse	11.20 p.m.
Jack Cornell murdered (according to police)	11.30 p.m. Fri 09 Apr – 08.00 a.m. Sat 10 Apr
Cartwright went back up to ewe pens (haven't asked farmhand)	01.00 a.m.
Cartwright says he returned to farmhouse again	01.50 a.m.
Cartwright apparently got up for breakfast	05.00 a.m.
Jack Cornell's body found by postman	12.15 p.m.

She sucked the end of the pencil vigorously, but it didn't help, it just made her feel slightly sick. No matter how long she stared at the two lists no stroke of inspiration or logical thought process revealed the killer. She began to wonder just how realistic those penny dreadful crime novels were.

She tickled Gladstone's ears and stared at Atkins' and Cornell's names on the page. 'Perhaps Cornell saw the murder at the quarry and that's why he was killed, Gladstone? He could have been a witness!' She shivered as she realised that on that basis she could be the next victim. Maybe Clifford wasn't overdoing his scaremongering this morning. She wrote 'Dead' next to Atkins' and Jack Cornell's names, but she was imagining writing it next to her own.

Eleanor shook her head. 'This is hopelessly tiresome, Gladstone. I hate to admit it but without Clifford to bounce ideas off, I'm not making much progress. I'm just going round in circles coming up with random theories. I need to thrash scenarios out loud with…' She cupped Gladstone's face. '… someone who is more interested in solving this than in liver biscuit treats.'

At the 'T' word, Gladstone jumped off the Chesterfield.

'To the kitchen with you, greedy chap.' Eleanor giggled. 'I have the perfect person to go and discuss the case with. Clifford is wrong, this is no time for caution.'

At the kitchen door she paused, holding Gladstone's collar. 'Good morning, Mrs Trotman. Thank you for breakfast.'

'Good morning, my lady. My pleasure, as always.' The cook smiled.

'Has Gladstone disgraced himself in the sausage stealing stakes recently?'

'No, my lady.' Mrs Trotman laughed. 'He hasn't managed to snuffle any in the last few days so he's not grounded from the kitchen at the moment.'

'Permission then to release the beast?'

'Of course.'

Leaving the cook to deal with the greedy bulldog, Eleanor ran upstairs to change.

CHAPTER 31

The chill of the morning air soon blew the woolliness from Eleanor's thoughts as she pedalled along the lanes. The stiffness in her shoulder from the crash was also all but gone. She rode up the hills with only minimal puffing and reddening. Even weaving round the worst sections of road, she covered the distance in just under an hour, which made her feel she was almost back to her old self.

'Ah, that's more like it!' she told the world in general as she leaned her bicycle against the metal railings and looked up at Chipstone's town hall. 'Now for some answers.'

'Lady Swift, what an absolute pleasure.' Mayor Kingsley put down the file he'd been waving in the clerk's face and took her hand. Eleanor smiled. 'My apologies for arriving unannounced, but I need your help.'

'A damsel in distress,' he exclaimed. 'You have come to exactly the right place. Perkins, tea, now! This way, my dear.' Closing the door to his office behind them, he turned to her. 'The air in our little rural paradise seems to suit you, you have quite a glow, if I might be so bold.'

'Such a beautiful county, Mayor Kingsley, and spring is such a lovely season.'

'Absolutely, my dear.' He gestured to a chair and slid into the one next to her. 'I'm always here for my loyal constituents, so how can I help?'

As always, after her initial rush of adrenalin, she had no real plan. The only thing that seemed obvious to her was that sitting around waiting for Clifford's dubious 'contacts' to come up with the answers they needed was not an option. She'd always looked after herself and, besides, she didn't consider Clifford charging off on his own and telling her to hide away meekly in the Hall as acting as part of the team. It was time to get answers and the mayor had been the only person, besides Clifford, who seemed to take her seriously.

A knock at the door interrupted Eleanor's reply. Instead of the rabbit of a woman who had served them previously, Perkins the clerk wheeled the trolley next to them. He stood awkwardly, waiting.

'Pour the tea, man,' Kingsley growled.

As Perkins closed the door behind him, Eleanor adopted her usual blunt approach.

'Mayor Kingsley, I believe there is a degree of corruption undermining the police and civil service here in Chipstone.'

'Corruption!' The mayor shot out of his chair with surprising speed for one of his bulk. 'Good gracious, my dear, whatever do you believe you've uncovered?'

Eleanor smiled to herself. *This was more like it!* Subtlety was all very well, but sometimes you just needed straightforward shock tactics to galvanise people. Something was rotten in the state of Chipstone, and she intended to find out what.

'Well, for starters, someone, somewhere is deliberately perverting the course of justice. Despite your assurances that you would monitor the police's progress in the case of the murder I witnessed, the whole thing has been hushed up.'

Kingsley stared at her. 'Are you referring to the murder at the quarry? Because, my dear, I admonished the police for not taking your report seriously and insisted they re-investigate. I confess, however, that I have been so busy with other matters, I haven't chased them up. I do apologise, but it is the burden of being overworked, an unavoidable evil in this role, I fear. But a cover-up, you say? What has brought you to that conclusion?'

'The fact that all traces of my initial report and subsequent trip out to the quarry with that buffoon Wilby have been removed from the police logbook.'

He raised his eyebrows. 'Gracious me, Lady Swift, that is a most serious allegation. I shall have it investigated immediately. And this time I will make it a priority to follow it up personally, you can be assured.'

'There's more. I believe the man murdered at the quarry was none other than Mr Atkins.'

Mayor Kingsley started. 'Atkins?' He frowned and then smiled. 'You are getting muddled, my dear. He was murdered at his home, I believe. A terrible business. I didn't really know the man, except in his work where he displayed a fine ethic and a strong dedication to duty. He will be hard to replace.'

Eleanor changed tack. 'Do you know this Cornell character, who the newspapers reported took his own life after apparently killing Mr Atkins?'

Kingsley frowned. 'It's not a name I'm familiar with. I think he was on the town's payroll but, honestly, my dear lady' – he shrugged and held his hands out – 'there are so many council workers.'

Eleanor changed tack again. 'Were you informed that Cornell's suicide note cited Mr Atkins as blackmailing him?'

Kingsley rubbed his chin. 'I believe I do remember the police report or the papers mentioning that.'

'Do you think Mr Atkins was capable of blackmail?'

Kingsley paced the floor. 'From my dealings with him, I would not have thought it likely, but you never really know people, do you?' He turned to Eleanor. 'Forgive me, my dear, but why do you ask?'

'Because I am sure that Mr Atkins was not blackmailing Mr Cornell.'

Kingsley eased back into his chair and took a sip of his tea. 'Really? That is most disturbing. How can you be so sure?'

Eleanor hesitated. The truth was, she still didn't have any firm evidence that the suicide note was fake. The gun oil being in Atkins' right, rather than left, hand suggested he had been murdered, but Jack Cornell's convenient confession that he was the guilty party seemed too pat, too orchestrated. And there was the riddle of why Cornell would have made Atkins' death look like an accident, only to confess to killing him in a suicide note. But actual solid, stand-up-in-court proof? How could she explain this tangled web of half fact, half wild theory to the mayor?

She cursed her impetuousness. Maybe Clifford had been right, maybe she should have waited back at the Hall for him to come up with some real proof? She swallowed hard. 'Well, my late uncle knew Mr Atkins and… er, according to Clifford, my uncle had the highest opinion of Mr Atkins. Clifford insists that it is out of the question that Mr Atkins would stoop to blackmail. And there's also a few… things that don't well… quite add up,' she ended lamely.

However, the mayor wasn't listening. 'I am sorry, my dear, but Mr Clifford? Your… *butler*?' Kingsley smiled thinly. 'I am not sure if the word of a mere butler can be relied on to vouch for a gentleman's character.' He hesitated, before saying, 'Lady Swift, may I be frank with you?'

Eleanor sighed. She couldn't blame him for not taking her seriously. 'Of course.'

Kingsley leaned on his desk. 'My dear lady, I applaud your dedication to the pursuit of justice, but I fear you may be in significant danger.'

Eleanor groaned. 'Thank you for your concern but I've already been warned off. Clifford was full of advice this morning.'

'Precisely my point.' Kingsley nodded slowly.

At Eleanor's confused frown he put his face in his hands, sucked in a deep breath and then looked her in the eye. 'My apologies to bring up such an unpleasant topic as your uncle's sad passing but, dear lady, there is no delicate way to say it.' He coughed. 'There is a possibility that his death was not due to natural causes.'

'What?' Eleanor was flabbergasted.

Kingsley sighed and put his hands on the table in front of him. 'It was not proven but Mr Clifford was under scrutiny for a considerable time. It was only the unfortunate lack of evidence which led to the investigation being closed down.'

'Clifford? But… but he was my uncle's wingman for years. He was at the Hall when I was a child. He can't have been suspected if my uncle was…' Her words dried up and her eyes filled.

'I am so sorry to be the bearer of bad news.'

Eleanor shook her head. 'And I'm sorry but I simply don't believe it. My uncle was too shrewd to be taken in. And besides, Clifford has been nothing but a loyal servant since my arrival.'

'Really?'

'Absolutely. Why, when someone tampered with the brakes on the Rolls, he practically saved my life.'

'Perhaps… or perhaps he made it look like he did. Mr Clifford is known to have a complicated past and a great many contacts that you and I would describe as "questionable", but which could also be described as downright criminal. I fought the urge to tell you all this on your last visit as you were so newly arrived, but now I fear for your safety.'

'Why on earth would he wish me harm?'

'Perhaps you are uncovering his most carefully laid tracks. He has been with you on your investigations so far?'

Eleanor nodded, sipping her tea to conceal her confusion.

'Don't you see, my dear? He has been with you every step and knows what you have discovered. What might he do to stop you finding out any more?'

Eleanor's face was ashen. *I know you toyed with him being a suspect, Ellie, but you never really believed it. Did you?* 'Clifford isn't a murderer!'

Kingsley shook his head slowly. 'I wish I shared your confidence. On the evening when you were at the quarry, where was your loyal butler?'

'He was out looking for me in the car.'

'And did he find you?'

Eleanor groaned. 'No.'

'So, his whereabouts at the time of the murder are unknown.' Kingsley nodded to himself. 'And who knew Atkins' personal habits as well as Mr Clifford? None of us who worked with him had any inkling of his home life. He was quite reclusive and fiercely private. I wager Mr Clifford knew a great deal though.'

Eleanor said nothing, but her face betrayed her thoughts.

'Lady Swift,' Kingsley said softly. 'How did you become alerted to the police logbook allegedly having been tampered with? A "discovery" of Mr Clifford's perhaps?'

Eleanor's mind raced. *Was it possible that she had been so blind?* She pictured her penny dreadful-inspired lists back at the Hall and now she could see plainly what she'd been unable, or refused, to see before – the name of the murderer.

And that name was Clifford.

Kingsley stood up and put his hands together. 'Lady Swift, will you permit me to provide a safe house for you to reside in until I can assure your safety?'

'What? Safe house?' Eleanor stared furiously at the mayor. 'Good gracious, no!'

Kingsley took her arm as she rose. 'Is Mr Clifford waiting outside for you?'

'No, he has gone to see his… contacts.'

Kingsley drew his breath in sharply. 'I see. Then if you return to Henley Hall, I insist that Perkins drives you in my car. But I do strongly urge you to let me ensure your safety. I will arrange for a member of the force to check on you regularly.'

She shook her head and, pulling her arm free, slid her gloves on and straightened her hat. 'Now I know what I'm dealing with I shall be fine, Mayor Kingsley. In my previous life I managed quite admirably. I foolishly let my guard down temporarily, that's all. Thank you for your time.'

'Perkins!' Kingsley bellowed from the open door. 'Car, now!'

Back at the Hall, Eleanor made her excuses to Mrs Butters and asked for tea in her room. Once the tray had been delivered and the door closed, she sat on the floor, leaning against the bed. Even Gladstone had been sent away with the housekeeper. She needed to be alone.

She buried her head in her hands, her mind switching from believing to disbelieving and back until she felt dizzy. It had to be wrong. Clifford couldn't have fooled her so completely. But what if he'd been fooling her uncle for all those years? She thought back to the day when she had arrived. Clifford had been so put out to see her. Was it because she'd disrupted his plans to murder someone that night?

And the brakes being cut on the Rolls. Had he arranged that himself as the mayor had suggested? Was it just an elaborate ruse to keep her from suspecting him? A cold-hearted plan that had involved him inflicting concussion and a battered shoulder on her?

And his mysterious contacts? She hadn't questioned who they were, but he hadn't volunteered the information either. Even the box Gladstone had uncovered in the quarry could very well belong to Clifford. After all, he'd been keen to stop the bulldog digging and he claimed he'd been unable to see the box even though she'd spotted it immediately. Which meant if the box was his, so were the notebooks, money… and gun!

Finally, what about his latest insistence she didn't leave the Hall? Was it for her own safety… or so he could find her if he needed to? She shivered. And he still hadn't returned. This was too much, how could she possibly know who to believe? Since her parents' disappearance she had learnt to trust no one, only letting her guard down once with the man she'd finally married, and that had been a monumental mistake. Had she done the same again?

She let her head flop back onto the bed. *There's only one way to find out, Ellie…*

Reaching under her bed, she scrabbled about for her soft-soled ballet pumps. At the door, she opened it a crack and listened carefully. The upstairs was silent and there was no movement in the hallway below. *Right, here goes, Ellie…*

CHAPTER 32

Downstairs, she listened again. Nothing. Holding her breath, she pushed the kitchen door open to be met by the soft sound of Gladstone's snores over by the range. She stepped towards the window and saw Mrs Trotman talking to the milkman, while Polly was fighting with the sheets she was trying to peg out on the washing line. Eleanor made the snap decision that she would just have to risk that Mrs Butters was somewhere out of the way.

She crossed to the other end of the kitchen and tapped gently on the door to the butler's pantry. This was the mysterious room leading between the kitchen and the dining room, allowing Clifford to magically appear with a tray at a moment's notice. Getting no answer, she turned the door handle and stepped inside.

Leaning against the door, she let it close with the softest of clicks. The arched windows on the opposite wall threw sunlight across the wooden countertops, which ran the full length of the room. Sets of silver tableware sat perfectly polished and arranged. Below this, was a long run of cupboard doors.

Willing her feet to move, Eleanor stepped to the first and pulled open the door. Acres of glassware filled the space. In the next three it was the same, only different sets of crockery. Good grief, her uncle would have needed to have thrown a party for the whole village to use half this stuff. The last door revealed sets of linen ware, all perfectly ironed and ready to go at the slightest hint of a spillage in the dining room. With a jolt, she remembered that it now all belonged to her…

With a deep breath, she focussed again on the task at hand. She turned in a full circle, noting that the two highly polished tables in the centre of the room each had drawers. But these revealed nothing more than a range of corkscrews in one and cigar cutters in the other. *Think, Ellie, he wouldn't hide anything incriminating in amongst the dinner service!*

Aside from the glass-fronted drinks cabinet, which she noted was locked, there was an oak tall boy, which opened with a nerve-wracking creak but only to reveal rows of decoratively labelled jars of preserves and a world of cheese, trapped in glass-domed kingdoms. That only left two doors. The larger of the two, she knew had to lead straight into the dining room. The other, therefore, had to lead to Clifford's personal quarters. *Ah, that was where she should be!* Grabbing a set of white gloves from the neat pile on the countertop, she slipped them on and grasped the handle.

It was only after she'd opened the door and peeped up the short flight of stairs that it struck her as odd that he didn't keep this locked. Good job though. Still, she had to take herself in hand and demand that her legs carry her up to the smart, bachelor-style sitting room. Snooping on one's staff was not her style.

A large writing desk filled the window recess, one pane slightly ajar on its stay, and two leather armchairs sat facing the stone fireplace. Two silver-framed photographs of Clifford with her uncle somewhere abroad were the only decoration, save for a wide mirror hanging above them.

At the far end, half-obscured by a jutting wall, a circular dining table was set with a blue cloth and two chairs. She noted one had a plump cushion propped against the back. Eleanor paused, had her uncle sat with his butler up here, invited into Clifford's private world? Two old friends, enjoying a brandy, chuckling over their adventures and sharing a late-night supper?

She shook her head. It didn't seem possible that Clifford could have taken her uncle in for all those years. She sighed. She knew so little about her uncle, how could she possibly judge?

She started with the drawers of the desk and quickly scanned all the papers, but nothing seemed in the least bit out of the ordinary, merely household accounts, archived letters to and from tradesmen and a copy of *Debretts Peerage and Baronetage*. The room was furnished with such elegant minimalism that she stared blankly round for a moment. Where could one hide anything?

Her eyes ran to the slim bookcase near the table. Going through each of the books and pulling on their spines in the hope of revealing a secret opening, revealed… nothing. Resorting to taking the lid from the copper kettle hanging on the hook over the fireplace, she chewed her lip. There had to be more. His bedroom! But where on earth was it? Spinning round, she noted one of the windows this end of the room had the curtains drawn. She gingerly peeped through.

Ah! Not a window but another short flight of stairs to Clifford's inner sanctum. With no idea what she would say if he found her peering under his mattress, she sprinted up the stairs. The cedar wardrobe held nothing but a perfect row of suits: morning, grey and black. She hurried through the pockets of the jackets and trousers to no avail.

A row of five pairs of highly polished shoes stood on a rack below but she could find no signs of sand or chalk from the quarry on the soles and no hidden compartments in the heels. Tapping the back of the wardrobe for a hidden panel did nothing but frazzle her nerves even further at the loud echo that bounced round the wooden-floored room.

Next she focussed her attentions on the single bed. It had a walnut-inlaid nightstand either side, a water carafe standing on one and an ornate oil lamp on the other.

The drawers were filled with a stack of clean handkerchiefs on one side and several pairs of spectacles and a set of thin metal rods she assumed were the set of skeleton keys he had used in the hut in the quarry on the other.

The bed was made with such military precision she hesitated before running her hand under the pillows and lifting the mattress. Nothing.

A few minutes later and she had resorted to lifting the circular rug in the middle of the room but this revealed nothing more than perfectly polished and dust-free oak boards. Off to the left was a small washroom, tiled in alternate green and white, complete with toilet, clawfoot hip bath and a ceramic basin. In the small corner cupboard, she found only shaving gear, a hand-held mirror, soap and a neat array of gentleman's nail clippers and combs.

Dash it! His rooms were just as inscrutable as his deadpan butler persona.

She sighed as she closed the bathroom-cabinet door quietly. Short of ripping up the floorboards or scouring every inch of the walls, she'd drawn a total blank. Money! The thought popped into her head. He had to have somewhere to keep his money; he wouldn't put that in the family safe in her uncle's study. She moved to the one painting hanging on the wall opposite the bed. A rather artless work of two cowboys watching the setting sun, astride sandy-coloured steeds. Artless and not the hiding place for a safe it turned out.

As she put the picture back, a thought struck her. She darted back into the bathroom and snatched up the shaving mirror. Then she sprawled on the floor and examined the underneath of the furniture and bed for anything taped out of sight.

Nothing!

Eleanor scrambled back up and resigned herself to being wrong about him. He really was as straight-laced and rigidly upstanding as he seemed. She went back to the bathroom cabinet to replace the mirror but tripped over the door threshold. 'No!' she blurted out as the mirror flew from her hand. Somehow she caught it. She lay winded on her back for a second before rolling over. 'Hello! What's this?' she whispered.

In the mirror she could see behind one of the feet on the hip bath where two of the wall tiles seemed to be slightly proud. Unless you were lying on the bathroom floor with a mirror, you'd never notice.

She lay back down and felt along the section of tiled wall until they came away. She nodded at the space that was now revealed. And the slim safety deposit box that just fitted in the hole.

She almost dropped the box at the sound of a voice drifting through the window. 'Polly, hang the bed sheets straight my girl. Mrs Butters doesn't want to spend her life pressing out creases!'

Eleanor stared at the box. She tried the lid. Locked, of course. Clifford's skeleton keys! After a couple of minutes that seemed like twenty, she heard it: the dink of a lock clicking back into its open position.

Holding her breath, she lifted the lid and gasped. Inside were seven oddly shaped gems.

'Garnets!'

She picked one up. It was certainly a garnet, like the one they'd found in the quarry, but… in the shape of a bullet?

For a fleeting moment, she thought of dropping it into her pocket but ironically Clifford's previous words flooded back to her: 'It would, after all, be a shame to alert the murderer to the fact that we have him on our list of suspects.' Slamming the lid of the box shut, she slid it back into the hole and replaced the tiles.

She licked her finger and ran it along the floor to pick up the telltale line of fine white plaster that had been dislodged. Hastily replacing the keys in the bedside drawer, she retreated down the two short flights of stairs into the main house.

Back in her room, she lay against the door to catch her breath. When her pulse had begun to settle, she moved into pacing the room. Why did Clifford have those garnets? Did he accidentally drop one in the quarry, or did he deliberately plant one there? Then again, the garnet she'd found in the quarry had been cut to fit in a jewellery mounting, the ones she'd just discovered in Clifford's room were cut like bullets.

She shook her head. *What to make of all this, Ellie?* She stopped pacing, the mayor's words coming back to her like an ice-cold dagger. 'My dear, he has been with you every step and knows what you have discovered. What might he do to stop you finding out any more?'

She stopped short and held her breath for a moment, as this time, the memory of Clifford's words came back to her: 'I have noted you are rather hard to kill, my lady.'

CHAPTER 33

Eleanor jumped as Mrs Butters called through the door, 'My lady?'

Calm down, Ellie!

'Come in!'

'Good gracious, my lady. Have you seen a ghost?' The house-keeper peered at Eleanor's pale face.

'No, should I have?' Eleanor snapped. 'I asked not to be disturbed, Mrs Butters.'

The housekeeper looked anxiously at her. 'I do beg your pardon, my lady, but with Mr Clifford not here and all the goings on I didn't think it best to send the gentleman away.'

'Gentleman?'

She handed Eleanor a card on a small silver tray: *Detective Chief Inspector Seldon, Oxford Criminal Investigation Division.*

She hesitated. *Maybe he would be bringing good news.* Taking the card, she brushed past Mrs Butters down the stairs and into the hallway where her visitor was waiting.

'Inspector, are you planning to stay long enough for tea?'

'Regrettably not, Lady Swift. May we talk in private?'

Eleanor gestured to the morning room and shook her head at Mrs Butters who was waiting at the base of the stairs for instructions.

With the door closed, Eleanor sat and motioned for the inspector to do the same. However, he remained standing.

'So, not a social call then? Do you come with the sombre news of more deaths and murder?'

DCI Seldon grimaced. 'Thankfully no, Lady Swift, no more murders… but I did promise to keep you up to date with… developments.'

'Do please come to the point, Inspector.'

'The fact is, Lady Swift, the Atkins case is closed.'

Eleanor jumped up. 'Closed! You've found the murderer then?'

He sighed. 'Mr Cornell has been deemed guilty of the murder of Mr Atkins. The suicide note—'

'That's what you were supposed to think,' Eleanor cried. 'You fell for it. Now there is a multiple murderer on the loose and no one is looking for him!' Her anger threatened to burn a hole through her skull and her cheeks as they turned crimson.

'Lady Swift, are you alright? Forgive me, but you look a little flushed.'

'More than alright, thank you. In fact, I am in superlative health and perfectly able to take care of myself.'

DCI Seldon looked at Eleanor's hands. For a moment she thought he might be about to reach out and take them in his. Instead, his continued in his usual gruff tone. 'Lady Swift, it is my official duty to repeat my warning that you shouldn't continue to investigate this matter any further. The case is, as I said, officially closed. Any attempts to re-open it by yourself will be seen as attempting to obstruct justice.'

'Obstruct justice!' She smiled coldly. 'Inspector, might I suggest that next time you decide to waste my time, you use the telephone and save yourself a journey.' She rose and gestured towards the door.

'Good day, Lady Swift.' He bowed stiffly and left.

Mrs Butters hurried in as soon as she had closed the front door behind the inspector. 'Forgive my interruption, my lady, but are you alright? I heard shouting.'

'Shouting? I could scream!'

'I'll… I'll be in the kitchen if you require anything.' The housekeeper scurried from the room.

Back in her bedroom, Eleanor was shaking with rage. 'How can the police be so utterly, utterly dumb? Or is the corruption really on such a grand scale that it goes all the way to the top? Maybe even to the inspector. Perhaps even Clifford is caught up in it… and…' She stopped pacing, her eyes widening. 'Maybe my uncle.'

Perhaps that explained why he'd kept her at arm's length all those years? Eleanor realised just how little she'd known about her uncle. *What a fool you've been, Ellie. The Hall can never be your home!*

She looked around at the books, marionette and doll's house. Her room seemed as stifling as it had the day she first arrived at the Hall. Jumping up, she ran down the stairs and out into the gathering dusk.

To begin with, Eleanor walked in silence, letting her legs take her wherever they would. She tried to block out her thoughts until she'd calmed down at least enough to control her breathing. Slowly in… slowly out. Her breathing was as ragged as… an elderly bulldog?

'Gladstone!'

The puffing dog caught up with her and collapsed at her feet, looking up at her with a look of devotion.

'I can see why dogs make better companions than people!' she muttered. 'Coming to the Hall has been the biggest mistake of my life… and I've made some monumental blunders before this. I mean, what was I expecting to find? A home? A new family? Love? Pah!' She shook her head. 'What a wretched mess.'

The only fleeting silver lining had been Lancelot, but he'd made no attempts to take things any further, in spite of his initial attentions. She decided he'd been toying with her like everyone else. 'Gladstone, I feel I'm the biggest fool that ever walked this earth.'

She stopped and shouted, 'Why, oh why, did I trust anyone again? Why, oh why, Ellie, will you never learn!'

Looking around, she realised she was halfway to the quarry where all this had begun. She shuddered. 'No more walking into the middle of nowhere. If we get caught up in any more murders, Gladstone, I'm going to pack us both onto the first steamer out of here and never come back.'

She spun round and set off towards the village with a lump in her throat. More murders or not, perhaps that was the best course of action. Were her dreams of finding a place to call home just that – dreams?

She let the steep descent carry her briskly into the centre of the village, past the sign welcoming her to Little Buckford. At the village pond Gladstone drank noisily while a gaggle of ducks quacked angrily at having their evening ablutions disturbed.

Eleanor's fury at the inspector's news hadn't diminished by the time she reached the small high street. Coming to, she realised that the last thing she wanted was to meet anyone. A street led off to the right, disappearing into the fading light. 'Perfect, that looks deserted. Come on, Gladstone. Help me stomp out all this anger before I explode.'

They turned up the street with Eleanor forging ahead, and Gladstone straggling behind her. But a few minutes further on, the road stopped, with a stone wall blocking their way. 'Oh, for goodness' sake, how hard would it have been to indicate this was a dead end back on the main road?'

On her right a narrow lane wound through some outbuild-ings and looked like it might lead back to the shops. 'This way, Gladstone!'

However, the lane was steeper than it had first appeared. 'Cobbles! How quaint and impossible to keep one's footing on.'

Twenty yards further, the rays of the setting sun blinded her. She shielded her eyes and tried to avoid turning an ankle on the uneven surface.

And that was when she heard it.

'Gladstone, shhh!' The bulldog stopped and pricked up his ears. 'Footsteps?' she whispered.

Looking around she could see only the blinding shafts of evening sun and inky patches of darkness in between. She set off again. 'I'm sure I…' Suddenly the shadows moved. A dark figure towered in front of her, with a weapon held aloft.

'Clifford!'

She dropped to her knees, defeated not by fear but by despair at the betrayal.

It isn't supposed to end like this!

She covered her head with her hands, but the blow never came. Instead, she heard a loud thump followed by a sharp groan. She sprang to one side and jumped up ready to defend herself.

'Clifford! Get away from me, you monster!' Her gaze dropped to his feet. 'Oh!'

Clifford half-bowed. 'Good evening, my lady.' He indicated the crumpled figure. 'He won't give you any more trouble now.'

'What the—?'

Clifford smiled. 'I admit it was a gamble that you would duck sufficiently before this gentleman succeeded in his intended task of cracking your skull with this.' He bent down and picked up a cosh that had rolled from the unconscious man's hand.

Eleanor gasped. 'Oh, Clifford, what a fool I've been. I thought you—'

'No need to apologise, my lady, an understandable error. Might I suggest, however, that we remove ourselves and this gentleman from here as quickly as possible? His associates may be close by.'

'Remove him? You can't take this thug back to the house, are you insane?'

'I believe he is merely an instrument of the real villain behind all this. However, with a little persuasion we may be able to loosen our captive's lips. The Rolls is parked nearby if we can just get him to it.'

'But we should go to the police. This man tried to kill me!'

'Actually, I believe his remit was only to render you unconscious, then kidnap you. As to the police, who do you suggest? The eminently trustworthy Sergeant Wilby?'

Eleanor nodded. 'You're right, but it's too dangerous to take him to the Hall. What about the staff?'

'I think you'll find the staff are more used to unexpected visitors than you might imagine. Mrs Trotman will see to him.'

Eleanor opened her mouth to object, but Clifford held up a hand.

'Really, we need to move. Now, my lady.' His voice was commanding.

Eleanor's natural survival instinct kicked in. She could discuss his un-butler-like tone later.

'There!' She ran over to a battered two-wheeled handcart, which was abandoned by the side of an outbuilding.

Clifford threw the cosh into the nearby bushes and joined her.

After a quick inspection, she said, 'It might make it to the bottom of the lane.'

'Possibly.'

'Let's give it a whirl anyway. What's so hard about pushing an unconscious would-be kidnapper through the streets on a dilapidated handcart without alerting anyone to our presence? Tonight can't get any more ridiculous, after all.'

'That's the spirit, my lady.' Clifford grunted as he hoisted the man from under his limp arms. Eleanor steadied the cart with one hand and grabbed a stray leg with the other. Once the man was onboard, Clifford took off his coat and wrapped it round the sprawled figure.

'Passable.' Eleanor grinned. 'But this is going to make a heck of a racket on these cobbles.'

'Fortunately, they finish a few yards before the houses begin. And there is a path we can take that will lead us straight to the car.'

'Gladstone!' Eleanor remembered the bulldog had been with her. 'Boy, where are you?' she whispered.

A snuffling came from behind her.

'Gladstone, it's alright, friend. It's only Clifford, come on. Got to be silent though.' She slid off his collar and tied his lead securely around Clifford's coat to tether their captive.

'Let's go!'

With Clifford pulling the cart and Eleanor steadying their comatose captive they made it down the steep slope. The only casualties were a few run-over toes and a large rip in Eleanor's coat as it snagged under the wheels.

'Right here, my lady. This is the back alley that will take us to the Rolls. It is a dirt path though.'

'Quieter than the cobbles at least,' Eleanor whispered. 'Good boy, Gladstone, keep going.' She patted his head.

The wonky cart's wheels struggled even more over the rough ground and threatened to collapse before they reached the end of the path.

When Eleanor finally saw the glint of the Rolls' silver-lady mascot, she sighed with relief.

'How can we get him in without being seen?' she hissed.

'If you can hold the cart still, I shall reverse the Rolls up the lane as if I am turning around. I'll jump out and we'll throw him in the back together.'

Eleanor did so while Clifford started the car. In a moment he had reversed the Rolls so it was adjacent to the end of the alleyway.

Between them they heaved the man into the boot. Shutting the lid silently but swiftly, Clifford spun round.

'Evening, Mr Clifford,' a voice called out in passing.

'Lovely evening, Mrs Jones.' Clifford's voice was impressively measured.

Once the coast was clear, Clifford eased the car out of the side turning and onto the high street. In a moment they were past the village pond and on the now dark run back up to Henley Hall.

Clifford held his fist up in triumph. 'Made it!'

Eleanor laughed. 'So is this what you and my uncle used to do to liven up your evenings? Assault and kidnap unsuspecting members of the criminal underworld.' She shook her head. 'And I thought I was going to be living the quiet life of a respectable country lady.'

She sat back in the seat, with the bulldog next to her. 'Gladstone, what on earth have I let myself in for?'

CHAPTER 34

'Well, I have to say I am impressed.' Eleanor smiled at Clifford as she adjusted the warm poultice on her shoulder.

'Indeed, my lady. Mrs Butters' potato, onion and herbal poultices are quite magical in their healing properties. I am, however, sorry I failed to consider your recent injury. Pushing a heavy handcart over rough ground was bound to aggravate the pain and stiffness.'

'Actually, Clifford, the poultice is working wonders, but that's not what I meant. The ladies haven't batted an eyelid over all our goings on this evening. Mrs Trotman looked positively delighted to be charged with keeping our guest fed and watered.'

Clifford smiled. 'Like yourself, my lady, the staff your uncle employed are made of stern stuff.'

The next morning the heart of the house was busy but serene. Mrs Butters stoked the crackling fire in the range, Mrs Trotman coaxed her dough into submission and Polly vainly tried to buff an array of silverware into sparkling perfection. Only Gladstone let the industrious team down, snoring in his quilted bed, with his nose pressed into a leather slipper.

Clifford held the kitchen door open and motioned Eleanor in.

'Ladies.' He nodded. 'How is our guest in the cellar holding up?'

Eleanor started. 'So, that's what you meant when you said Jack Cornell was a former "guest" of my uncle?'

Clifford nodded.

Polly tittered and then blushed at Mrs Butters' pointed look. Mrs Trotman dusted her floury hands on her apron. 'Well, sir, there are no complaints so far.' The ladies all laughed.

Eleanor was confused. 'No complaints?'

Mrs Trotman answered. 'The thing is, my lady, our current guest was kind enough to say he's never eaten so well or been so well attended to.'

'He's supposed to be our prisoner!' Eleanor said.

'Quite so, my dear, quite so.' Mrs Butters smiled. 'And there's no better way to break a man's spirit than through his stomach. I reckon we could have him sitting freely up here with us and he still wouldn't go nowhere.' More laughter echoed round the kitchen.

She couldn't help feeling they were all being rather casual about the prospect of having a dangerous criminal locked up in the cellar. 'Has he confessed to who put him up to kidnapping me?'

'The ladies wouldn't presume to ask,' Clifford said. 'Not yet. They know these things take time. A lackey's first thought is to remain loyal to his paymaster, notably to ensure the security of his kneecaps and loved ones. On this occasion, however, I fear we may not have the luxury of waiting for our velvet glove approach, and Mrs Trotman's fine fayre, to loosen his tongue.'

He stepped across the kitchen and into the scullery. Behind him, Eleanor nodded at the door that led off into the larder. 'I remember sneaking in here a lot.' She smiled mischievously. 'When you weren't looking, of course.'

He paused with his hand on the handle. 'It took a great many extra trips to the village, my lady, to keep up with your penchant for stealing sweets.' He gave her a rare smile.

She watched with widening eyes as he opened the door of the store cupboard and pushed aside a cake tin. Taking a key from his pocket, he turned it in a hidden lock and swung the entire back wall forward to reveal a set of stone steps.

She stared at him for a moment, dumbstruck. 'I can see that once this murder business is out of the way, I shall have to insist on a full guided tour of the house.'

'Very good, my lady.'

At the end of the short flight of steps she could see an extra steel door had been fitted over an old oak one. The steel door, however, lay back against the wall, not closed and certainly not locked. She raised a questioning eyebrow.

Clifford lowered his voice. 'It is a psychological phenomenon your late uncle shrewdly observed, my lady. The man interned will respond positively to the subtly reduced confinement measures. That is, he will note that after a few days of his incarceration, only the standard household door stands between him and his freedom. He begins to feel trusted and in turn begins to trust his captor. Unfortunately, given we have little time, I have speeded up the process by leaving the steel door unlocked from the outset.'

She frowned. 'What happens if he doesn't respond and makes a dash for it?'

He waved vaguely. 'It is a risk, but there are certain hidden measures in place for such an eventuality. None of our "guests" have escaped yet.'

Ellie lowered her voice. 'This all sounds very sophisticated. I thought we were just going to slam into him with threats unless he squealed on whoever set him up to kidnap me?'

He patted the pockets of his morning-suit jacket. 'Thankfully I appear to have left my blackjack and knuckleduster upstairs, my lady. Shall we?'

Her eyebrows rose as he knocked on the oak door before turning the key. 'Good morning,' he called out.

'Hullo?' a deep voice answered back.

She stepped into the room which had been plainly furnished but, in her opinion, over comfortably so for a homespun cell. In a reupholstered wingback chair by the fireplace, a giant of a man spilled out over the sides. On seeing her, he lumbered to his feet and doffed a non-existent cap.

In the dark and pandemonium of the night before, she'd had no chance to really see her attacker. Now he was standing in front of her, she couldn't help thinking whoever had moulded this man's features had done the bulk of it with a boxing glove. And finessed the edges with a heavy plank of wood. His nose spread sideways, flattened out of shape and his brow dominated the entire top half of his perfectly square face. This left his deep, brown eyes buried under heavy lids and his protruding jaw, somewhat hidden by sagging jowls.

'Miss.' He nodded at her, then looked to Clifford. 'What's going to happen to me, guv?' The man spoke in a deep voice with a broad cockney accent.

'Well, one of two things actually.' Clifford turned to Eleanor and gestured towards two chairs arranged so that they faced the first. 'Either you will be polite enough to answer our questions or—'

'Or you'll dob me into the bluebottles.' The prisoner had been waiting for Eleanor to sit and now he slumped in his chair, his gorilla arms hanging over the sides.

Clifford turned to Eleanor again. 'The police. Where this gentleman comes from they are often referred to as "bluebottles".'

Their guest grunted. 'Busy beaks in blue uniforms, always swarming about causing trouble.'

She sat straighter. 'I rather thought "trouble" was your remit, Mr…?'

He eyed her sideways. 'Oh alright, seems I ain't got no choice.' He slapped his chest with a thud that echoed round the room. 'Cooper, Ambrose Cooper.'

'Delighted to meet you, Mr Cooper. Now that wasn't so hard, was it? How about you give us the rest of the gen on why you tried to kidnap me?'

Clifford nodded. 'And mind your Ps and Qs, a lady is present.'

Ambrose shifted awkwardly in his seat, staring at his enormous hands. 'It weren't meant to come to that, honest. Kidnapping ain't normally my game.'

She snorted. 'You hardly expect us to believe you, a hardened criminal, do you?'

The man frowned. 'I was a Joe. But that was before.'

Clifford leaned towards her. 'Cockney rhyming slang, from the heart of London: Joe Rook – Crook.'

'Of course.' She flapped a hand as if this was old news.

Clifford leaned back in his chair and folded his hands. 'Mr Cooper, kindly explain why you tried to kidnap her ladyship and on whose orders?'

'It's complicated.' Ambrose ran his hand across his bull neck. 'I got told I needed to do a job or else…' He faltered. Clifford raised one eyebrow. Ambrose sighed again. 'Or else people I know, good people, would suffer.'

'You were threatened? Is that what you're saying?' Eleanor asked.

'Yeah. I got threatened that I had to do the job or the others would go down for a long time.' A flash of anger crossed his face. 'And they'd done their time and was going straight. We all were.' He looked from one to the other. 'I don't speak lah-di-dah, otherwise I'd say it different, wouldn't I?'

'We understand you perfectly,' Clifford said. 'You are suggesting that your friends would be implicated for a crime, or crimes, which they did not commit but would be held as guilty for. Am I right, Mr Cooper?'

'Yeah. 'Cos who'd believe them? Wouldn't stand a chance, all three's got a record, one of them longer than your arm.'

'So, to protect your friends, you agreed to kidnap Lady Swift,' Clifford said.

Eleanor tilted her head. 'So who set you up, Mr Cooper? Who was it who threatened your friends?'

He held her gaze. 'Couldn't say.'

Clifford slid forward in his seat and added an edge to his voice. 'What a shame. It seems then that you will have to pay your full dues for preying on a helpless woman. Your full dues… or maybe more?'

Ambrose started out of his chair. 'Now see here.'

'No!' Clifford leaned in to Ambrose's face. 'You see here, Mr Cooper. Strange to you though it may seem, I understand entirely where you've come from. I even sympathise that your efforts to go straight were thwarted by someone who wanted a lackey to do his dirty work. However, the matter rests that you attempted to attack a woman, and that is unforgivable. I am offering you one chance to redeem yourself. I suggest you take it before I change my mind.'

Ambrose sunk back into the chair. 'But I can't!'

Eleanor flapped a hand. 'Oh, let him make his choice, Clifford. It'll be several years before he gets out of prison. Then, if he's lucky, his paymaster will have forgotten that he was going to take Mr Cooper's kneecaps as souvenirs for squealing to the judge to reduce his sentence. I'll go and ring the detective inspector. He'll be here before lunch, I'm sure.'

'Stop!' Ambrose wrung his hands. 'Please, miss, I didn't mean to yell at a lady, any more than I meant to kidnap her… you. I didn't know what to do, honest.'

'Indeed.' Clifford sat back in his chair. 'But you know what to do now, don't you, Mr Cooper?'

'I'd tell you who made me do it if I could, really, guv. I never met him. Just got messages.'

'How?'

'Notes, paper notes, nothing fancy.'

'Have you got any with you?' Eleanor asked.

'Nah, burnt them every time. It don't do to leave evidence, that's how they catch up with you.'

Clifford picked up the thread. 'What did the note that told you to kidnap Lady Swift say?'

Ambrose sighed. 'It said to grab the lady, by any means, but not to hurt her too much and deliver her to the crossroads way out past the end of the village.' He spread his hands. 'Honest, guv, I done me best but the likes of me can never get away from being brought up wrong. We was fools to think it could ever be different. Didn't work for Honky.'

Clifford's brow creased. 'Honky? You knew Jack Cornell, didn't you!'

CHAPTER 35

'That's right. Poor blighter, oh sorry, miss.' Ambrose smiled at Eleanor but she was staring at Clifford with her mouth agape.

'Clifford?'

'Apologies, my lady, I should explain. Cockney relies on simple rhymes and obtuse associations. "Corn" rhymes with "horn" and "hell" with "bell", so "Cornell" becomes "Horn bell". However, to disguise it further, the noise a horn makes is substituted for the word itself, so horns honk, hence "Honky". Thus "Cornell", "Honky Bell". Simple really.'

Ambrose stared between them. 'It ain't complicated, not like you made it sound. Just comes natural like. Used to be a way to talk without the bluebottles knowing what you was saying. But then they started to cotton on, so we had to make it a bit more' – he grinned at Eleanor – 'sophisticated, like.'

Eleanor nodded. 'Understood, Mr Cooper. But tell us how you were acquainted with Jack Cornell.'

He looked unsure for a moment but then seemed resigned to his lack of options. 'I met Old Honky when I was doing time with me mates in Wormwood Scrubs.'

Eleanor looked to Clifford for a translation.

'It isn't rhyming slang, my lady. Wormwood Scrubs is in fact the name of a prison, near Hammersmith in London.'

Ambrose thumped the arm of the chair. 'Terrible place it is. We swore we'd never go back, and we'd help each other stay on the straight and narrow. Ain't easy, you know.'

'I imagine not.' Clifford spoke slowly. 'Mr Cooper, we believe Jack Cornell did not commit suicide. He was murdered.'

Ambrose's jaw dropped. 'Done in, you say?'

'Yes,' Eleanor said. 'And we suspect it was by the same person who forced you into trying to kidnap me.'

'Blimey! Oh, sorry, miss.' He rubbed his forehead. 'Old Honky done in? But what for?'

Clifford shook his head. 'That is what we are trying to find out. Help us, Mr Cooper, for Jack's sake if nothing else.'

Ambrose nodded slowly as if in shock. 'I honestly thought his plan would work. He got accepted onto that programme where you get help to find a job and a place to live. Help to have your bad past all forgotten like. He should a been on his way up.'

Clifford nodded in agreement. 'But somewhere, somehow, someone tricked and manipulated him. Just as they did you.'

'Did you see Jack recently?' Eleanor asked.

'About two or three months ago. He wasn't looking so good, weight of the world on his shoulders.'

'We suspect Jack was being blackmailed. He must have been getting notes like you did.'

Ambrose shook his head. 'He never said nothing about it.'

'You seem very sure, Mr Cooper,' Clifford said. 'The suicide note that was found with him said he had been blackmailed.'

'Suicide note? Old Honky wouldn't a left no suicide note! He could read a bit, numbers and things, but he never learned to write.' Clifford and Eleanor shared a look. They'd both suspected that Cornell's suicide note was a fake, but now they had firm evidence. Ambrose was still talking. 'He could just about sign his name. Looked like it had been signed by a spider with a set of broken legs, mind.' Ambrose dragged himself from his chair and stood unsteadily before them. 'Suppose you're going to ring the police now.'

'Not a bit, Mr Cooper.' Eleanor grinned. 'I'm going to return to the kitchen and ask Cook to pop down with some of her pastries and a pot of coffee.'

Ambrose shook his head. 'Don't really understand why you ain't turned me in yet, but mighty kind, miss.'

'Well, Mr Cooper, we're hoping you may be able to help us further. We may be back to pick your brain on how to trap the man responsible for all this misery later.'

'Whatever you says. If I can help catch the b—, sorry, miss, catch the lowlife what murdered Honky, I'll be proud to do it.'

Back in the kitchen, Clifford pulled on his gloves. 'I have another contact, a petty villain your uncle also helped back onto the straight and narrow. There is a possibility he may be able to furnish us with a clue as to the identity of the real brains behind all this now that Mr Cooper has told us what he knows. I will be back as soon as I can.'

Left alone with her staff, Eleanor realised they were waiting for her direction. After the perils of the previous days, she felt she'd earned an evening off from sleuthing. It really could be quite draining! 'Well, it's been a funny sort of day, ladies. So, being new to country house rules…' The three women rocked with laughter. 'I think it calls for a celebration! How does one celebrate with one's staff?'

Mrs Butters answered, 'Well, my lady, in a grand house them as is downstairs never stops working. So if the lady of the house is to hobnob with us, she'll have to pull on an apron and muck in.'

Eleanor grinned. 'Let the hobnobbing begin!'

The housekeeper smiled. 'Polly, get her ladyship a fresh apron from the linen cupboard, clear away the silver and start on them vegetables. You remember what Mrs Trotman said we're making for tomorrow?'

'Yes, Mrs Butters.' Polly nodded. 'Potatoes, peas and corn.'

The cook tutted. 'Celery, onions and tomatoes. We're making slow-braised brisket, child. And finishing the fish. Where is your memory?'

Polly pulled an apologetic face at Eleanor, who gave her a reassuring shrug.

Mrs Butters brought two bottles of wine from the pantry and placed them next to the cook. Mrs Trotman added a generous splash from one bottle into the pan she was stirring on the range. As she tied on the freshly starched apron Polly handed her, Eleanor's nose started tingling at the mix of delicious aromas circling the kitchen.

'One moment, Polly.' Eleanor took down four glasses from the shelf. Mrs Butters poured them each a wine, adding half water to Polly's glass and topping up Eleanor's generously.

With the fish wrapped in paper, Mrs Trotman dispatched Polly to the cool pantry. 'Place them carefully on the bottom shelf, my girl.' The cook grinned at Eleanor. 'Doesn't seem altogether fair to keep the fish in the cellar as usual, my lady, not with our gentleman visitor down there.'

'Well, at least he'll have some company.' Eleanor giggled.

The next hour passed with entertaining anecdotes of dinner party disasters and eccentric visitors to the Hall from the cook and the housekeeper. The second bottle of wine had been opened and the ladies' faces were glowing a soft pink. Giggles turned to roars of laughter as they moved on to good-natured chit-chat about the more colourful characters of the village. Eleanor's stomach rumbled. She'd completely lost track of time.

'Supper's almost ready, fifteen minutes,' Mrs Trotman called, sipping from her glass as she chivvied Polly on with finishing the multitude of pots and pans in the sink. 'I was planning a platter of cooked meats, minted salad potatoes and a basket of tarragon and onion bread, hot from the oven. Would that suit you?'

Eleanor's eyes lit up. 'Sounds heavenly. And the company will make it all the more so.'

The three women exchanged a quiet smile of delight, which Eleanor pretended not to see. They were clearly enjoying her company as much as she was theirs.

Mrs Trotman wiped the table while Mrs Butters laid four place settings and collected the ladies' glasses from around the kitchen.

The housekeeper clicked her fingers. 'I'll tell you what would go perfectly with the platter, Mrs Trotman, is that dandelion delicacy you conjured up last year.'

'I was thinking more of the parsnip perry, that was one of the more successful experiments.'

'Let's try a bit of both,' the housekeeper suggested.

The cook rose and beckoned to Polly to follow her to the pantry. They returned, each carrying a large bottle of homebrew and more glasses.

Mrs Trotman then made up two extra plates of food, arranging each selection precisely but generously. Taking one of the plates and a bottle of beer from the dresser she disappeared for a few minutes. On her return, she settled back in her seat, her eyes sparkling.

A jug of water was added to the array of plates and cutlery and the ladies looked at Eleanor.

'Oh, I see. Err… dive in!'

The busy clink of knives and forks and the splashing of wine into glasses filled the kitchen. In the taste test the parsnip perry won, as Mrs Butters was outvoted by Eleanor and Mrs Trotman, while Polly abstained for fear of offending the cook or housekeeper.

As the meal progressed, the ladies begged Eleanor to regale them with stories from her adventures, which she delighted in doing. She felt more relaxed than ever and beamed round the table at the company, who were 'ooh-ing' and 'ah-ing' at her every tale.

'My stars, what incredible stories!' Mrs Butters said.

Just then the back door opened and Joseph the gardener came in backwards, pulling his boots off with the edge of the step. He jerked to a stop mid-turn at the sight of the four rosy-cheeked women and the row of bottles and glasses.

'Err, good evening, my lady.' He bobbed to Eleanor. 'Ladies.'

'Don't look like a rabbit caught in the torchlight, Joseph. I made you up a hearty plate in case you didn't feel like joining us girls,' Mrs Trotman said.

'Ta, Mrs Trotman. Perhaps I won't join you, if that's alright, my lady? Don't mean to be rude.'

Eleanor stopped eating long enough to reply. 'No problem at all. I wouldn't fancy taking on a table full of tiddly women either. Perhaps I should join *you*?'

Joseph's face showed such alarm that Polly had to thump Mrs Butters on the back to stop her choking. The housekeeper patted the maid's arm in gratitude and waved Joseph away. 'Enjoy your supper, muddy boots.' She smiled affectionately. 'Leave us to the taste testing.'

'Oh no, you're not on the parsnip?' Joseph shuddered and looked at Eleanor. 'Sorry, my lady, weren't my fault. I grew them for the plate, not the glass.' Grabbing his supper and beer, he shot back out into the darkness in his socks, pulling the door closed behind him.

Mrs Butters coughed and turned back to Eleanor. 'So back to this Rajah gentleman. Tell us more about the palace.'

Polly held her knife and fork in mid-air, her mouth slack with wonder. 'Oh, yes do, my ladyship, it sounds so beautiful.'

CHAPTER 36

Eleanor's stomach gurgled. Gladstone tilted his head sideways and stared at her.

'Oh, boy, I'm too old or too out of practice for drunken evenings any more. Ow, my head!' She put her face in her hands to block out the light. The truth was, she rarely drank to excess, but the events of the last few days had taken its toll and she'd needed to let her hair down.

'Good morning,' Clifford boomed as he entered the room with a silver tray.

'Good… morning, Clifford. Are you having trouble controlling the volume of your voice?'

Clifford smiled innocently. 'No, my lady. Do you have a problem with your hearing this morning?'

Eleanor glared at him from between her fingers and groaned. 'How was I to know Mrs Trotman's parsnip perry was so lethal?'

'Indeed. And the dandelion homebrew. Forgive me for saying so, my lady, but I fear the real mistake, was to finish with the chestnut liqueur.'

'What chestnut liqueur?' Eleanor's stomach lurched. 'Oh help, I don't remember us moving on to that.'

'It's very good,' Clifford noted. 'Robustly sweet, not too oaky and deceptively strong. Best added as a dash to a fine roux, rather than quaffed with gusto, perhaps.'

'I'm sure it was only a snifter,' Eleanor lied, even as her head and stomach violently disagreed. 'How are the ladies?' she ventured.

'In fine form apart from a slight bleariness to the eyes.' Clifford offered her the glass on the tray. 'Rest assured, my lady, this will make it all go away.'

Eleanor took the glass gingerly. 'What is it?' She sniffed the murky liquid and peered up at him. 'Is this some hideous concoction of my uncle's or are you really trying to kill me this time?'

'A little of both, my lady.' Clifford gave a half-smile as he noisily clanged the lids of the breakfast salvers.

Eleanor downed the liquid in one. 'Oh dear, that was disgusting!'

'It is the penance one accepts for over-indulgence. It is also the miracle cure that will allow you to be back to your usual form in a trice.'

'Wonderful,' she moaned. 'But what's in it? Please tell me it's not sheep's eyeballs or herring innards?'

'No, my lady, although your uncle was a fan of both Mongolian and Baltic cuisine. It is in fact lime, garlic, Angostura, tomato, a secret ingredient of your uncle's and, of course, a hefty shot of the hair of the dog.'

'Which dog?' Eleanor groaned into her glass.

'It is the country expression for another shot of the liquid culprit of the hangover. Which presented me with a conundrum, my lady. Should I add a shot of the parsnip, dandelion or chestnut?'

'Alright, alright.' Eleanor flapped her hand and pulled her morning robe closer round her.

'However, Mrs Trotman has fixed you the perfect chaser. Two rounds of bacon sandwiches to restore your electrolytes.' Clifford continued doing something unbearably loud on the other side of the room.

Mrs Butters appeared just then with a large tray, bearing the promised bacon butties, a large jug of water and two white tablets.

The women exchanged a sympathetic grimace before Mrs Butters left the room.

Swallowing the tablets, Eleanor offered Clifford a seat. 'I do declare, Clifford, I already feel a tad brighter. Maybe it is a miracle cure. Anyway, I'm dying to hear your news. I trust by your uncharacteristically public exuberance your contact proved his worth?'

Clifford nodded. 'Indeed. I have gleaned two significant facts from him.'

Eleanor mumbled incoherent encouragement for him to continue through a mouthful of salty, crisp bacon and soft, white bread.

'Are you familiar with the Second Chance Programme?' Clifford poured her a weak black tea, which she accepted with a smile, still munching.

'Sounds vaguely familiar, what is it?'

'Well, Mr Cornell was a Second Chancer. Second Chancers are, as one might deduce from the name, persons with a criminal past who are offered the chance to reintegrate back into society after being released from prison. Ex-cons,' he added for clarity. 'Ostensibly, the programme seeks to aid people with a minor criminal background. Interestingly, our Mr Cornell completed five years for armed robbery.'

Eleanor frowned. 'Hardly a minor offence, Clifford?'

'Indeed. It seems that he was nonetheless accepted readily into the programme. It could just be that someone saw that Mr Cornell was genuinely trying to go straight and bent the rules. Or…'

'Or?'

'Or someone wanted Mr Cornell where they could use him.'

The greasy bacon Eleanor had just finished devouring muted her low whistle somewhat. She wiped her mouth. 'What about the item we found at the quarry?'

'Yes. It seemed judicious to leave the item where it was for the moment. However, I also had a contact run a few checks on the smaller item you found next to it.'

'The stone? Was I right about it being a garnet?'

'Quite right, my lady.' Clifford pulled the polished, semi-precious gem from his waistcoat pocket and placed it on the table. Eleanor picked it up and held it to the light, turning it in her fingers.

'It's almost as pretty as a ruby.'

'To the untrained eye, yes. But you might be surprised to find out one of its more common applications.'

'It's a bit early for twenty questions but I'll give it a bash. It's too big for an engagement ring, that would be positively gauche. Earrings, brooch or bracelet?'

'Cold!' Clifford smiled.

'Belt buckle or Indian headdress?'

'Way colder!' He sighed.

'Necklace.'

'Warm.'

She rubbed her forehead. 'How about a decoration of some kind? A medal?'

'Hot, with a little largesse.'

'Err, a ceremonial chain?'

'Bingo!'

Eleanor slapped her forehead and instantly regretted it. She waited for the throbbing to go down. 'Mayor Kingsley!' She shuddered. 'But he didn't strike me as a murderer. He was so… helpful.'

'A result of your self-professed shortcomings in judging character when it comes to men, perhaps?'

Eleanor ignored the remark. 'Mind you, the garnet could easily have been planted by Cartwright or Sergeant Wilby to throw suspicion on Mayor Kingsley.'

Clifford nodded. 'Very true.'

'And anyway, even he wouldn't be vain enough to wear a mayoral chain when hiding that box and its contents in the quarry, would he?'

'No, my lady, but the stone could easily have been dislodged elsewhere and fallen into a pocket or fold of Mayor Kingsley's clothing, only to be dislodged again by him retrieving the said box.'

'True, and he accused you of being the murderer. Surely proof enough?'

'Again, not, necessarily, my lady. Your uncle and Mayor Kingsley never saw eye to eye.' At her look he continued. 'It is a long tale, perhaps best left for another time.'

She thought of the garnets she'd discovered hidden in his room. Might that be part of the tale? Now she was convinced Clifford was on the side of truth and justice, there was obviously an innocent explanation, but she wasn't about to confess to searching his rooms. That would have to wait until after they'd caught the murderer and she'd worked out how to broach the subject. Instead, she shrugged. 'If you say so, Clifford. So it's possible Kingsley was just trying to get back at my uncle?'

Clifford nodded. 'Or indeed, he might even have believed what he said. Maybe Mr Cartwright or Sergeant Wilby have been spreading rumours unknown to me? There was a certain amount of… mystery surrounding your uncle's death. That I fear, again, may have to wait until we have concluded this current business.'

She drew a deep breath. 'There is a lot I need to discuss with you, but for now we need to keep our focus.'

Clifford nodded. 'Well said, my lady. And Mayor Kingsley is not the only person who could have used Mr Cornell. There is also the possibility that Sergeant Wilby was the one putting pressure on him. In Sergeant Wilby's position, it would be easy to have Mr Cornell sent back to jail. As you observed, the head of police in these small rural communities holds as much power as anyone.'

'Absolutely, Clifford. Not forgetting, of course, that our man Cartwright is still up there with Kingsley and Wilby as a suspect. He is the only person we can directly link with Jack Cornell. I saw them together with my own eyes the day after the murder.' She looked down at her, now rather congealed, bacon. Still, waste not and all that. She popped it in her mouth. 'So who's our murderer, assuming, of course, he is even among our suspects?'

Clifford cleared her plate. 'That, my lady, is what we need to ascertain next.'

Eleanor jogged up the stairs, brimming with excitement. Gladstone had caught her mood and bounded up beside her. Catching her foot in the hem of her robe, she fell up the last few steps, banging her head against the bannister, and ended up spreadeagled on the landing. To express his concern, Gladstone offered several slathers of his tongue to her nose.

She had hoped her clumsy enthusiasm had gone unnoticed, but she peeped up and saw Polly's giraffe legs jiggling in front of her.

'You alright, your ladyship?' the maid whispered, blushing as she bent down to offer her mistress a hand up.

Eleanor held her finger to her lips and winked, making Polly giggle. 'More haste, less falling over,' she whispered back. Together they got her up off the floor and installed in her room in front of the mirror. 'Marvellous!' Eleanor peered forlornly at the bruised egg blossoming on her forehead. 'Very fetching, not!'

Back downstairs, Clifford was waiting for her in the morning room. He passed her a small tube of ointment and nodded, gesturing to her forehead.

'I can't get away with anything when you're around,' she grumbled good-humouredly. 'There really are no wasps on you.'

'Flies, my lady. I believe the Americanism you are alluding to is "There are no flies on me."'

She peered at the miniscule writing on the label.

'It's arnica, my lady. Best applied as soon after the cause as possible. I thought you might like to reduce the swelling.'

After applying a dab of the cooling salve, she clapped her hands together.

'Thank you, Clifford. Now all we need to catch our killer is to find out who among our suspects bites. And then once we've got the blighter—'

'Find some actual evidence that would hold up in court, my lady? Assuming we could get it to court, given that the local constabulary seem to be either in the killer's pay, or number the killer among them.'

Eleanor threw her hands up in frustration. 'Mere details, Clifford. We need to get a move on before there's another murder!'

'Perhaps two, my lady, if we are insufficiently prepared?'

'Agh! I understand your natural caution, Clifford. That doesn't stop me wanting to bang your head against this walnut dresser.'

'Oak, my lady. And if we are to defeat such a ruthless opponent as the murderer has proven to be, I believe we need to act as a team.'

Clifford's words made Eleanor forget her frustrations. She'd never been part of a team before. Not really. Even in her job she had always acted independently or led the way. She relented. 'You're right, Clifford. Sorry for wanting to wallop your head against something very hard and unforgiving.'

'Apology accepted.' Clifford nodded. 'I understand, and admire your desire for action, but I also promised your uncle to keep you safe.'

'Okay, Clifford, as a newly initiated team player, I'm willing to be persuaded.'

'Thank you. Now, what we need is a plan that combines the best of both of us. Your flair for the… unexpected.' Clifford frowned at Eleanor's mismatched wardrobe choice. She was wearing a turquoise cashmere sweater fitted over blue twill trousers and brown satin pumps with a silver beaded silk scarf finishing the ensemble.

'What?' she huffed, looking herself up and down.

'And,' Clifford continued unabashed, 'my flair for the logical.'

'It could work, Clifford. The killer seems so arrogant I'm sure he'd underestimate a mere woman and…' Eleanor thought back to the mayor's words.

'A mere butler, my lady?'

'Yes, Clifford. A mere woman and a mere servant. Two classes undervalued and underestimated for generations, joining together to make a formidable team.'

Clifford tilted his head. 'I see you have the beginnings of an idea, my lady.'

Eleanor smiled. 'Yes, Clifford, one you'll love as much as the killer will hate it. It's time to turn the tables!'

CHAPTER 37

'Around a dozen meat pies, you say? Let's see…' Mrs Trotman thought for a moment. 'Fifteen minutes to prepare, forty in the range and ten to cool. What does that make?' She glanced at the clock. 'How about an hour and a bit, my lady?'

'Perfect, thank you. Sorry it's such short notice.' Eleanor beamed. 'Oh, and, Mrs Trotman, if you could wrap them well, I'll be taking them in my bicycle basket.'

On her way back through the hall, Eleanor bumped into Clifford, who was looking grave.

'What's wrong?' She frowned.

'My lady, I have a doubt. On reflection, I fear this plan is too dangerous.'

'Nonsense, Clifford, we've already discussed this. As a seasoned campaigner I'm sure my uncle would have recommended attack as the best form of defence.'

'He was also known to observe that "the better part of valour is discretion", my lady.'

Eleanor continued on her way upstairs. Leaning over the balcony rail she called down, 'Dickens?'

'Shakespeare,' he replied as she disappeared.

With the wind behind her, Eleanor flew down the road from the Hall and on into Little Buckford. Unfortunately, she also ended up flying into Mr Penry. Yanking on her ineffectual brakes, she skidded into a parked van, dropped her bike and ran over to him. 'Mr Penry, I'm so sorry!'

The butcher heaved himself up and straightened his cap. 'Heavens to Blodwen! A healthy pursuit they say, the bicycle, but I'm not so convinced, m'lady. Seems mighty dangerous for the pedestrians along the way.'

'Gracious, Mr Penry, how can I apologise enough?' She looked him over in concern.

'Oh, no need for that. Save for my pride, there's no harm done.'

Eleanor laughed. 'Well, if you're absolutely sure, I will continue, but with more caution for those on two feet rather than two wheels.'

With a wink and a cheery wave the butcher continued across the street to his shop, calling behind him, 'The guilty flee with no one chasing them, m'lady.'

'Let's hope so!' Eleanor muttered as she remounted and tried to make up for lost time. As Clifford had taken the Rolls, she had been left with only her bicycle to complete the first part of their plan. At the edge of the village, she glanced at her watch.

Come on, Ellie! She stood on the pedals as the rise steepened. *If you miss Lancelot, the whole plan falls apart.*

With her legs and lungs on fire, she wobbled into Joe's taxi yard. She had been informed that Lancelot had rented a barn there and moved Daphne, his precious plane, in.

But there was no sign of him or Daphne.

'Anybody home?' she called as she dismounted.

'Over here, miss.'

She turned to see a well-rounded rump bent over an engine. Hurrying over, she got straight to the point. 'Have you seen Lord Fenwick-Langham? Is he still here?'

The rump straightened up into a gnarly face with fewer teeth than gaps, but a warm smile. 'Lady Swift. Apologies, I didn't see it was you. I had me head stuck in this rascal of a motor. Driving me to distraction, it is.'

'How… naughty of it. Forgive me changing topic, but I'm desperate to see Lance— Lord Fenwick-Langham. Is he here?'

'Nope, afraid not. He left ten or so minutes ago as it happens.'

Eleanor groaned. 'Did he say how long he would be?'

'Said as how he was just popping into town and then he'd be back to have another bash at that sticky linkage on his plane.'

'Mind if I wait?'

'Help yourself.' Joe smiled, pointing to a seat that had been ripped from a car and propped up against the wall of the nearest barn. 'Tea?'

Before she could take him up on his offer, the unmistakable roar of a motorbike rang through the lanes.

'Lancelot!' Eleanor cried. She pulled her uncle's fob watch from her jacket pocket. 'Cutting it very fine, my friend,' she muttered.

Lancelot turned into the yard and on seeing her, started unsteadily circling her.

'Stop!' she yelled over the din. 'Urgent business.'

Lancelot stopped beside her.

'What ho, Sherlock.' He grinned, pulling off his helmet.

Eleanor was a little put out at his nonchalance. 'Surprised to see me, Goggles?'

'Not a bit, old fruit.'

'What!'

Lancelot tapped his nose. 'Sandford sent word you couldn't make it through the afternoon without clapping eyes on me.'

'Fibber! Stop distracting me.'

He ruffled his tousled fair hair. 'I am quite the distraction, I know.'

'This is serious, Goggles. I need your help. And somewhere quiet to talk to you,' she whispered.

Lancelot gave a mock salute and swung his leg off the bike, making her sway as he nudged against her.

'Come into my lair, my dear.'

She blushed, as she realised she was wishing he could stay right where he was, pressed up against her. Throwing his helmet on the motorbike's tank and an arm around her shoulder, he spun her, and then paused. 'Oh, the crash in the Rolls. Is your shoulder all fixed up now?'

'Absolutely,' she lied, enjoying the feel of his touch. *Keep your mind on the task, Ellie.*

At the door of a barn opposite the entrance to the yard, he stopped and gave the handle a sharp tug. 'Bit rickety but it does the job.' He gestured her inside.

She squinted into the gloom. 'I can't see a thing.'

'Hold on a tick.'

Eleanor could just make out the shadowy outline of Lancelot as he jogged to the back wall. There was a rusty squeal and then a creak that should have heralded the fall of a mighty oak tree.

'What the…' Eleanor started, but then the barn filled with light as Lancelot secured the two enormous doors back against the outside wall.

Eleanor gasped. 'No! Lancelot, what have you done to your plane?'

'No need to worry, old girl.' He pulled off his jacket. 'It's just the steering linkage.'

'But she's in pieces.' Eleanor groaned, staring in dismay at the array of parts laid out on a smart picnic blanket beneath the engine bay.

'She'll be fine, Daphne's come through worse. Why the theatricals, Sherlock? That's not like you.'

Eleanor whipped round on her heel, fuelled with agitation. 'But I need…' However, she lost track of her words at the sight of Lancelot's white shirt streaked with oil, which had soaked through in parts, leaving it almost transparent. His sleeves were rolled up tight, and his sun-kissed arms were exposed.

'You need…?' he said softly, stepping in close.

'I need… to keep my mind on the job,' she heard herself say, even though she was yearning for the exact opposite.

'Bally shame that, Sherlock,' Lancelot whispered as he tucked a few of her stray curls behind her ear. He gazed into her eyes. 'Romantic spot and all that.'

'Romantic?' She caught her breath. 'Lancelot, this is a dilapidated old barn.'

'True, but I haven't had you to myself anywhere so private. I've been thinking about you ever since you accosted me in old man Cartwright's field.'

'He prefers Thomas… Really, you've been thinking about me?' Eleanor said dreamily.

'Sherlock.' He took her arms gently. 'What does a man have to do to let a girl like you know how he feels? You're an impossible creature! Chocolate boxes and flowers aren't going to cut it with you, are they?'

'Aren't they?' Eleanor was quite partial to chocolates. Flowers she could take or leave, although it did rather depend on who gave them to you, but that was beside the…

'I've never met a girl like you before. You're… well, you're… peculiar.' He laughed. 'Irresistibly so. Every time I meet you, you're splattered in mud, or your hair's stuck to your face… Or you're chasing murderers.'

She looked down at his arms holding hers. 'It's funny. I came here to leave all that craziness behind and… and it sounds awfully gushy but, I came to find myself. My life. My roots. I've been wandering round the world trying to make sense of what this odd life is all about.' She looked into Lancelot's eyes. 'I used to think it was love, but that hasn't gone so well, if I'm honest.'

Lancelot grinned. 'Know all about that, old thing. And I guessed when you told us about your short-lived marriage at luncheon the other day that there was more to it than that.'

She nodded. 'I was young and foolish, what can I say?' She looked into his steel-grey eyes. 'Maybe I still am. Foolish, that is.'

In the distance she heard a church clock strike the hour. *Dash it!* Time was running out. She wrenched herself back to the present. 'Look, Lancelot, I know who the killer is. Well, okay, not yet, but I will by tonight!'

Lancelot stepped back. 'Right, ho! I say, top-notch sleuthing! What's the next move?'

'We need to stop him. He's already killed twice, maybe more, and tried to kidnap me, to boot.'

Lancelot put his hands on her cheeks. His eyes smouldering with anger. 'Did he, by Jove! Then I think it's time he had what's coming to him.'

Eleanor ignored the emotion in his voice and the way it made her feel inside, and glanced at the plane. 'I shouldn't have relied on Daphne being available.'

Lancelot's eyes twinkled. 'Don't worry, Sherlock, what's one more trip with haphazard steering?'

'Lancelot no, that sounds horribly dangerous!'

'Perhaps, but what's your alternative? You don't happen to have a spare plane about your person, do you?' He pretended to search her, patting his hands gently down her sides to her hips.

Eleanor felt light-headed. It was all she could do to keep her focus. 'If you're sure, but promise me two things?'

He stopped and cocked his head.

'Don't fly if it's really dangerous... and... oh dash it, Goggles, can we finish that other conversation when this is over?'

He squeezed her hand. 'Honestly, Sherlock, I can't wait.'

CHAPTER 38

The scenery en route to Chipstone passed in a rural blur, as Eleanor's mind was so fixated on Lancelot.

Reaching the town's outskirts, she paused at the first grocery store. After looking up at its smart green-and-white-striped awning with a sceptical expression, she pedalled further down the high street. The next food store she reached was more of a general supplies outlet. On the pavement, sacks of potatoes mingled with bottles of paraffin. Brooms and carpet brushes hung next to long strips of lard and a selection of pigs' trotters. This was more like it. Eleanor rested her bike against the rough brickwork and stepped inside.

'Good afternoon,' she greeted the couple behind the counter. The wife nudged her husband in the ribs. He stared at Eleanor but seemed unable to speak.

'Oh, you great lummock!' the woman tutted. To Eleanor she gave a warm smile and tugged at the wilder strands of her grey hair. 'Good afternoon, madam, how can we be of service today?'

Eleanor spotted the fruit scones on the counter. 'A dozen of these. They look delicious.'

'Ten, eleven, twelve… and one for Saint John.' The woman deftly swung the corners of the bag over themselves, securing the ends.

'Saint John?' Eleanor asked.

'The last one's free for friendship.' The woman smiled. 'Saint John, Patron Saint of friendship, you see. May you never eat alone, my dear.'

'Gracious, thank you very much.'

'Twelve buns, that'll be half a shilling, madam.'

Eleanor peeped into the bag. 'Did you bake them yourself?'

'No.' The woman laughed and pointed at her husband. 'He's good for a few things. Baking is one of them, thankfully.'

Eleanor giggled. 'Perhaps you'd be kind enough to help me with something else. I need to find someone. Maybe you might know them?'

'We've been stood behind this counter for twenty-seven years, hasn't we, Frank? There's not many folk we don't know. Who is it you're looking for?'

'A young boy, well he's probably about ten or so.' Eleanor stumbled on her words, realising how vague she sounded. 'He's called Alfie, I believe.'

'Alfie Sullivan?' The woman looked to her husband with concern. 'Ida's lad? He's a good kid, usually.'

'Oh lummy. He's never been in trouble before. Must have got in with the wrong crowd. It'll break Ida's heart.'

Eleanor wondered what on earth she'd said to give them the impression the boy was in trouble. Then it dawned, why else would a 'lady' be asking the whereabouts of a simple, working-class boy? What business would she have if it wasn't to accuse him of a snatched purse or pickpocketed jewellery?

She beamed. 'Young Alfie is a most delightful child. He's not in any trouble.'

The woman sighed. 'Well, there's a relief, isn't it, Frank? Our Alfie's been a diamond to his mum, she's always saying so. Especially since his dad passed away.'

Frank shook his head. 'Shouldn't have doubted the little fellow.' He looked up at the shop clock. 'Now then, given the time, I would say he'll be in one of two places. Either at Barnes' paint factory, or up at the blacksmiths stoking the fire and stacking up the old horseshoes for melting down.'

His wife interrupted, 'Or I'd bet he'll be setting up tin cans to wallop over with pebbles.' She smiled at her husband. 'Me and Frank used to do that when we was kids his age. Row of empty tobacco tins snaffled from behind the pub, all lined up for pelting. Remember, love?'

They gazed fondly at each other.

Eleanor cleared her throat. 'Barnes' and the blacksmiths are both at the other end of town?' They nodded in unison. 'And if he's playing tin-can tumble?'

Frank smiled. 'Over at the kids' den, I suspect. They've got themselves a right little camp in the woods. Past Barnes' chimney and just up the slope a way. You'll see a fort made of sticks, proper moat they've started digging and all.' He chuckled at the thought.

'Thank you for all your help, and for the buns. And for Saint John's blessing.' Eleanor hurried out to her bicycle.

Jumping into the saddle she couldn't help but feel her plan hadn't allowed for the delightful but slow pace of rural life. She was seriously behind schedule. Barnes', the blacksmiths or the woods? She plumped for the woods.

She rounded the far end of the high street, negotiated the cobbles past the brewery and kept on going up the slope. And then she carried on some more. And some more again.

'This is hopeless,' she groaned, pulling her bicycle wheel out of yet more fallen branches.

'Need a hand, lady?' called a boy's voice.

'Alfie!' She spun round with a relieved smile. 'Oh, you're not…?' She looked at the small freckled, red-headed boy who was facing her.

'He's not here, miss. But whatever it is, he didn't do it.'

'What a good friend you are, standing up for him. But there's been no trouble. I have a… job for him.'

'Job! Five minutes, miss.' He started off down the slope then pointed off to the right. 'Meet you at the fort.'

With the incredible speed of youth, he was gone. Eleanor peered up to where he'd pointed. A tattered red flag fluttered in the light breeze between the trees.

Leaning her bicycle against an old beech tree, she unhitched the basket, noting that its contents had miraculously survived intact.

Wobbly handwriting greeted her as she walked up to the fort: 'Fort Chippers. Nock furst!' This was scrawled on a rag and tied to a home-made gate of whittled saplings.

Beyond the sign, a bunch of enthusiastically built hazel shelters followed the vaguely circular defences along the perimeter of the camp. In the centre, there was a circle of logs with a taller one at each of the four corners.

'Aha, this must be the council chamber,' she mused, perching on one of the lower logs. To the right were a stack of cans, a heap of pebbles and some home-made bows and arrows. She put the basket on the ground and waited.

She didn't have to wait long.

'I can't believe you did that! Ladies don't go tramping about in the woods. Fancy sending her up to the fort, you turnip!'

'Well, she was almost there. She'd have found it anyhow.'

A few scrambling noises followed and two curious faces peeped between the last trunks hiding the entrance to their camp. Eleanor was relieved to see she recognised one of them.

'Hello, Alfie!' Eleanor waved. 'I knocked, but there was no one to report to.'

Alfie slapped his friend on the arm and swung the gate open, whispering, 'I told you it had to be her.' He pulled his cap off and nodded to Eleanor. 'Afternoon, miss. Are you lost again?'

'No, Alfie, I'm hoping you can help me.'

'Course we will. If it ain't rude to ask though, the sarge did say as you had a job.' Alfie chewed his bottom lip.

Eleanor was confused. 'The sarge? I don't think I've met…'

'Sorry, miss.' Alfie pointed to the other boy: 'That's Billy. I'm the cap'n, he's the sergeant.'

'Right. Thank you, Billy, er, Sarge, for fetching the captain, much appreciated.'

Billy nodded, rooted to the spot like a star-struck rabbit. 'No trouble, I knew he was at Barnes'.'

Eleanor stood up. 'I do indeed have a job for you. And I wish to pay you for your help.'

'A penny!' The boys chorused to each other.

'And something to keep you going while you're helping me.' She pulled off the chequered linen cloth that covered the basket and tilted it forward so they could see inside.

Their eyes widened. 'Are those meat pies, miss?'

'For your families, and fruit scones as an extra thank you.' She'd guessed that some of the young lads' families would rarely be able to afford such luxuries.

'Whatever it is, we're your men!' Alfie cried. They stood to attention and saluted.

Eleanor saluted back. 'Thank you, Captain and Sergeant. Our alliance is now officially formed. I trust you have more troops though, and reliable ones? Around a dozen ought to do it.'

Alfie seemed to do some complicated arithmetic in his head. 'Not a problem, miss.'

Eleanor took twelve pennies from her purse and dropped them into Alfie's hand. Then she dropped another in muttering to herself, 'And one for friendship.'

Handing the basket to Billy, she leaned in. 'Now, Alfie, you've just come from Barnes' so this should be right up your street. First of all, though, the most important thing to remember is this: If anyone catches you or your companions, you are to tell them that Lady Swift forced you to do it. I threatened to go to the police with a story that you stole my valise, okay?'

They both nodded vigorously.

'Right, I wouldn't normally encourage such behaviour, but these are exceptional circumstances. Now, gentlemen, here's what I need you to do…'

Mrs Butters trotted down the steps of the Hall to meet Eleanor as she dragged her bicycle up the last section of the drive.

'I'd say you've had a busy day and no mistake, my lady.' The housekeeper smiled and took the handlebars.

'Oh, Mrs Butters, I'm getting too old for scrambling up hills and playing soldiers. And for having my heart wrung out, again.' She sighed.

Mrs Butters patted Eleanor's arm. 'You need a cup of tea and a plate of Mrs Trotman's pastries. They're just cooling now.'

'Apricot?'

'Oh, she's been busy. There's a tray full. Rhubarb and ginger, lemon curd and cherry chocolate.'

'Sounds heavenly.'

'Will you take tea here by the range, my dear?'

'What? Oh yes, if I'm not in your way. My, those look amazing.' Eleanor peered at the cooling pastries and then sunk into the chair and dropped her hat and gloves on the table.

Clifford's voice made her jump. 'Your coat, my lady?'

'Clifford! How many times. Please take up trombone lessons so that you can herald your arrival. I swear your ability to appear from nowhere will be the death of me one day.'

'Let's hope not, my lady. But perhaps a herald's trumpet or a sackbut might be more appropriate?' He smiled and caught her coat as she stood up and let it slide off her shoulders.

'Mr Clifford, I've set you a tea place to join her ladyship here at the table. Mrs Trotman will be back on the hour and Polly and I have the linen to attend to. Will that suit?'

'Perfectly, you've done more than enough. Thank you, Mrs Butters.'

After hanging Eleanor's coat, Clifford poured them each a refreshing cup from the fine china pot.

'I need to make those calls,' Eleanor said through the steam of her tea. 'Is everything in place your end?'

'Indeed it is, my lady. The recruits you arranged were hard at work when I arrived. I merely had to curb their natural over exuberance and focus them on the task in hand.'

Clifford passed her the platter of pastries to choose from.

'Excellent. I've been granted honorary membership into Chippers Fort as well, you know.' She imitated Alfie's accent, 'The cap'n and the sarge gave the say so.'

Putting her cup down, she picked a particularly chocolatey pastry.

Clifford looked at her quizzically.

'And yes, I did catch Lancelot.'

'I can see.' Clifford went to the sink and dampened a fresh handkerchief from his pocket. He held this out to her as he sat back down.

'What?'

'Your cheek, my lady.'

She rubbed her cheek and then groaned as she looked down at the cloth streaked with oil. 'Oh, dash it, Clifford! I've been pedalling round the county, asking for directions… oh no, the couple in the shop. They must have thought I was on a most peculiar errand going about covered in oil, asking for young boys.'

'Perhaps, although they would have been correct.'

Eleanor stared at the cloth. 'You know, Clifford… I… I might be falling for Lancelot.'

Clifford took the oily cloth. 'Perhaps that could be our next plan.'

'What, to snare Lancelot? Clifford, you're too funny, that's something one's best girlfriend would come up with in sixth form!'

'Thank you, my lady. But if we are to succeed in our present endeavour…'

'Of course, enough of all that. I'd better telephone.'

Revived by the magic of sweet treats and tea, Eleanor was primed and ready. Clifford informed the staff that her ladyship was not to be disturbed and joined her in the snug, closing the door behind him.

Eleanor stared at the receiver, suddenly feeling less confident. 'Clifford, do you think it will work? I mean…'

Clifford turned towards her. 'It's a risk. There are a lot of variables that we cannot allow for. Will the killer believe that the man he sent to kidnap you, having failed, did not dare return to tell him for fear of his wrath? Did he see you talking to young Lord Fenwick-Langham today?'

'Or young Alfie?'

'Well.' Eleanor picked up the receiver. 'I suppose we'll never know unless I ring. Here goes, fingers crossed!'

Fifteen minutes later, she put down the receiver for the third time.

Clifford gave a hearty round of applause. 'Bravo, my lady! A fine performance.'

'Thank you, Clifford. Let's hope it was convincing enough.'

'It only needed to be convincing enough for the three men you rang to believe that we are about to uncover irrefutable evidence that will identify the killer.'

'I'm not so sure Cartwright believed my tale, though. I know he gets my goat, but I don't underestimate him. Or Wilby. No one can really be that incompetent, surely it must be an act. And Mayor Kingsley seemed to waver towards the end.'

'Possibly true, my lady, but given the conundrum we have presented them with, what choice do any of them have if they are the killer?'

'Absolutely. Whatever happens we'll be prepared.'

'If I may be so bold as to suggest your efforts deserve a brandy?'

'Or maybe two, Clifford?'

As he poured the drinks in the sitting room, she tried to quiet the nagging doubt in her mind. Had she really been convincing enough? Had they covered all eventualities?

For her and Clifford's sake, and for the two men already murdered, she hoped so. As she took the proffered glass, she took a deep breath.

There was no turning back now.

CHAPTER 39

The darkness would have been less disconcerting if it had been as inky black as it always was in the romantic novels she devoured. In them, the hero would inevitably be searching valiantly in the impenetrable blackness to find and rescue his lover. Yet here she was, in real life, trying to trap a murderer, surrounded by grey shadows that continually shifted and reached out to grab her. She shuddered and pulled her jacket closer round her shoulders. *Get a grip, Ellie!*

The purr of a car broke the silence. She peered out as much as she dared. She could just see the outline of a vehicle. It didn't look or sound like Cartwright's tractor, but then again he'd hardly turn up on something so conspicuous, just as Kingsley would hardly turn up in the mayoral Rolls or Wilby in a police car.

She stiffened as the headlights flashed across her hiding place. Tyres crunched to a stop. The engine died.

Eleanor blinked hard trying to make out something, anything, in the gloom. The blood pounded in her ears. The sound of the driver's door clicking open made her stiffen again. Soft footsteps walking… away from her.

She slowly let out the breath burning in her lungs. Then she heard it… scratching and scraping, followed by the metallic clink of a spade.

'Ah!' whispered a familiar voice.

Whatever happened now, they had their killer.

She stepped forward, her legs trembling. She was no coward, but she wasn't a fool either. Neither Clifford nor her were arrogant enough to underestimate their foe. Or to pretend that their plan couldn't go wrong, fatally wrong.

'Looking for something?' She silently cursed the waver in her voice.

The man jerked upright. 'What the devil are you doing here?' In a flash he regained his composure. 'You're supposed to be at the brewery, my dear, I was on my way to meet you.'

'Really?' She cocked her head and nodded at the damp sand stuck to the knees of his trousers. 'And yet here you are scratching about in the dirt like a grubby urchin, just as I knew you would be.'

It was a small lie. She'd told each of the three men she telephoned that she and Clifford had learned that there was an item hidden in the workman's hut at the quarry that would prove that Atkins and Cornell were murdered by the same man. And, more importantly, who that man was. She had asked all three men to meet her at the old brewery in town. Whether they came or not, didn't matter. What she and Clifford were counting on was only the murderer would know that the evidence was real. And even if they half suspected it was a bluff, they would have no choice but to go straight to the quarry and remove the evidence before she and Clifford unearthed it.

She just hadn't known who, if anyone, it would be. But now she did.

Mayor Kingsley frowned. 'Has no one ever told you that deception is most unbecoming for a lady?'

'Often. Anyway, did you find what you were looking for?'

A malicious grin split Kingsley's face. 'Oh, absolutely.' He placed the metal box on the table.

She nodded at it. 'You've Gladstone to thank for finding that, you'd obviously forgotten where you'd put it. It's still locked,' she added innocently.

He took a small key from his waistcoat. She watched with apparent disinterest as he took out the two small, red notebooks, followed by the bundles of money. He placed them in his pockets and reached into the box again.

She recognised the last item, a Browning pistol, which was now aimed at her.

She sighed. 'How predictable and...' From her pocket, she removed a handful of bullets and threw them out the door in to the dark. '... useless without these.'

He cursed, flinging the weapon at her head. She ducked, and the pistol clattered harmlessly against the hut wall behind her.

So when she lifted her head she was somewhat disturbed to find herself staring into the barrel of another gun.

Seeing her expression, Kingsley smirked. 'Yes, that's right, my dear, I brought a spare! Always be prepared. Quite the boy scout, wouldn't you say?'

She shrugged, eyeing him warily.

'Now, where is he?'

'He?'

'Don't be coy, your butler. Let's hope he's not stupid enough to think he can outwit me.' He pointed the gun at her heart. 'I'll only ask you once more, where is he?'

She sighed. 'He's at the brewery apologising to a couple of gentlemen for dragging them out for no purpose in the middle of the night. You see, unlike yourself, Mayor Kingsley, neither of them it turns out, are murderers.'

Kingsley's eyes narrowed. 'Do you expect me to believe he let you come here alone? Now don't try my patience, my dear.'

She raised her hands in mock surrender. 'Okay, he bailed out, would you believe? Really, you can't get the staff these days.'

'Mr Clifford,' Kingsley yelled into the darkness. 'Don't try my patience either. Show yourself now or you will need to find a new employer.'

After a short pause, Clifford stepped forward from the shadows, with a shotgun draped in the crook of an arm. 'My sincere apologies, my lady.'

Eleanor shrugged.

Kingsley pointed his pistol at Clifford and waved him to stand next to Eleanor. 'Without the shotgun, Mr Clifford, if you please.'

Clifford placed the weapon on the table and joined her.

Kingsley turned his attention back to Eleanor. 'Now, my dear, tell me what you know. Or think you know. But a word of advice, if you try any shenanigans, I'll spoil that pretty dress of yours.'

'How distressing, I'm rather fond of this dress and bloodstains are such a nuisance to remove. And besides, you've already tried twice and bungled it both times. Once by having the brakes of the Rolls cut and once by attempting to have me kidnapped.' Her tone was casual, but her heart and thoughts were racing.

Kingsley smiled thinly. 'Third time lucky, then? Now, answer my question.'

Eleanor shrugged. 'Where would you like me to start? Let's see,' she started, counting on her fingers. 'There's the quarry murder, Atkins' "accidental" death, Cornell's "supposed" suicide.' She stopped and looked up at him. 'You do realise you're a monster, don't you?'

'Kind words, my dear.' Kingsley slicked his hair back. 'But what leads you to suspect I had anything to do with them?'

'Well, for a start we traced the garnet we found to your mayoral chain. We checked this out and rather coincidentally it seems that the mayoral chain was recently repaired, so we were pretty sure the garnet was dropped by you. Then there was Cornell's easy acceptance into your Second Chance Programme, which was suspicious given that his crime sheet should have prevented him from ever being considered. Oh, and Cornell's fake suicide note.'

Kingsley's brow furrowed. 'What makes you think it was fake? Such a miserable specimen of humanity was bound to take the loser's way out.'

Eleanor bristled, but forced her voice to stay level. 'It was obviously fake because Cornell wasn't being blackmailed by Atkins, I'm sure of that. And I have it on good authority Cornell couldn't write beyond signing his name, so how could he have written that suicide note? And he didn't kill Atkins either, so why would he commit suicide?'

'Ah, now that is where you are wrong.' Kingsley laughed at Eleanor's obvious surprise. 'You disappoint me, my dear, I imagined you to be brighter than that. Perhaps Mr Clifford can guess the correct version of events?'

She looked at Clifford. His eyes flickered for a moment and then he nodded. 'Of course. Given Mr Atkins' high profile in government and his connection, however loose it might be, to Mayor Kingsley, I presume Mayor Kingsley realised it would be too risky to personally kill Mr Atkins. So he used Mr Cornell to carry out the killing, but I am sure Mr Cornell did not do it willingly.' His eyes widened slightly. 'Of course, *you* were blackmailing him.'

Kingsley smiled smugly. 'The key is to understand what motivates men. Once you do, you can use that knowledge to make the most virtuous of men commit the most vile acts. Initially Cornell had no idea who was blackmailing him, but as you guessed, it was me. I'd been blackmailing him for some time. In fact, I have quite a nice sideline going in blackmail.'

Eleanor nodded to Kingsley's pockets. 'That explains the bundles of money and the entries in those little red notebooks we found in the box you'd buried here.'

'Exactly. I need to note down my victims' dirty little secrets. It not only provides a nice side income, it provides me with a useful lever if I need something done. In the case of Cornell I had evidence of an armed robbery he had committed, but was never caught for. The blackmailer, that was me, of course, said unless Cornell paid him a tidy sum, he would make sure he was locked up again, this time for good.'

Eleanor gasped. She was slowly piecing the puzzle together. 'You tricked Cornell into thinking Atkins was the man blackmailing him, didn't you? Atkins was about to find out about your shady dealings – that's why you wanted him dead, isn't it?'

Kingsley waved the gun. 'Enough, Lady Swift. Atkins was sent from Whitehall to investigate rumours of corruption. He had the authority to offer immunity from prosecution in return for information. Fortunately, everyone in my pay was unwilling to talk, but it was only a matter of time before he discovered some of my alternative business arrangements—'

Eleanor snorted. 'Some of your blackmailing, you mean!'

Kingsley shrugged. 'So I had to… dispose of him.'

She frowned. 'But how could you be sure Cornell would kill him?'

Kingsley tutted. 'Simple really, I steadily bled Cornell dry by increasing the amount I was demanding in blackmail payments. Then I sent him a final letter, addressed from the blackmailer, of course, telling him he had twenty-four hours to pay a tidy sum or the evidence would be passed to the police. Of course, I knew he couldn't pay. Naturally, being in my Second Chance Programme and trusting me, Cornell asked me what to do. I said I'd try and find out who the blackmailer was. Later I rang Cornell and told him I'd found out the blackmailer's identity and had arranged to meet the blackmailer that night.'

'At the quarry,' Eleanor and Clifford chorused.

'Exactly. I told Cornell he could go instead of me and appeal to the blackmailer. I made sure Atkins would be there by sending him an anonymous letter saying I had evidence of the corruption he was investigating, but I was too scared to meet anywhere public.' Kingsley's lip curled. 'Atkins was such a devoted and virtuous public servant that he had to go despite any misgivings. And despite Cornell having some fanciful idea of redeeming his past crimes and going straight, once the blackmailer had demanded more than he could pay, he had no choice but to kill Atkins or go back to jail, this time for good. The only thing I didn't foresee was Cornell trying to cover up the murder by taking Atkins' body back to his house and making it look like an accident.'

Eleanor shook her head. *That explained it!* 'I couldn't get it out of my head why Cornell would go to all that trouble to kill a man and make it look like an accident only to confess a few days later. Now I understand. Cornell covered up Atkins' murder so well, the police were fooled into thinking it was an accident, which is obviously what Cornell hoped. But it messed up your plans, didn't it? You wanted Atkins' death to be recorded as murder so when you killed Cornell and left a fake suicide note in which Cornell confessed to killing Atkins, it would be an open-and-shut case. And to that incompetent, though now I realise, not corrupt, Sergeant Wilby, it was.' Understanding dawned in her eyes. 'And it was you who tore the quarry murder entries out of the police logbook, not Sergeant Wilby.'

Kingsley shrugged. 'As you know, it is fairly easy to distract our local police. And I thought of changing my plan, but it seemed best to continue with the original idea. I relied, as you noted, on the police's ineptitude. And in that respect, I was right.'

Eleanor frowned trying to follow the whole thread. 'So you thought it was just a matter of time before Atkins uncovered your blackmailing, so you fooled him into unwittingly meeting Cornell that night at the quarry. Once Cornell killed Atkins you then took Atkins' papers on the corruption case from his house and destroyed them – that's why Atkins' desk was empty when we searched his house. Then you murdered the only person who could incriminate you, Cornell, and faked his suicide note.' Eleanor looked at Kingsley with a mixture of fear and awe.

'Finally, my dear, you catch up!' Kingsley took a step backwards. 'However, unfortunately, for you and Mr Clifford, too late.' He raised the gun. 'Being a busy man, you understand, I normally have underlings to do this kind of thing – people like Cornell. However, I rather enjoyed killing him. You see, I'm tied to a desk most of the time, so it's good to be hands on sometimes. For you and your loyal butler, I'm also going to make time to personally pull the trigger. And I'm going to enjoy it even more than I did with Cornell.' His finger tightened on the trigger.

CHAPTER 40

The hut door flew open. Half a dozen armed constables surrounded them. DCI Seldon stepped forward. 'Drop the gun, Kingsley! You're under arrest.'

To Eleanor's grudging admiration – and horror – the mayor didn't even look around. Instead, he kept his eye, and gun, firmly trained on her.

'A little surprise for me, my dear?' He tutted and shook his head. 'I don't think so.' He raised his voice. 'Inspector, much as you think you've got me over a barrel, I'd say it was the other way around. I have no qualms about putting a bullet in this interfering witch's head, so I suggest you call your men off or I'll shoot her in a heartbeat.' He shrugged. 'Your choice.'

DCI Seldon swallowed hard. Keeping his eyes on Kingsley, he motioned to his men. 'Lower your weapons.'

'Good decision.' Kingsley grabbed Eleanor around the neck. The hard barrel of his gun drilled into her temple. 'All of you, line up over there. Hands over your heads. You too, Mr Clifford.'

DCI Seldon gestured to his men to do as Kingsley instructed.

Kingsley crooned in her ear, 'Now, be a good girl and you might make it through this.'

Her feet stumbled over each other as he dragged her out to his car. Things weren't going quite according to plan, she thought ruefully. *Just keep cool, Ellie!* He opened the driver's door and shoved her in roughly.

'Drive! And remember what I said – I will shoot you in a heartbeat.'

She thought of trying to disarm him, but knew she'd never reach the gun in time. Briefly she also wondered about confessing that she couldn't really drive, but one look at his face told her he'd just believe she was stalling. Instead she graunched the gears, put her foot down and skidded the car out onto the road.

But then, her heart skipped… *was that? Yes!* Above the roar of the car's engine, came the unmistakable drone of a plane. Daphne! Lancelot was there, just as they had planned. She stared straight ahead, praying Kingsley wouldn't notice.

Her elation was short-lived as it dawned on her they hadn't counted on the killer taking her hostage. DCI Seldon was supposed to wait until whoever turned up had confessed and then jump out with his men and arrest him. In case the killer got away, Lancelot was to be patrolling the skies, ready to intercept.

The plane banked sharply, dive-bombing the car. Kingsley looked up, confused by the noise. A dull whoomph sounded on the road ahead. He peered through the window at the patch of blue on the road surface. 'What the—?'

THUD! A second paint bomb hit the bonnet and splattered over the windscreen. Kingsley swore as Eleanor tried to clear the screen with the wipers.

The plane came in for a second run. This time she glimpsed Lancelot leaning out of the plane, clutching a handful of the paint bombs Alfie and his troops had manufactured under Clifford's guidance that afternoon at the fort.

THUD! A direct hit this time. Their view turned red as the bomb exploded against the windscreen.

THUD! THUD! THUD! Red morphed with green, then blue as a barrage of bombs rained down. The windscreen wipers gave up the fight and jammed across the screen.

'I… I can't see anything!' she shouted to Kingsley.

'Keep driving!' Kingsley commanded, peering up at the sky. 'I've had enough of this clown!' Taking his gun from her temple, he aimed at Lancelot hanging out of Daphne, another clutch of paint bombs in hand.

No way! She wrenched the wheel away from the plane. Kingsley rocked backwards, the sound of the shot ringing in her ears.

Then everything slowed down. She saw Lancelot's plane dive bomb towards the ground as the paint bombs he'd been holding exploded around the car. The last clear patch of screen disappeared in a kaleidoscope of colours.

Then they hit something very hard indeed.

Kingsley was out of the car first. He stumbled around to the driver's door. 'Get out!'

'Give me a moment… my ribs.' The impact of the crash had jerked her onto the gear stick. She wondered if her ribs were broken, or just bruised.

He stepped forward, his face purple. 'Get out or I'll kill you right here!'

She let go of her shoulder. 'Okay, I'll get out right…' The driver's door slammed into Kingsley's wrist, sending the pistol flying. '… now!'

He doubled over, clutching his wrist, his face white. 'You… you've broken my wrist, you stupid woman!'

'Stupid?' Eleanor pointed the pistol she'd scooped up at him. 'Who's the one holding the gun and who's the one holding their wrist? I thought so.'

He lunged at her. She sidestepped him, bringing the gun down on the back of his head. His body slumped to the ground. Taking a step back, she kept the weapon trained on him, but he seemed to be out cold.

A police car skidded to a halt behind her and DCI Seldon and his men jumped out. On seeing the unconscious body at her feet, he stopped and looked at her with respect.

'Lady Swift, it seems that once again, I'm not needed.'

Eleanor grinned. 'Oh, I don't know. You could take this gun, my ribs are aching a tad.'

'It would be a pleasure.'

Relieved of guard duty, she turned to find Clifford standing at her side.

'Clifford, I've told you about creeping up on me like that. Especially when my nerves are a little… frayed.'

'Apologies, my lady, but I had to thank you.'

Eleanor was puzzled. 'Thank me, Clifford, for catching the killer? Most of it, if I'm honest, was your idea.'

He coughed. 'No, my lady, although I must congratulate you on keeping your head when our plan went a little… awry. I meant thank you for saving me the inconvenience of finding a new employer.'

She laughed. 'Well, you were the one who told me I was hard to kill.' She started. *Lancelot! Where was Lancelot?*

Just then a familiar voice rang out. 'I say gang, what a wheeze!' The voice came from the adjoining field. 'Didn't Daphne do a spiffing job?'

'Goggles!'

'Sherlock! A chap could do with a hand over here, you know.'

CHAPTER 41

'Come in, Mrs Butters. I'm awake.'

Stepping into Eleanor's bedroom, the housekeeper gasped. 'Out of bed, m'lady! Doctor Browning was very insistent. Proper bed rest, he said, and he stressed the "proper" bit too, mind. What would Mr Clifford say if he found you halfway up on your feet?'

'The great thing about reaching a certain age, my dear Mrs Butters, is that one is too old to be told off.' Eleanor giggled and instantly clutched her ribs. 'Okay, bad idea, ouch!'

'Forgive me, m'lady, but I don't believe a young'un like you has quite reached that magic age yet. Now, back into bed with you.' Mrs Butters yanked on the top blanket. 'And I'm not sure the good doctor would approve of a great, lummocking bulldog lying alongside you. Suppose he rolls over and lands on your ribs?'

Before Eleanor could reply the housekeeper slapped her forehead. 'Oh, the visitor! I really am all over the place this morning.'

'Visitor?' Eleanor groaned and then glanced up. 'Is it Lancelot… er Lord Fenwick-Langham?'

'No.' Mrs Butters gave a wry smile at Eleanor's crestfallen face. 'It's the Detective Chief Inspector.'

'Seldon? Of course, he needs my statement.' Eleanor peered at her grey silk pyjamas and then at the housekeeper.

Mrs Butters opened the wardrobe. 'How about that beautiful wool shawl of your mother's, secured with a brooch? I'll brush your hair and you'll pass for a lady who is supposed to be convalescing.'

*

Ten minutes later, Eleanor had negotiated the stairs with the support of Mrs Butters' arm. In the drawing room, she held a finger to her lips before her guest could speak.

'Inspector, how good to see you. Forgive my appearance and hushed tone but I'm hiding from Clifford.'

'Hiding from your butler? Is he still trying to kill you?' DCI Seldon laughed and then leaned forward as Eleanor clutched her side. 'Oh gracious, shall I call someone?'

'No, I just can't laugh. Really, it's nothing, merely a scratch.'

'I spoke with Doctor Browning as we passed in the town earlier and he described your injuries as anything but a scratch. He also said…' DCI Seldon looked down at his hat. 'That an independent spirit heals twice as quickly in his professional opinion.'

'I imagine he said something closer to a "stubborn-minded spirit", but I appreciate your delicacy in recounting his words. You're here for my statement, of course?'

'Actually, no, that can wait a day or two. I'm here to collect your… er, "guest".'

'Guest? Oh Ambrose. I forgot all about him still being detained in the cellar! How did the ladies take the news – not well, I suspect?'

'There was a fair amount of wringing of hands. There's every chance he'll get off lightly though. We've traced Kingsley's operation and the whole dastardly thing is based on blackmail, your "guest" was probably threatened into kidnapping you as he said.'

'Have you got enough to send Mayor Kingsley to jail for a long time?'

'We've only just started unravelling his criminal activities, but we already have enough evidence with his confession and the money and notebooks you found to convict him of murder and blackmail to start with.'

A thought struck her. 'You know, with all the excitement of capturing Kingsley, I'd forgotten about Cartwright's meeting with

Jack Cornell. And his practically denying towing that car out of the mud the day after the murder. Cartwright obviously isn't the killer, but I'm still in the dark as to his dubious activities.'

DCI Seldon grunted. 'Well, I can clear up one aspect. It seems Cornell always intended to make it look like an accident. On re-examining Mr Atkins' property, we found evidence that on the night of the storm he hid his motorbike near Atkins' house as he knew he'd need to move fast after the murder. Then he walked to the quarry and laid in wait until Atkins drove in and entered the hut. He then shot him, as you witnessed. What you didn't see, was Cornell then placing the body into Atkins' car and driving to the dead man's house.'

'Ah!' Eleanor nodded. 'That's why there was no body. And so it was Atkins' car that passed me? That's why it seemed strangely familiar. I never thought anything about it at the time, just a car on a dark road. The motorcycle was different, he obviously saw me but didn't stop, while I assumed the driver of the car simply couldn't see me at all.' She frowned. 'Also the car passed me very soon after the shooting, so I didn't really think it could be the killer with the body.'

It was Seldon's turn to nod. 'Cornell moved fast, I'll give him that, but then he planned it well. Once he'd arranged the body in the house, he simply collected his motorbike and shot back to the quarry and removed all evidence of the murder. His only bit of bad luck was to almost run you down in his haste.'

'And the car that got stuck in the mud, Inspector? The one Mr Cartwright towed out?'

Seldon grunted. 'Just a local lad in a hurry. He realised he'd forgotten a package he was supposed to be delivering and tried to use the quarry lane to turn around without slowing down. He lost control of the car and ended up stuck. Apparently Mr Cartwright charged him handsomely to pull him out.'

Eleanor laughed. 'I see, that explains the stuck car. But there's another thing that's been bothering me. Jack Cornell obviously knew Cartwright quite well?'

A cough at her shoulder made her start. 'Clifford?'

'I apologise for interrupting, but perhaps I can answer the riddle of Mr Cornell and Mr Cartwright's relationship. And about Mr Cartwright's "nefarious dealings"?'

Eleanor nodded. 'That I'd love to know!'

'It seems a few days ago Mrs Trotman was in Brenchley's. She was inadvertently hidden from view by a giant display of Persil, the "amazing oxygen washer" as I believe it has been dubbed.'

Eleanor smiled at Clifford's inability to recount anything without, as she saw it, superfluous information.

'She overheard Mrs Mount whispering to Mrs Jefferson that she'd gone all the way up to Pike Farm this week only for Mr Cartwright to tell her he couldn't supply her regular order of game, what with the police trampling all over the quarry and his land since it was shown, by yourself, my lady, that a murder had indeed occurred there.'

DCI Seldon's face cracked into a grin. 'So, Cartwright was selling illegal game from poachers.'

'Indeed, Inspector Seldon, and the man supplying the game was—'

Eleanor raised a hand. 'Let me guess, Jack Cornell?'

'Exactly, my lady.'

DCI Seldon laughed. 'And you had Cartwright pegged as the murderer!'

Eleanor huffed. 'At least that clears that up. And explains why Cartwright is no friend of our upstanding butcher.'

Clifford nodded. 'Indeed, not only would it have offended Mr Penry on a moral front, for he is a very religious gentleman, but also on a business one. I imagine Mr Cartwright's activities cost him customers.'

'Well, until the police cease their investigations, they'll have no choice but to go to Penry now.'

'It would seem so, my lady. However, standing here discussing such matters isn't helping you recover. I believe Doctor Browning recommended rest. It would be a shame to ignore the good doctor's advice.' He turned to DCI Seldon. 'We are obviously immensely grateful for the first-rate medical attention Lady Swift has received. I fear, however, if she sustains any more injuries, the household accounts will suffer dreadfully when the doctor sends in his bills. We may have to economise.'

Eleanor snorted. 'Nonsense, I'm fine!'

'Indeed, my lady. What else explains your playing havoc with the meal schedules, running the housekeeper's errands, making merry with the staff in the kitchen and… entertaining visitors in your pyjamas?'

They both turned at the inspector's roar of laughter.

Eleanor grinned. 'I am delighted that you are here to witness the disgraceful insolence I am subjected to. Perhaps in the future you will record my complaints in case I ever wish to press charges.'

'Of course, Lady Swift.' DCI Seldon held her gaze. 'I've learned to pay attention when you have something to say.' He glanced at the mantelpiece clock. 'Forgive me, but I really should be going.'

Five minutes later, Mrs Butters popped her head round the door, and spoke in a voice tinged with sadness. 'Excuse me, m'lady, Mr Clifford sir, they're taking him away now.'

Eleanor and Clifford joined the solemn gathering in the hallway. Polly had a hand on Mrs Butters' shoulder, and a tissue to her eyes while Mrs Trotman hung back. Ambrose Cooper stood between DCI Seldon and a uniformed officer, with his hands cuffed.

The prisoner grunted. 'Can I say something?'

'As I said when I read you your rights, anything you say, will be taken down and may be used as evidence in court,' said DCI Seldon.

'It's nothing to do with that. I just wanted to thank these ladies… for their kind hospitality. Ain't never been treated so well. Never eaten so well neither.'

He smiled at Mrs Trotman who darted forward and placed a parcel into his cuffed hands.

'Well, he won't be eating so well where he's going, Detective Chief Inspector, this should tide him over for a while.'

DCI Seldon groaned. 'Thank goodness there's no one to see this.' He turned to the constables. 'If any of you utter a word about this, I'll have your badges.'

DCI Seldon led Ambrose out of the door. As the inspector passed Eleanor he paused. 'I wish you a speedy return to full health, Lady Swift. And… perhaps we can meet less… formally next time?'

CHAPTER 42

With the inspector and their guest gone, a peculiar sense of loss hung in the air. The ladies had returned to the kitchen, and it was just her and Clifford in the drawing room. As he turned to leave, Eleanor blocked his way. 'Clifford, I wanted to wait until we were alone to say thank you for... well, everything.'

'It was a pleasure, my lady.'

'And... and to apologise.'

'Apologise, my lady?'

'Yes. When... when I thought you were, you know...'

'Trying to kill you?'

'Yes, that. Well, I sort of snuck into your...' She blushed at the memory.

Clifford coughed. 'If you are confessing that you entered my rooms and searched them, I am already aware of this.'

She stared at him. 'How? I mean I was as stealthy as a cat. Clifford? You're... laughing!'

Regaining his customary butler-esque demeanour he pulled a spotless, starched handkerchief from his waistcoat pocket and wiped his eyes. 'It is my turn to apologise. You have many talents, my lady, but "stealthy" is not a word I would associate with any of them. If Polly were not strictly forbidden from entering my rooms after that last episode' – he shuddered – 'I would have imagined that she had run amok in them. As it obviously wasn't her, that left only one possible culprit.'

'Look here, dash it, I was trying to apologise!'

He gave a half-bow. 'Apology accepted.'

She folded her arms. 'It's all very well being so understanding after the event, but I… well, I found garnets in your room just like the one we found at the quarry! I mean, what was I to think?'

He nodded. 'I agree, my lady, I would probably have drawn the same conclusion. However, it is just a coincidence, not that strange a one either. Garnets actually have many uses most people are not aware of. The ones you discovered are actually your uncle's. They were a gift from the leader of a Hunza tribe in Kashmir. The tribe believed that bullets made from garnets were a stronger weapon against one's enemies than those made of lead.' He hesitated, then seemed to make up his mind. 'Your uncle retired early from a successful army career because of his increasingly strong sympathy for self-rule for the Indian Subcontinent. After leaving the army he continued to support those who seek independence, including the tribe in Kashmir that gave him these bullets to protect him from his enemies. Both Christians and Muslims have used garnets as a talisman since the Crusades.'

'Is that why…?' Eleanor tailed off.

Clifford's voice was soft, his words genuine. 'That is why those garnets, along with much else, is hidden away. My lady, your uncle loved you very much, but his life was too dangerous to have a young niece living with him. He feared for your safety.'

Tears ran down Eleanor's cheeks. She didn't brush them away. 'Oh, Clifford, I thought he didn't care about me.'

'He cared more than he knew how to say, my lady.' Clifford handed her his handkerchief and then winced as she blew her nose hard into it.

'Thank you.' She sniffed. 'I mean for telling me. I'm so sorry… I briefly doubted you. Now I feel terrible.'

Clifford sighed. 'Your uncle and I were master and servant, that much is true, but away from the eyes of the world we were also friends. He confided in me his worries and confusion over how to raise a child. With no guiding feminine hand, he worried that you might founder in the care of two old bachelors living a life totally unsuited to a young girl.'

He closed his eyes and swallowed hard. 'It was I who suggested a boarding school for you, my lady.' Clifford stared at her. 'We wanted you to have a proper education among girls of your own age. Above all, we wanted you to be safe.' It was his turn to sniff. 'I'm so sorry, we underestimated how much you needed… love above all that.'

Eleanor offered him back his handkerchief. With a smile, he pulled another from his waistcoat pocket and wiped his nose.

It had been years since Eleanor had properly cried but Clifford had just opened the latch to her heart and her tears rained down. She stared through them at the man in front of her. He was clearly wrestling with his own emotions, and with his years of guilt.

She cleared her throat, her voice trembling. 'Thank you for everything you did for my uncle… and for me. After the disappearance of my parents, I resented being sent away to boarding school, but only because I didn't know the truth.' She momentarily managed a laugh through her tears. 'Despite everything, Clifford, I think you and my uncle made the right decision. Just imagine how I would have turned out if I'd spent my days with you two on your adventures. I would surely have ended up as a tomboy hooligan with a penchant for dressing as a cowboy.'

Clifford smiled. 'If I may correct you, my lady, I believe that in Dodge City you actually did dress as a cowboy, or cowgirl, as I suppose the correct term is.'

Eleanor gasped. 'Clifford! My uncle really did keep tabs on me!'

Clifford gazed into the distance. 'Many, many evenings were spent in enjoyable recollection of your latest exploits.' He looked down at his lap. 'Your uncle always said you were a marvel and that you would go on to do great things.'

Eleanor wiped her eyes and looked down at her lap too. 'Well, perhaps that was my uncle's only failing then.' She hesitated and then sighed. 'Between you and me, Clifford, I think I've made a bit of a hash of my life so far. Dabbled at lots of things. Travelled for years to keep from having to face the fact I didn't know what to do with myself. And…' She bit her bottom lip. 'I'm absolutely rubbish when it comes to men.'

Clifford startled her with a roar of laughter that filled the room.

'Forgive me, my lady, but your uncle noted the very same. He remarked on more than one occasion that he needed to study the art of matchmaking to save you from the terrible affairs of the heart you kept charging into.'

Eleanor laughed and then stopped as a thought struck her. 'Okay, Clifford, I can understand why my uncle sent me to boarding school now. But once I turned eighteen why didn't he send for me? He and I could have had this exact same conversation all those years ago.'

Clifford took a long breath. 'In your uncle's final moments he confided that his deepest regret was not having made you a greater part of his life once you became a young adult. He feared…' His voice broke. Eleanor bent forward and stared into his eyes until he had regained his composure. 'He feared you would reject him.'

'Reject him! I spent my whole childhood wishing he was a greater part of my life.'

'I know, as did he. But behind his fierce love, there was a fear that he hadn't done the right thing by you. He said it had eaten him up for years, wrestling with the idea of contacting you but fearing your reaction might be indifference… or worse.'

'Oh, Clifford, what a mess. And now I can't tell him that I would never have rejected him.'

'My lady. If I may ask permission?'

She raised her hand. 'No, Clifford, you may not ask permission. It's my turn to ask for permission… permission to hug the life out of you.'

For the first time since arriving at the Hall, his stiff butler's demeanour slipped.

'Permission… granted, my lady.'

Eleanor found the ladies as ever, working away industriously in the kitchen. 'Ladies. I believe we need to have words' – they looked up anxiously – 'about how we best go about having a celebratory lunch!'

They giggled in relief and patted each other's arms. She held up her hand. 'But, I now know' – she put on her best imitation of Ambrose – 'that them what is downstairs never stops working, so if the hoity-toity lady of the 'ouse wants to join in, she'd better pull on an apron…'

'And muck in!' chorused the cook and housekeeper.

Several hours later up in her bedroom, she found an uninvited guest. 'Gladstone, old chum, how did you get in here? I thought we shut you out when I went downstairs.' She sat on the bed and patted him, laughing as he rolled onto his back. 'Honestly, that belly. You must be part pig, surely.'

Her foot knocked against something on the floor. Her walking shoes! What the…? She was sure she'd left them in the wardrobe. Bending down, she could see a small card folded inside one of the shoes.

Be yourself, everyone else is already taken.' Oscar Wilde.
'Oh, Clifford!'

Half an hour later she stepped from her room, feeling content with her choice of attire – a calf-length, green silk tunic with delicate straps and matching beaded shawl. She held a satin clutch purse but abandoned it on the lamp table as she passed. *No need of accessories, Ellie, you'll do as you are.*

Clifford was waiting for her at the bottom of the stairs.

'Thank you for your note,' she said. 'I went for ballet pumps, although the walking shoes were tempting.'

'Either would have been a fine choice, my lady.'

'You know, you are a true gentleman, Clifford, a true old-fashioned gentleman.'

'And you are a true lady, a true modern lady. Tell me, will there be more like yourself in the future?'

'Absolutely, Clifford.'

'Then I look forward most heartily to that.'

The rumble of tyres sounded on the gravel drive.

'I do believe the car has just arrived, my lady.'

From the hall table he picked up a silver tray and held it out to her.

'A package? For me, Clifford?'

Clifford nodded at the long, green, silk-covered box, tied with a delicate bow and embossed with the unmistakable Harrods logo. Lifting the lid, Eleanor gave him a puzzled look. She parted the folds of the tissue paper and gasped.

'Forgive my presumption, my lady, I ordered ivory white.'

Eleanor took a pair of long, satin gloves from their box. She ran her finger over the finely monogrammed 'ES'. Her shoulders shook with emotion as she slipped them on and mouthed a heartfelt, 'Thank you, Clifford.'

They waited on the steps as Lancelot struggled out of the driver's door, with his right arm bandaged heavily.

'Sherlock, you look… stunning.' He held out a powder-blue wrap with his good arm. It was the softest cashmere she had ever felt.

'Gracious, Goggles, that's so thoughtful. Thank you.'

He grinned. 'Wasn't sure about the colour, old girl, but I'm pretty sure that Holmes chap wore a blue scarf. Or maybe it was a blue jacket? Anyhow, I just needed to bring you something to warm you up for… that conversation we never finished.'

'It's perfect.' Eleanor slid into the passenger seat and giggled. 'After all, blue and green should always be seen with a lady between. Shall we?'

A LETTER FROM VERITY BRIGHT

Thanks so much for choosing to read *A Very English Murder*. I hope you enjoyed reading it as much as I did writing it. If you'd like to follow more of Ellie and Clifford's adventures then just sign up at the following link to be the first to know when the next book in the Lady Swift series will be available. Your email address will never be shared and you can unsubscribe at any time.

www.bookouture.com/verity-bright

And I'd be very grateful if you could write a review. Reviews help others discover and enjoy the Lady Swift mysteries as well as providing me with helpful feedback so the next book is even better.

Thank you,
Verity Bright

🐦 @BrightVerity
📘 veritybrightauthor
🖥 veritybright.com

ACKNOWLEDGEMENTS

Thanks to Maisie Lawrence, my editor, for her amazing patience and insights and for believing in Ellie, Clifford and the ladies of Henley Hall. And a huge thanks to the whole team at Bookouture who made *A Very English Murder* possible.

Printed in Great Britain
by Amazon